PRAISE FOR CAPIT.

C000161040

Draws You I.

"Fantastic book! It draws you in like a Venus fly trap and takes you on a ride. Definitely a good read!"

Like a Bar of Chocolate, You Can't Put it Down Until Finished

"Good well thought out book, kept trying to put it down but had to keep reading, looking forward to next two books!"

A first...

"I don't usually choose to read this type of book. This is, in fact the first. It definitely held my attention throughout, and I liked the interaction of the main characters. I recommend this one."

A Great Zompoc!

"The thrills and spills were nonstop in this latest instalment. A new twist to the tale was introduced and battles continue to rage across London! I look forward to book 4!"

Lance Winkless was born in Sutton Coldfield, England, brought up in Plymouth, Devon and now lives in Staffordshire with his partner and daughter.

For more information on Lance Winkless
and future writing see his website.

www.LanceWinkless.com

By Lance Winkless

THE CAPITAL FALLING SERIES

**CAPITAL FALLING
CAPITAL FALLING 2 – DENIAL
CAPITAL FALLING 3 – RESURGENCE
CAPITAL FALLING 4 – SEVER
CAPITAL FALLING 5 - ZERO**

THE Z SEASON – TRILOGY

KILL TONE
VOODOO SUN
CRUEL FIX

Visit Amazon Author Pages

Amazon US - Amazon.com/author/lancewinkless
Amazon UK - Amazon.co.uk/-/e/B07QJV2LR3

Why Not Follow

Facebook www.facebook.com/LanceWinklessAuthor
Twitter   @LanceWinkless
Instagram @LanceWinkless
Pinterest www.pinterest.com/lancewinkless
BookBub www.bookbub.com/authors/lance-winkless

*ALL REVIEWS POSTED ARE VERY MUCH APPRECIATED,
THEY ARE SO IMPORTANT, THANKS*

CAPITAL
FALLING 4
SEVER

Lance Winkless

25/5/2022

Lance Winkless

This book is a work of fiction, any resemblance to actual persons, living or dead, organisations, places, incidents and events are coincidental.

Copyright © 2021 Lance Winkless

All rights reserved.

Published by Lance Winkless

www.LanceWinkless.com

Chapter 1

Retreat, retreat, the word repeats inside Jason's head over and over on a loop, toying with his sanity. He had agreed with Tyrone's suggestion to 'retreat' instantly when the word first fell out of his comrade's mouth. The word had given Jason a glimmer of hope and a chance of survival, knowing there was never any dishonour in withdrawing when faced with an overwhelming enemy. Even the most determined and renowned commander is forced to retreat on occasion, aren't they? And nobody is ever going to benefit from a brave but futile counterattack by two isolated squaddies, low on ammo and without any prospect of support.

Jason shakes his head vigorously to try and snap himself out of the haunting trance that has taken hold of him. The visions of death and slaughter threatening to overwhelm him. His bullet entering Den's blood-splattered forehead as his comrade began to turn into a monster on the floor of the school's staff toilet, sitting at the forefront of Jason's visions.

Dislodged dust and debris fall from his helmet and the sickening cycle in his head is finally broken, even if the image of Den's dead face will never leave him. A stinging sensation in his eyes welcomes him back to reality as acrid smoke wafts across his face, to also coat the back of his throat. Despite his discomfort, Jason manages to concentrate on his surroundings. The devastated street immediately puts his nerves on edge and his finger rushes to find the reassurance of his rifle's trigger, the images before his eyes equally traumatic as the visions he has just exorcised.

"Where do we retreat to?" Jason asks Tyrone, standing silently next to him. His mate's eyes are distant and fixed on the charred black crater where the doomed Warrior armoured vehicle had stood before it was vaporised only moments ago.

"Back the way we came?" Tyrone answers despondently, his focus gradually pulling away from the horror and onto Jason.

"I'm not sure about that mate. I don't think we'll be welcomed back there. They made it crystal clear that we have to push forward no matter what. The only thing waiting for us there will be a bullet," Jason replies.

"They're not gonna shoot us. We're not deserting, we just need to regroup."

"Are you sure about that? We could be infected for all they know." Jason points out.

"What do you suggest then?" Tyrone insists.

A chilling scream rings out from behind Jason before he has a chance to answer Tyrone. Immediately, Jason twists to turn in the direction of the blood-curdling noise, his rifle raising to aim as he drops to his knee to take up a firing position. Black smoke from the explosions and burning buildings hangs in the air distorting his view, insisting on blowing into his eyes to irritate them further.

Where the fuck did it come from? Jason thinks as he struggles to focus on anything in his immediate vicinity. Never mind seeing into the distance where the crater sits and the obliterated houses burn. He raises his arm to eye level in the hope that his sleeve will soak up the moisture that his tear ducts are producing to allow him to see clearer.

Jason's dust contaminated sleeve is rough as it moves across his eyelids, smearing water over his cheeks which cool as it evaporates when his arm lowers back to grip his rifle. His vision improved marginally; he scans again in the dense smoke to find where the scream has come from.

"There!" Tyrone announces from next to Jason, where he has taken up a covering position. His finger pointing.

Jason's eyes dart in the general direction of the pointing figure, but his eyes are filling with water again and his focus blurs. Blinking deliberately to try and clear his vision as his rifle points aimlessly, Jason's heart thumps in fear and anticipation.

"I'm not seeing it," Jason confesses.

"Two o'clock, a woman in a nightdress," Tyrone tells Jason.

Jason finally sees the movement and redoubles his efforts to bring the ghoul in a white flowing gown into focus. A chill runs down Jason's spine as the middle-aged woman, dazed and confused, stumbles in amongst the rubble littering the street. Her bare feet bang into chunks of brick and onto splintered wood, but she seems oblivious to the pain her raw feet must be suffering. She must have climbed out of one of the devastated houses that line the street, Jason decides. Miraculously escaping from one nightmare and finding herself in another.

Deep red blood flows from an unseen wound in the woman's blonde matted hair, the red liquid streaks down the left side of her face to soak into the thin dirty white fabric of her nightdress. The poor woman's mouth gapes open, perhaps to beg for help but nothing escapes from her throat, her shock having stifled any new screams. All she can do is reach out, palms up ready to welcome any assistance or help, but none is offered in time to save her.

3

Shadows move behind the stricken woman, drawing closer to her through the heavy smoke. The infected beasts are beginning to rise once more, the devastating explosion only temporarily halting their compulsion to feed.

Jason's finger hovers over his rifle's trigger as he takes aim at the closest shadows behind the forlorn woman. There are far too many shadows for the meagre amount of ammo in his magazine to deal with, however. He knows it would be futile to open fire and probably suicidal to engage the enemy here and now.

"We gotta get out of here!" Tyrone insists from beside Jason. Reaffirming what they must do.

A shadow bursts out of the smoke only feet away from the stumbling woman. The beast screeching as it launches itself into the air. More creatures appear out of the smoke to try and regain their advantage and to strike first but they are too late. The first beast hammers into the woman, knocking her sideways off her feet and she falls heavily into the road. The puff of dust that rises around her as she thumps into the ground doesn't disguise the torrid images of the beast's continued attack.

A forceful tug under Jason's armpit and the shout of "Move!" brings Jason out of his shocked paralysis and scrambling to his feet. Tyrone virtually drags Jason, still at sixes and sevens, across the road and towards the street opposite their position. Even as Jason's feet flounder beneath him, Tyrone drags him forward. Jason's eyes still fixate on the bloody slaughter of the doomed woman.

"Snap out of it!" Tyrone orders as he drags Jason up the kerb and off the road, closing in on the new, quieter street ahead. Jason's eyes widen further with fear as they lock onto numerous creatures enveloping the piece of road where the woman had fallen. The dreaded beasts continue on in his and Tyrone's direction.

"They're coming!" Jason shouts.

"I fuckin' know mate, get your shit together or we'll be next on the menu," Tyrone barks.

Tyrone's words sink in instantly and the haze that has been clouding Jason's mind finally lifts. *I am supposed to be the squad leader*, Jason tells himself, *start acting like it!*

"Sorry mate, that woman made me zone out for a second there," Jason finally responds to Tyrone, running ahead of him, boots striking the ground hard.

"I know the feeling," Tyrone replies over his shoulder without breaking his stride.

"We've gotta find some cover and quick," Jason says, stating the obvious.

The chilling screech that follows them up the street feels like it is almost on top of Jason, and he takes a fearful glance over his right shoulder as he runs. His worst fears are realised as he gets a glimpse of the horde of baying creatures careering along the pavement directly at them. "Here they come," Jason hears himself cry out, as his mind spins again, his eyes racing to find an escape.

The tightly packed houses on each side of the road offer no possibility of an escape route and the long street seems to go on forever in front of Tyrone. Jason knows instinctively that they will be cut down as they run before they can reach any junction and the shelter it may offer. There is only one option, and that is to fight.

"Covering fire!" Jason shouts as his legs come to a sudden stop and he spins around to face their pursuers.

At least ten fearsome creatures are immediately behind them and Jason is immediately firing his SA80 rifle even as he lowers to one knee to steady his aim. He puts all his faith in his brother-in-arms Tyrone, that he will not abandon him and will take up the fight alongside him. Only for a millisecond does Jason think he has miscalculated and that Tyrone has carried on running, taken his chance to escape, leaving him as a sacrifice to aid his retreat.

Bullets whizz past Jason's head as Tyrone unleashes a burst of automatic fire into the midst of the attacking creatures. Bullet's whack into the beasts, hitting torsos and heads, dropping some to the ground. Jason remembers their operational briefing and aims high, trying to make headshots to neutralise the beasts. Some, but not enough of his bullets do hit their targets to eject brain matter into the air, dropping the creatures to the ground.

The beasts are almost upon them when Jason changes tack and lowers his rifle in a desperate attempt to keep the horde at bay. He sprays bullets into the legs of the oncoming creatures, aiming for their fragile shins. Bones are shattered and the squealing beasts suddenly fall into the hard tarmac below them and into a pile, only feet away from Jason's stooped position. Evil and haunting eyes stare up at Jason. As their arms reach their clawed hands forward, the beasts still only having one overriding purpose, and that is to feed.

Behind the pile of squirming bodies, rounding the corner, another large pack of terrifying creatures appears, far too many to fight. Whether they have been drawn into the hunt by the sound of the automatic gunshots or whether they have sensed the fresh flesh on offer, Jason doesn't know. Right now, it is immaterial, the hunt is on once more and the two squaddies need to evacuate the area, immediately.

Jason's legs push him back to his feet and he turns to make a break for it, his stomach dreading seeing the long road in front of them again.

"Run for it!" Jason shouts hysterically at Tyrone, wondering why his comrade hasn't bolted already. Tyrone must know that every second counts, that the odds of them reaching the end of the street are wafer-thin as it is.

"This way!" Tyrone screams, causing Jason to grind to a halt in disbelief.

Before Jason can demand, *what the fuck* Tyrone is playing at, Tyrone is running at the solid-looking wooden green door of one of the houses only feet away from them.

Jason's head spins in anguish at the actions of Tyrone. The creatures are closing in fast and Jason doubts that even Tyrone's hulking stature is going to make an imprint on the solid door. And what about any person who might be sheltering inside? There could be women and children inside and Tyrone is trying to break down their only defence.

Tyrone smashes into the door with all his might, his shoulder the battering ram. He is bounced backwards straight off the heavy door, barely rattling it in its frame. A low whining sound of pain escapes from somewhere inside Tyrone as he staggers back, but he looks fiercely at the door again and prepares to charge.

Jason's stomach drops when Tyrone staggers back again; their chance to run has gone, they are out of time. Deathly screeches are only meters away as Tyrone moves to take his third run at the door. *Fuck this,* Jason thinks as he raises his rifle. They are committed, and there is no escaping the oncoming zombies, not by running down the road at any rate.

Tyrone lurches at the unforgiving door, his eyes bulging with determination. Jason fires two rounds at the polished brass lock shining on the face of the dark green door. His bullets disintegrate the brass housing of the lock, and wood splinters around it just as Tyrone's hefty shoulder smashes once more against the green paint.

This time, the door bursts open under Tyrone's assault, catapulting him through the entrance. He disappears like a shot, falling forward off his feet to crash inside. Jason doesn't pause to congratulate himself or to wonder if Tyrone has injured himself. He sees from the frantic movement in his peripheral vision that the baying horde is all but on top of him.

Jason bolts for the doorway, terror coursing through him, expecting an attack as he reaches for the doorframe to pull himself inside. His movement only just takes him out of the grasp of the lead creature, which, committed, flies past his back. Others follow, stumbling over themselves and falling to the ground.

Inside, Tyrone's momentum has taken him a couple of meters into the dim hallway of the house. He is flat on his face, dazed, and trying to push himself up, his rifle across the back of his head where it landed. Jason ignores him, turns away from his fallen comrade and takes hold of the door to slam it shut as approaching shadows dim the hallway still further.

The door, painted white on the inside of the house, bangs into its frame but there is nothing to stop it from flying open again. The brass lock is useless, only prevented from falling to the floor by a few wooden splinters that cling onto it. Jason turns again and slams his back against the door, bracing his feet against the laminated floor of the hallway. He prays that he can hold the door closed when the inevitable assault against it comes.

Jason's legs strain not to buckle as the beasts crash into the door almost immediately with an almighty force. His back vibrates against the wood as the door is hit multiple times and it jerks inwards. The crashing against the door suddenly stops, but the pressure against it increases and his legs threaten to give way, his knees beginning to bend. Daylight seeps through the increasing gap between the door and its frame as the force becomes too much for him to hold back. Gritting his teeth, Jason's thigh muscles contract and with all his strength he pushes back, desperately trying to keep the deathly creatures and their screams out. The force is too great, however. Even as he manages to straighten his legs, his feet begin to slip against the laminate flooring; he cannot hold the beasts back.

Suddenly, a shadow moves over Jason and inexplicably, he hears the door bang back against its frame as it closes. Jason's feet stop slipping forward and he inches them back into position as Tyrone takes some of the strain.

"Use your rifle to jam it!" Jason cries out as he sees Tyrone's rifle swinging beside him.

Tyrone understands immediately, and whilst keeping his one shoulder pressing against the door, he pulls the rifle's strap over his head. Quickly pressing the muzzle of the rifle into one of the ornate cut-outs in the surface of the door, he then jams the butt of the rifle against the floor. Finally, Tyrone kicks his foot against the rifle's butt to wedge it in place.

"I've got it," Tyrone announces, "go check the back, look for an escape route!"

"Are you sure you've got it?" Jason demands.

"Yes, go!"

Jason nervously releases the pressure he is applying to the door a little at a time, his legs trembling from their excursion as the muscles relax. Hoping for now that Tyrone has indeed got the door secure, Jason rises from his bracing position.

His legs sapped of strength, Jason staggers away from the door, his rifle pointing forward, gripped in both hands. He can feel the strength quickly returning to his legs as he moves forward down the hallway, and his senses begin to take in his surroundings. There is one room off the hallway, which must be the lounge, and another at the end, which he can see is the kitchen.

"Is there anybody here?" Jason shouts out as he moves down the hallway, ignoring the lounge and moving straight towards the kitchen. His training is telling him to check the lounge, to check his blind spots, but the front door could give way at any moment, even with Tyrone's bulk against it. Jason ignores his training; they need to get out of this house as soon as possible and he heads directly for the kitchen.

At the end of the hallway are the stairs to the floor above, and Jason eases his rifle up and around the flight of stairs, but all seems still up there. "Is anyone here!" he shouts again but there is no reply from anywhere in the house.

"Get a move on," Tyrone barks at Jason in a strained voice. Jason glances back at his mate and the urgent look on Tyrone's face has Jason quickly pointing his rifle at the entrance to the kitchen.

Through the entrance and to his right, Jason finds a gleaming modern kitchen area and a cosy looking, fashionable dining area to his left. Opposite him is a glass wall of bi-fold doors reaching almost entirely across the back of the house. Beyond the glass is the greenery of the house's ample garden.

Rushing over to the glass wall, Jason searches for the means to exit into the garden but the handle he finds at the end of the glass doors is locked tight and there is no key in sight. With no option, he raises his rifle ready to shoot out his second door lock in only a matter of minutes. Stepping back and preparing to aim, something catches Jason's eye—another door, almost hidden on his right at the back of the kitchen. *It must be a utility room*, Jason decides, and he pulls the muzzle of his rifle around and moves quickly towards it.

Jason is right; behind the inconspicuous door is a narrow utility room with appliances lined up under a long work surface littered with discarded laundry. There is no door to escape through, but there is a large window at the end of the room which even Tyrone will fit through, if it will open.

Nerves tingle inside Jason's belly as his hand closes around the window's handle. *Please don't let it be locked,* he begs when his hand twists. The handle levers up and the window pushes outwards to Jason's great relief. Air flows through the opening and Jason tastes the now familiar smoke contaminating it.

"Let's get out of here," Jason tells Tyrone after grabbing a chair from the dining area. Tyrone's relief is obvious when Jason begins to jam the chair against the door and the floor to allow Tyrone to retrieve his rifle.

"That won't hold those fuckers for long," Tyrone remarks, his shoulder still heavily pressed against the front door.

"We only need a few seconds. On the right in the kitchen is a door leading to a utility room. There is a window out to the garden at the end which I've opened. We can block the door behind us with the dryer or the fridge."

An almighty boom suddenly vibrates throughout the entire ground floor of the house, stunning both men, who look fearfully at each other.

"What the fuck was that?" Jason asks almost under his breath in shock.

"The front window. They're smashing into the front window! You ready?"

"As I'll ever be," Jason responds.

"Lead the way then, go!" Tyrone orders, pushing Jason unceremoniously away.

Jason doesn't protest and bolts for the kitchen, his hands sweating against the grip of his rifle, his stomach burning with fear. Tyrone bides his time, holding his weight against the front door until Jason is crossing the threshold into the kitchen. Not trusting the dining chair to secure the door alone, he doesn't want any obstacles in his way when he makes his run for it.

Just as Tyrone pushes himself off the front door and makes his break for it, another sound crashes through the house, the sound of smashing glass. Tyrone sees the creature hitting the floor of the lounge out of the corner of his eyes as he tears past the lounge's doorway. He doesn't turn to look at the floundering creature or to see the other creatures scrambling and bursting through the new opening, and he motors straight into the kitchen.

"This way!" Tyrone hears Jason shout from his right and he swerves for the narrow door that Jason disappears into. More bangs and crashes sound out, this time the noises coming from inside the house. Tyrone knows exactly where they are coming from and the accompanying snarls and screeches accosting his ears confirm the creatures are in the hallway, close behind him.

"Shut the fucking door!" Jason shouts as Tyrone crashes into the wall opposite the door of the narrow utility room. Tyrone spins around and does exactly that and applies his weight to it while Jason heaves at one of the white appliances from under the work surface.

The tumble dryer clatters across the floor under Jason's force as he manoeuvres it over to the door. Tyrone has to stretch and make a bridge with his body to allow Jason to get the dryer under him and up against the door. He doesn't dare take his pressure off the door by removing his hands from it, not until it is blocked.

With the tumble dryer in place, Jason doesn't rest until he has manhandled the fridge into position behind the dryer forcing Tyrone to finally move out of the way. The two appliances fill the gap between the door and the wall opposite, both men feeling momentary relief that the door cannot now be opened, and they look at each other, panting from their efforts.

"It never ends," Tyrone says breathlessly as the first bangs hit the utility room door.

"Don't I fucking know it mate," Jason responds.

"Was there any food in that fridge?" Tyrone asks and they both look at each other again, wide-eyed.

Chapter 2

"What you reckon?" Jason asks Tyrone, who is peering out of the window at the end of the utility room as Jason puts his last piece of ham into his mouth. The ham is four days out of date, dried out and probably on the turn, but his stomach gratefully receives the meagre offering, nevertheless. The fridge was bare apart from the clingfilmed ham, some squishy tomatoes, and an equally squishy half a cucumber.

"We need to get to the end of the garden and over the fence in double time," Tyrone responds. "The glass doors in the kitchen won't hold those things, they'll be through those just like the lounge window as soon as they see us."

"And then?" Jason presses.

"Who knows what's waiting over that fence in the other garden, but we can't hang around. We'll have to keep climbing over the fences, play it by ear and be ready for anything."

Tyrone turns away from the window to join Jason looking at the map of London they have spread over the work surface and on top of the discarded laundry.

"What else can we do?" Tyrone asks looking down at the map.

"The best we can hope for is that they arrest us when we reach the perimeter, if we reach it," Jason says.

"All we can do is try, there really is no other option."

"No, no there isn't," Jason says. His qualms about retreating to the perimeter when Tyrone mentioned it earlier have been overridden by recent events. If they run into another squad, replenish their ammo and join up with them to carry on the mission, then they will. But if they don't, then their only option is to take their chances and retreat to the perimeter on the North Circular Road.

"Shall we then?" Tyrone asks.

"Give it five, I'm feeling a bit lethargic after that hearty meal," Jason jokes.

"Come on mate, let's go while we have the light. It won't last much longer and it looks like the weather is deteriorating." Tyrone smiles as he puts his helmet back over his short-cut afro hair.

"Yep, I'm ready," Jason says before turning on the tap over the basin next to him to take one last swig of water.

"Mate, you've just pissed in there!" Tyrone moans.

"I swilled it out," Jason points out.

"Very considerate of you. I'll leave them a note to reassure the owners," Tyrone says and they both laugh.

Jason climbs out of the window first, making sure he stays pinned up close to the adjacent wall when his boots touch the ground. He makes sure that he isn't seen through the windows by the creatures. The gap is a tighter fit for Tyrone, but he squeezes out and pushes the window closed behind him before pressing his back against it.

The two men glance at each other, nod and then push themselves off the house. Jason takes the lead as the two men storm across the slabbed patio, launching themselves off the low wall at the end to land on the grass beyond. They don't break their stride on landing and neither of them looks back to see what is happening at the windows behind as they sprint over the grass.

The first boom against the glass doors sounds out as they reach a few feet from the fence. Launching themselves again, they jump off the grass as they near the fence, their hands gripping onto the top of the wooden panels as they land against it. The top of the fence is rough against their hands as they swiftly haul themselves over in a well-drilled motion.

As soon as they land on the grass on the opposite side of the fence, their rifles are up, gripped in their hands. Both pointing across their new surroundings and looking for targets. There is no sign of life… *or the undead*; the house at the top of the garden looks deserted. The only things present are a child's swing and a plastic slide. As they scan their new surroundings and without a word being said, both men pull in their rifles and break left ready to traverse the next fence to reach the adjoining garden.

Halfway over the next fence, an explosion of shattering glass hits their ears as the zombies smash through the bi-fold doors and out of the house. Suddenly, their jaunt across the improvised garden assault course takes on a sinister new reality.

Jason scans the next garden on his way over the fence. It is empty, so he dispenses with raising his rifle on landing and sprints straight across the grass. Tyrone follows suit, the sound of cracking wood behind them and high-pitched cries forcing them on.

Three fences later, Tyrone almost lands on top of a heavy breathing Jason, bent over with his hands on his knees. He takes up a firing position next to Jason, down on one knee to cover his out-of-breath comrade. Things have gone quiet behind them, their pursuers having either given up the chase or lost the scent. *Hopefully, both*, Tyrone thinks as his lungs work overtime to replenish his body's oxygen.

His rifle's muzzle moves across the garden as Tyrone takes in their new surroundings. The house at the top of the garden is dark inside, and initially, Tyrone thinks it too is deserted. Then suddenly, he has a pair of eyes in the crosshairs of his rifle. Low down, staring out of the back patio window, a child stands staring at him. The boy of five or six years stands motionless, his eyes wide as if he has seen a ghost.

"There's a boy inside the house," Tyrone informs Jason who now stands next to him with his hands on his hips, his breathing calmer.

"Yes, I see him," Jason replies.

The little boy's mouth moves as if he is trying to say something to the two soldiers who have suddenly appeared at the end of his garden. It is not the soldiers he is talking to, however. The boy's words bring movement behind him and a man moves into view behind the glass, followed by a worried-looking woman.

The man pulls a boy who must be his son away from the window and puts him behind his legs, only for the boy's head to pop sideways around the side of the legs. Neither of the parents seem to know what to do, they just stand behind the glass staring at Jason and Tyrone.

It is Jason who takes the initiative; he puts his hand to his mouth and moves his mouth in an eating motion.

"Always thinking with your stomach," Tyrone teases.

"I'm bloody starving mate."

"Me too, to be fair," Tyrone agrees.

Behind the glass, the man looks at the woman for a moment and they talk. Below them, the boy's mouth moves too, hopefully encouraging his parents to feed the two soldiers. Turning back to Jason and Tyrone, the man nods and that is all the invitation the two men need.

"I'm going to ask you to stay out there, if that's okay?" the man says through a gap he has opened in the patio doors.

"Yes, we understand," Jason replies. "This is Tyrone and I'm Jason. Sorry for dropping in like this, things got a bit out of hand."

"Indeed," the man says. "I'm David, and my wife will make you some sandwiches. Is ham okay?"

"Our favourite," Jason replies with a wry smile.

"You talk funny," a little voice says from behind his father's legs.

"Bob, don't be rude," David tells his son.

"That's okay," Jason says. "I'm from Scotland, that's why I talk like this," Jason tells the boy, looking down at him.

"What's Scotland?" Bob asks.

"Bob, be quiet!" his father says. "Go and see if your mother needs any help."

"Dad, I want to talk to the army men."

"Now, Bob!"

Bob sulks off into the house, giving David a chance to asks Jason and Tyrone what is going on in his city. They tell the worried-looking father and husband what they know, which doesn't ease his worries any. The only advice they can give the man when he asks what he should do, is that they should stay locked inside their house. Try and ride it out and wait to hear what the government says.

David's wife passes out a plate stacked with sandwiches for the two men, who, now seated on garden chairs, devour the pile quickly. They wash the food down with glasses of water they have been given. Bob watches them eating intently through the glass, eyeing their rifles with wonder.

The sandwiches eaten, Jason and Tyrone discuss their next move. Debating whether to carry on over the fences and through the gardens or whether to go through David's house and carry on through the streets.

"I'll ask if we can go in to recce the street out of their front windows," Jason tells Tyrone. "If it looks clear, we'll go out the front door. There's still loads of fences to go and we'll be knackered by the time we reach the end of the road."

"I think you'll have to insist," Tyrone replies looking a bit too comfortable in his garden chair.

Jason gets up off his chair, picks up the empty plate and glasses and approaches the patio doors. Inside, David sees Jason coming and gets up off his sofa, where he has been keeping an eye on his unexpected visitors.

"Thanks, they were just what the doctor ordered. Please thank your wife," Jason says as the patio door opens, and he hands over the crockery.

"Our pleasure, will you be off now?" David asks.

"Yes, but I need to ask another favour. We need to come inside and check out the street, to see if we can use it instead of climbing over fences."

David looks apprehensive by the request, glancing back to his wife. "Okay," he finally says, "but can you leave your weapons outside?"

"I'm afraid that won't be possible, but we won't be inside for long. You have my word," Jason replies as Tyrone approaches Jason's back as if to enforce the issue.

Without saying another word, David pushes the door open and stands aside. Jason steps quickly across the threshold before he changes his mind and Tyrone follows him in. An excited Bob is whisked up off the floor by his mother, who immediately sits back down on the sofa, holding her wriggling son tightly so that he cannot escape, no matter how much he protests.

Jason nods a greeting to David's wife and smiles at Bob, who must be in total awe of the two burly soldiers in full combat gear and with guns towering over him in his house.

David brings up the rear as Jason and Tyrone head straight across the lounge which runs the length of the house. He hovers behind the two intruders in his home as they take up positions at the front window overlooking the street.

"See any movement?" Jason asks.

"Nothing, it's deadly quiet out there," Tyrone answers, immediately regretting his use of the word deadly, what with the young boy in the room.

"Agreed, let's move then," Jason says, turning to their host. "Can you let us out of the front door please?"

David leads them out of a door on the left. Neither of the soldiers says a word to David's wife or Bob as they go. Their heads are elsewhere, psyching themselves up, ready to head back out into harm's way.

There is a slight pause at the front door as Jason and Tyrone do a weapons check. David looks on nervously as the weapons make unfamiliar metallic sounds that echo around the enclosed space, his hand hovering over the front door latch.

"Ready?" Jason asks, workman like.

Tyrone nods and David automatically turns the latch and opens his front door.

"Good luck," David says as they leave, and they return the words to him before David shuts the door behind them.

The street is eerily quiet, despite the constant sound of gunfire that hangs over the city. A smoke haze clogs the air, making the day appear later than it is. The closing in weather, only adds to that illusion. Dark clouds are beginning to form overhead, and a breeze is building to distribute the smoke to every corner of their surroundings.

The street they find themselves on is not as tightly packed with houses like the one they escaped from, one street over. The houses here have modest front gardens and driveways to offer them cover as they move. On the flip side, however, cover for them also means cover for the enemy.

"Let's get on with it," Tyrone says quietly as he stalks forward behind his rifle, past a car parked on David's short driveway and towards the road.

Jason falls in behind him, covering Tyrone's back. He is aware of David watching them move out from behind his front window and for a moment, he wonders what is in store for David and his family. Jason doesn't dwell on the family's fate for more than a passing moment though, his concentration needed elsewhere.

At the end of the driveway, both men pause, hiding behind any available cover that will give them a good vantage point to scan the street ahead. They mean to go left out of the driveway, in the opposite direction to where the Warrior vehicle was attacked and then destroyed.

Jason gives Tyrone a thumbs up to signal all clear and he then chops the air in a forward motion. Staying low behind his rifle, Tyrone eases himself out into the open and onto the pavement.

Feeling exposed as he follows Tyrone out into the open, Jason wonders if perhaps they should have commandeered the car, sat idle on David's driveway. He quickly disregards the thought though; it wouldn't have been right to effectively strand the family where they are. Also, a car, although quicker would draw more attention. At least on foot, they can try to stay inconspicuous, using their training and senses to stay out of danger.

Quietly, slowly, and steadily does it, Jason thinks to himself as they progress along the pavement. The muzzle of Tyrone's rifle zigzags through the air like a bumblebee looking for nectar as it searches every crevice and blind spot for signs of the enemy. Jason's boots creep forward sideways, behind his comrade as he watches their rear.

Tyrone makes good progress with Jason in support, and none of the undead creatures has shown themselves as they approach the end of the street. The only faces they see are the ones looking out of the houses they pass. Men, women, and children watch them as they edge by, from a good proportion of the houses. None of the haunted faces moves to open their front doors to try and converse with the two soldiers creeping along their road. The residents daren't come out into the open, they hide in the sanctuary of their homes and Jason doesn't blame them, not one iota.

Jason signals for Tyrone to take cover in the driveway of the last house on the street before the road junction next to it. Tyrone nods his understanding, having already taken a step towards the cover, the two men in sync.

"You read my mind," Jason whispers under his breath as the two men become hidden behind the sparse foliage decorating the end of the house's driveway.

"It takes it out of you, doesn't it? My arms are burning, and my back is stiff," Tyrone answers.

Jason's are too; holding a rifle out front and stalking forward becomes very tiresome over long distances. There are only two ways to negate the strain; take a breather or train harder! Jason consoles himself in the fact that they would have had to stop anyway to recce the junction before crossing it, as he agrees with his comrade.

There is no need to get the map out to check their route, as both men know in which general direction they need to head from studying the map while they were in the utility room earlier. A quick check of a compass tells them they need to cross straight over the junction and keep heading in the same direction.

"I don't like the look of this weather," Tyrone says as they scan the junction.

"Me neither. Let's move out, it looks clear ahead," Jason replies.

"It looks too quiet to me," Tyrone points out as the muzzle of his rifle rises, and his legs push him up to move out.

Jason feels the same apprehension as he follows Tyrone out from behind the bush and they step out into the junction. There is no cover on the crossroads and both men crouch even lower, moving in double time as they begin to cross the wide junction.

Less than halfway across, with the two men out in the open, a roaring noise quickly begins to build from behind them, from the direction of the street they have just left. Neither man looks back to see what the noise is, they both instinctively know what the sound is immediately. Cursing their luck that the sound has arrived at the most inopportune moment, they pick their speed up to get across the road and to cover as fast as they can.

Tyrone reaches the cover of the car first and Jason's back slams against the same parked car as he ducks behind it while the noise builds to a crescendo. Jason only gives the two approaching helicopters a cursory look as they fly above the road that the two soldiers have had to meticulously stalk down in only a matter of seconds. In that quick glance, he sees that the lead helicopter has a strange-looking piece of kit hanging from below its belly.

Tyrone sees the same, but neither man can afford to be staring at the sky to get a better look at the object. Their eyes are on the streets around them and searching for any sign of the enemy.

The two helicopters pass overhead of their position. The whirring of the machine's engines and the roar of their rotors buffeting into their eardrums with a vengeance. The assault doesn't last, and within seconds the cry of the helicopter begins to fade and move away from their position.

The soldiers stay low behind their rifles, their backs pinned against the car. Neither man is in any hurry to show themselves, waiting until the disturbance passes and things settle down again.

Their patience doesn't pay off, however; the helicopter may have moved off but not far. The buzz of their engines still whines in the distance, and there is another noise that wasn't present before, a disturbing noise that is getting louder.

"Do you hear that?" Tyrone asks from beside Jason.

"Yes, I fucking do, can you see anything?"

Tyrone doesn't answer Jason's question; his concentration is focused on the sights of his rifle, his eye squeezed against it. A vein pumps in the side of Tyrone's neck, Jason notices as he glances back. Tyrone's neck is pushing forwards with his rifle, hoping that those couple of extra centimetres will improve his view.

"They're coming, straight down the road," Tyrone announces, referring to the same road they have just crossed from.

"How many?" Jason asks quickly, almost tempted to move his sights away from his zone to see.

"A shit load, and they're moving fast, so we need to go. Are you clear, because I'm not sure that's where the noise is coming from?"

"Yes, clear, let's move," Jason responds, but he can only see a short distance in front before the road disappears around a bend. He can only tell his comrade what he can see, and the other road, the one they planned to take, which is on his left, is definitely clear.

Jason hurries forward and low, then left around the back of the parked car. He doesn't take his eyes off the bend until it quickly leaves his line of sight as he steps onto the pavement of the road they had planned to take.

Tyrone follows Jason towards the back of the car, but just as he goes to turn left, he sees movement ahead coming around the bend in the road.

"Contact," Tyrone announces, just loud enough for Jason to hear, whilst trying not to draw attention from the stream of the undead that is rounding the corner. *With any luck, they won't see me before I'm out of sight*, Tyrone thinks desperately.

A wave of fear shudders through Jason when he hears Tyrone say the word 'contact'. Even though the bend is now out of sight for him, he can't help but look around at the road behind him. The mistake hits Jason like a hammer when his concentration returns to the area in front of him, where it shouldn't have left, and his fear turns to terror.

A large male beast has appeared as if from nowhere on the pavement not more than ten feet in front of him. The shock makes Jason's legs go weak and he almost falls over himself trying to stop himself from careering straight into the fearsome creature.

Jason is slow to react, his arms sluggish in positioning his rifle to aim at the zombie in front of him. Jason peers at the beast as he struggles to get his arms to work. His shock deepens from the evil eyes that stare back, which weakens the muscles in his arms further.

Slowly, he manages to get the rifle into some sort of firing position, and he centres his aim, but there is no hope of a headshot. Luckily, the beast is also surprised by its sudden encounter and its face is only now turning from that surprise and into fearful determination to attack. The vital short delay from the beast enables Jason to squeeze the trigger on the SA80 that his arms can barely hold steady, just as the creature moves to attack.

Jason's rifle rings out as the bullet exits the muzzle, but his confidence that the bullet will hit its target is sorely missing. The creature's arms raising towards its prey as its shadow shortens on the pavement towards Jason.

Dark black blood ejects out of the back right shoulder of the beast as it lurches forward, Jason's bullet managing to at least hit its target. The impact of the shot forces the creature's body to recoil sideways, a deathly scream escaping its hideous mouth.

Adrenaline finally enters Jason's bloodstream, and he feels the strength the chemical brings to his flagging muscles. His newfound vigour doesn't come a moment too soon, and all the bullet has done is increase the beast's anger. It regains its momentum forward and reaches to take hold of its prey. Jason's reflexes finally return, and the rifle pulls back snugly into his shoulder and he fires it again.

Jason sees the second bullet pierce through the grey matted skin of the beast's forehead and instantaneously, the back of his attacker's head erupts. The creature drops like a stone to the ground, its body thudding against the pavement that its ejected brains splatter across.

A figure flies past Jason's right hand side almost in a blur. "Fucking run!" Tyrone screams at him, not slowing to assess Jason's situation. A fresh dose of adrenaline courses through Jason's veins, the tap now fully open. His legs react immediately to Tyrone's scream and they fling him over the dead zombie's body in front of him to chase after Tyrone.

Motoring after Tyrone, Jason has learnt his lesson and doesn't risk looking back over his shoulder; he knows what is there. His legs swerve to follow his comrade as Tyrone breaks right, off the pavement and into the road to sprint down the middle of it where there are no obstructions. The turn gives Jason a glimpse of what they are running from and the horror fuels his legs to lift higher and stretch further.

Meters behind them, ploughing down the road after them, is an army of the undead. The fleeting look does not give Jason a chance to estimate how many creatures are coming for them, but it's a darn sight more than they barely managed to escape from through the green door. That near escape feels like a distant memory that happened days ago, but it didn't; it was only hours ago, and now they are running for their lives again.

Tyrone's bulk starts to slow him down, Jason can see that he is struggling, and he knows he is huffing to keep up his speed. Jason's legs are tiring too, their fix of adrenaline almost exhausted, as the tap has suddenly been turned off. He isn't racing him, but finds himself drawing level with Tyrone, and worryingly, the other members of the race are starting to gain on them.

An exit, we need an exit, Jason's mind screams and his eyes dart in every direction to look for one as his legs begin to give way. *There*, his eyes fall on an opening just past the last house on the right, next to a long wall that continues to follow the road down, instead of along the houses. The narrow opening looks like an alleyway, but he can't be sure and they haven't time to investigate. There is no choice; it's their only option.

"Opening, two o'clock," Jason shouts and Tyrone sees it immediately. He too isn't sure about the opening or where it could possibly go, but his legs are about to stall. There is no choice but to gamble and let Jason take the lead. Tyrone changes direction slightly, aiming for the gap.

Jason shouts again, and this time the word does give Tyrone some confidence; he has never been happier to hear the word 'grenade' in his whole sorry life.

Ripping the grenade from his combat vest, Jason's hands jerk out the pin as his boots hit the ground. The discarded pin falls, clattering against the tarmac. Then, as they draw nearer the opening, Jason lets Tyrone take the lead. He moves behind Tyrone's badly swaying body. Carefully gripping the explosive in his hand, he moves it around to the small of his back where he simply opens his hand to release the grenade.

Jason hears the grenade's lever spring away from the outer body and then hears the lump of metal, with its explosives, bang against the road where it bounces and bangs once again.

Tyrone disappears through the bricked opening that is peppered with overgrown grass and weeds. Jason follows him in at speed, not daring to slow in case he has miscalculated his timings and the grenade goes off before he is behind cover. His hands reach out to push him off the wall of the opening to help him turn the corner. Feeling his palms graze against the rough surface, he just manages not to slam into the wall.

Just registering a path and daylight ahead, Jason feels a wave of relief just as the grenade explodes. His hands rise above his head in reflex as the supersonic shockwave rushes past the opening, even though he is behind cover. The ground beneath his feet shudders, but within seconds, Jason is looking ahead to see where they need to go. He knows the explosion will have hardly made a dent in the number of undead pursuing them, but hopefully, it will have been the diversion they need to lose the horde. The opening was only small after all.

Chapter 3

"Move!" Jason orders. Tyrone, heavily panting and bent over is a few feet farther down the alleyway, which is walled with brick down each side. Tyrone's face is glistening with sweat as he straightens his back, and Jason's is too; he can feel the sweat running down it. Both men break into a fast jog towards the daylight ahead of them.

Wailing screeches from behind force Jason to look back. His head turns towards the opening of the alleyway, his body ready to stop running and to turn and shoot, should it need to. A cloud of smoke and dust is blocking most of the light entering the alleyway, but shadows move in the haze, he is sure of it. Jason's head quickly turns forward to check his direction before it goes back again. Nothing is behind him; the shadows are going straight past the opening, carrying on their hunt down the road.

Relief puts a new spring in Jason's step and he quickly catches up to Tyrone, who he had fallen behind whilst looking back.

"I think it worked, I think they are going straight past the opening," Jason tells Tyrone from behind.

"Thank fuck for that. My legs couldn't have kept going much longer at that speed," Tyrone pants.

"Mine neither," Jason replies.

"Well done mate, that was a close one," Tyrone congratulates.

"Too fucking close," Jason agrees.

"What now?"

"I don't know, let's see where this leads to," Jason answers as they near the daylight at the end of the alleyway.

"To the pub hopefully," Tyrone says flatly. "I could murder a pint."

"Me too mate, me too," Jason agrees.

Nearing the end of the alleyway, they stop running and begin their approach to the exit. Jason takes the left and Tyrone the right as they stalk deliberately forwards, prepared for anything.

Beyond the exit is a lush green expanse of grass which is dotted with trees that sway heavily in the growing wind. Rain is coming, heavy rain and possibly worse; Jason can feel it. *They could be in for a storm, which is just our luck right now,* he thinks.

"What you reckon?" Tyrone asks.

"It's wide open, isn't it? Not much cover," Jason replies as he looks at his compass.

"Yes, but I can't see any zombies, which is always a bonus."

"A big bonus," Jason agrees. "We need to head that way," he says, pointing in a direction parallel to the road they have just escaped from.

"Maybe a change of direction might be advisable? That direction could lead us straight back into the arms of our undead friends," Tyrone suggests.

"I don't think we got much choice mate. South is back in the direction we came, and east will take us deeper into the city, away from the perimeter," Jason points out.

"Fuck's sake." is Tyrone's only input to Jason's reasoning, as his focus moves to the direction Jason had pointed to.

"Let's move out. I've got a feeling this weather is going to shift soon."

"It doesn't look good," Tyrone agrees as he steps out of the exit and onto the grass.

Houses in the not-too-distant view tell them that the park isn't excessively big. Tyrone estimates it will take ten minutes or so to cross it and he quickly picks up his speed into another fast jog. He aims for a cluster of trees branching up from the ground close by, wanting to get out of the open and to cover in quick time.

Jason follows him across the grass which snags into his boots and is overdue a cut. Tyrone takes up a position behind the fattest tree trunk in the cluster of trees aiming his rifle beyond, where Jason joins him.

"What the fuck is that?" Tyrone asks looking out from behind the trunk.

Jason doesn't need to search for long before he sees what Tyrone is referring to. Stood about halfway across the clearing is a dark green tower, approximately three meters in height, with some apparatus mounted on top. The man-made structure looks completely alien in its surroundings and the lifting straps that dangle from the top prove that it is a new arrival.

"I've seen that before," Jason says. "That is what the helicopters were transporting when they flew over us."

"What is it? It's not a piece of kit I'm familiar with."

"Me neither mate, I haven't a clue," Jason agrees.

"It could be some kind of monitoring station?" Tyrone suggests.

"Possibly? Whatever it is, it won't help us, let's get moving."

Jason moves first this time, pushing himself up off the tree trunk and venturing out into the open, again moving forward in quick time. Tyrone doesn't delay in following and they both begin to move across the clearing that the structure stands idly in.

"Here comes the rain," Jason announces when he feels the first cool drops of water hit his face as he runs.

Despite the tower offering the only cover until the trees on the other side of the clearing, neither man takes a path to make use of it. They give it a wide berth, eyeing it with suspicion as they draw closer to it.

"Contact, eleven o'clock!" Tyrone says quietly, panic in his voice and dropping to the grass below.

Automatically, in a well-drilled manner, Jason follows suit. Dropping to his knees and then forward onto his belly, his rifle pointing at eleven o'clock, fear tightening his stomach.

He immediately sees the enemy ahead, emerging through the trees on the far side of the clearing. Three creatures amble aimlessly out into the open and Jason realises that Tyrone has managed to spot them before they themselves have been seen. Jason's fear subsides; they have the upper hand and the element of surprise.

"Hold fire; let's see what they do, as they might pass us by," Jason whispers with the lead creature in his rifle's sights.

Both men hold position, tracking the undead with their rifles. The beasts continue their amble across the top of the field, but they move at a snail's pace. *Come on*, Jason thinks as the rain begins to fall more heavily, *get a bloody move on!*

The three creatures don't pick up their pace, but they do change direction, turning their backs on Jason and Tyrone's position to head away from them. Jason decides they can't afford to wait any longer and begins to rise off the grass.

"Come on, but stay low," Jason tells Tyrone.

Jason covers Tyrone as he begins to rise off the dampening grass, his aim not leaving the targets. His eyes scan right around the perimeter of the park, the dark shadows under the trees widening and closing in on him. Rain thumps against Jason's helmet and distorts his vision, causing the shadows to flicker. Wind blows through the trees, turning them this way and that, every swaying branch threatening to reveal the army of the undead's position that Jason's petrified body is sure hides patiently amongst the trees.

"What is it?" Tyrone asks, his voice echoing in Jason's head. "Jason?"

"It's nothing, I just got spooked for a second," Jason replies.

"You and me both; I'm totally creeped out. Let's get out of the open and find some cover," Tyrone says.

The only cover is in the trees, in the shadows, where the undead are waiting for us, Jason's mind races, his feet rooted to the spot.

"We can't stay here mate, we've got to go," Tyrone reasons, seeing that his comrade is struggling.

Jason blinks, trying to break the spell that the haunting, dancing trees have cast over him. Rain drips from his eyelashes to run down his cheeks, and his vision blurs, filled with swaying tree branches. Jason blinks again and this time when his eyes reopen, he makes sure they are looking at the only tangible piece of sanity he can possibly find: Tyrone.

"Let's move," Jason hears himself say. His leg wrenches his foot, to prise it off the grass that it is stuck to. His mind wavers again as his foot rises and then suddenly his mind snaps. His whole brain is filled with sound, a deafening high-pitched sound, his whole body vibrating under its assault.

Jason's mind somersaults and his body sways as if he might faint, the sound overwhelming him. *Is this what madness sounds like?* he asks himself, loud guitars and drums, the guitar's riff all too familiar to him. Is he back at barracks with his squad, getting psyched up before they move out with AC/DC blasting out over the speakers? Or is it his mind playing tricks on him, playing out the song Thunder in his crazed mind as the storm moves in?

Hands grab onto Jason's combat vest and they shake him violently. He sees Tyrone's wide panicked eyes staring straight at him and his mouth moves seemingly shouting. Faintly, Jason hears Tyrone's shouts intertwined with the unrelenting music.

"It's a trap," he shouts, 'the tower, it's a trap for the zombies."

Jason's mind races, calculating what the hell is going on and finally reality bites back. The tower, placed in the middle of the clearing, blasting out AC/DC's Thunder has been put there to attract the undead to it. Tyrone is right. It's a speaker stack, a honey trap, and that can only mean one thing.

"We gotta get outta here, this place is going to be overrun!" Jason shouts back at Tyrone whose face shows some relief in amongst his panic that his mates head is finally back in the game.

Jason's eyes dart back to the three creatures that were wandering away from them. He knows before he looks that they will be coming back in their direction, and he's right. All three of the beasts have turned and are coming at them fast across the grass.

The trees, no matter how much dread they bring to Jason, he knows they are their only possible salvation. He forces himself to look back at the bouncing trees, dancing in time to the overpowering heavy rhythm of AC/DC. This time, it isn't the trees that fill him with dread; it is the figures emerging from the shadows beneath them. These figures aren't crowds of people making their way to the rock concert; they are crowds of the undead ready to feed.

Shots ring out from Tyrone's rifle, adding to the cacophony of sound as he fires at the three creatures closing in on their position. Masses more are coming though, Jason sees, and he spins in the opposite direction towards where they had entered the park.

Jason hears Tyrone shout something, but he can't hear what he says above the blasting speakers. Creatures stream through the opening of the entrance they had come through, back beyond the clearing. *There will be no escape that way*, Jason's terrified mind tells him. He can't see an escape from the park in any direction.

Whichever direction the two soldiers turn, hordes of the undead chasing across the field, fighting amongst themselves to be first to reach the honey pot. Tyrone releases another volley of bullets at the closest pack of creatures, but the meagre number of bullets in his magazine is wasted. Within seconds, the two men will be overwhelmed and ripped to shreds.

Jason spins to face the monolith, the source of their torment, its dark green wooden façade vibrating. Jason fires off the hip as soon as he faces the target. Bullets pierce through the flimsy façade, splintering it before doing their work on the monolith's innards. Immediately, the music's volume is reduced drastically and as Jason moves the rifle's muzzle across and up, the cursed sound is finally cut.

"On me," Jason shouts to Tyrone.

Tyrone, overjoyed that the incessant music has finally ceased, turns to see Jason jumping up on the structure behind him. Grabbing onto one of the lifting straps that dangle from its top, Jason starts to pull himself up.

With the undead surrounding them, Tyrone doesn't need asking twice and jumps for the other length of strapping.

Deathly screeches ring out from every direction, almost on top of them. Tyrone's hands grip the fabric strap and he yanks himself up, one hand over the other to pull himself higher. The wet fabric threatens to slide through his grip with every grasp, but he makes good progress and is quickly nearing the top. A steel scaffolding bar crowns the summit of the tower and Tyrone's powerful arms pull on it to lift himself up and over the edge.

There is a small shelf around the top of the tower, barely wide enough to hold Tyrone, but he squeezes his knees onto it and looks around to find Jason.

The tower shudders as something crashes into it, and Tyrone realises the undead have reached the base of the tower as he wobbles on top of it. His hand gripping another scaffolding bar mounted near the centre surrounding the equipment positioned there, Tyrone leans over the side to where Jason was climbing.

A cry of help greets Tyrone as his head peers down over the side. Jason's petrified face stares up at Tyrone, his hands desperately trying to grip the lifting strap, but they slip on the wet fabric. Below Jason, the undead have closed in around the tower and are thronging at its base, dead hands reaching up to grab hold of Jason's boots. Jason has lifted his feet up and out of the creature's reach, but it has put him in a sitting position against the side of the tower and unable to climb.

"Grab my hand," Tyrone orders, reaching over the side to try and reach his comrade.

Tears escape Jason's terrified eyes and Tyrone sees that he is too afraid to let go of the strap. Reaching down further, as close as he can get without releasing the scaffolding bar, Tyrone stares into Jason's eyes.

"Jason, take hold of my hand. Do it now."

Jason's face changes to one of acceptance. He knows that he must reach out for Tyrone, and suddenly his left hand releases the strap to reach up. Tyrone stretches out to grab Jason's hand; their fingertips touch and then Jason's right hand slips.

Jason stares at Tyrone as he falls away from him, their eyes locked together for what will be an eternity. "Noooo," Tyrone screams as his mate falls away from him and into the throng of creatures below.

Dead hands and arms pull Jason into them, and heads dart forward to sink their gruesome teeth into Jason's flesh as Tyrone stares in utter shock. Jason's throat releases an unholy scream as the teeth sink into him and he is pulled deeper into the pack of baying creatures. Tyrone sees Jason disappearing into the mass of undead and he must lift his eyes away; he cannot witness any more.

Tears well in Tyrone's eyes as he looks up to the sky where his tears are lost in the rain. The tower rocks again and with the sound of death encircling him, Tyrone screams at the heavens above.

Alone, stranded and surrounded by the undead, Tyrone's despair is interrupted. A buzzing sound enters his ears, and he forces his head down, bringing his face out of the heavy rain. He turns towards the source of the noise, but the rain makes it difficult for him to see anything.

Gunfire explodes at Tyrone's back and his head ducks in reflex. The rapid fire continues relentlessly and Tyrone's head inches up to see where it is coming from. Through the rain, a shadow moves, red tracer fire spitting out from its belly. Howling wind buffets Tyrone, threatening to cast him off the top of the tower. This wind isn't caused by the weather, however; it is coming from the rotors of the helicopter closing in over the tower.

The gunfire suddenly stops as the helicopter approaches, easing directly over the top of the tower. Tyrone swerves out of the way as something drops down, nearly hitting him. It clatters against the scaffolding bar he is gripping onto to stop himself from being dislodged by the downdraft.

Focusing, Tyrone sees the rung of a ladder swaying in front of him and suddenly understands. He quickly grabs onto the rung before anyone changes their minds about picking up the stranded squaddie from the middle of the undead horde.

He doesn't know how, but Tyrone manages to climb up the ladder, fighting against the downdraft, the wind, and the rain, almost to the top. His strength almost spent, someone grips the back of his combat vest to help haul him up over the edge and into the helicopter's hold.

"We've got him," a voice shouts above the din and Tyrone feels the floor beneath him tilt. "You're one lucky bastard," the voice says as Tyrone is pulled up and into a seat. "You were about to be vaporised."

"What?" Tyrone manages to blurt out.

"Here, look," a man in a helmet says into his ear then leans back, points his two fingers at his eyes and then directs Tyrone's vision out of the hold.

Tyrone follows the man's direction and looks out of the open hold door. Already in the distance, he sees the small park, in the middle of which, he can just make out, is the tower surrounded by a mass of bodies.

A few seconds pass and a white light erupts at the epicentre of the park directly where the tower stood. A massive fireball instantaneously engulfs the white light and a mushroom cloud begins to form above the whole scene.

Moments after the explosion hits, the helicopter tilts again and Tyrone's view of the explosion is cut off.

"A drone strike," the man shouts at Tyrone, but all he can think of is his mate, Jason.

Chapter 4

Spiralling this way and that, the flames catch me in a trance as they flicker higher on their eternal dance, the heat from the fire drying out the skin on my face. Fire has always held a fascination for me, ever since I was a child and it nearly bit me more than once when I was young; a memory of me, hidden in the garden playing with matches crosses my mind. I am burning a stray thread from the bottom of my pyjama leg when a whoosh of blue flame travels up the outside of the material, burning through the build-up of fluff. I jumped out of my skin and luckily, nothing more than the fluff caught on fire. Straight after my scare, I quietly went to put the matches back, with a smell of singed hair following me. I didn't mention my fright to anyone, especially my mother.

A loud crackle explodes out of a damp log, its ember shooting up into the air. The ember joins the countless others pluming out of the top of the fire. My head eases back to watch them rise into the night sky before they are lost in the twinkling stars where their fuel is exhausted. Perhaps there is an all-knowing being watching our plight from above? If there is, I hope they are enjoying the show!

"Hey soldier, are you away with the fairies again?"

"I'm afraid I might have been," I reply, pulled back to reality by Catherine's voice.

41

"Here, I got you a fresh beer," Catherine says handing me a bottle as she takes her seat next to me on the tree trunk in front of the fire.

"Great, thanks. I was just thinking, you know."

"I certainly do, Andy. There is so much to think about, but I thought we were going to try and have a night off?"

"I know, I'm sorry. Are the girls okay?"

"Yes; they're still watching the film, snuggled up on the settee."

"She's such a lovely girl Stacey is, isn't she?"

"Yes. Is that what you were thinking about?" Catherine asks.

"Amongst other things. I feel so sorry for her, and useless."

"Don't be silly. You tried to reach her parents and if there was anything more you could do for her, you would." Catherine volunteers.

"I know," I say, but do I? We circled their building a couple of times and gave it a cursory look, but no more. Karen and Jim could easily still have been holed up inside and it's possible they still are. We flew off at the first sign of trouble; could we have done more, gone inside to look for them, even?

"Try not to beat yourself up about it, it was out of your control," Catherine soothes. "Things are feeling down today because it's quiet after the others left yesterday and we don't know what the future holds. We've got to come to terms with it and form a plan for the future."

"It certainly is quiet around here without Dixon." I smile.

"Yes, he's definitely a character, alright. Funny how Emily took to him."

"And him to her," I laugh. "He didn't seem the type."

"A soft centre under that rugged exterior," Catherine jokes.

"Definitely," I reply.

"I hope Josh and Alice aren't too much longer," Catherine says.

"I'm sure they won't be. Josh is driving after all, so he can't drink too much. I'm sure it's done them good to go to the pub for a while, take their minds off things."

"You could have gone with them, you know. I wouldn't have minded staying here with the girls," Catherine says.

"I know you wouldn't have. I didn't want to go; I'd rather be here with you and Emily."

"Ah Andy, you're just a big softie too," Catherine teases me.

"I don't deny it," I reply. "Might have done Stacey good to have a change of scenery though."

"No. I think she is best here with us for the moment. It's very early days for her."

"Yes, you're right, of course," I agree.

"How are you feeling about your appointment at the hospital tomorrow?" Catherine asks, taking my hand in hers.

"I haven't given it much thought, to be honest," I answer.

"Oh, come on, you must have," Catherine insists.

"Not much, no. I've had other things on my mind. I think it will be a waste of time," I say, looking at my feet.

"Typical man. Surely, you're interested in what they can tell you about what's happened to your body? Something has changed since you fought off the infection. There's a reason why the Rabids don't attack you."

"I am interested. I just don't hold out much hope that it's going to change much. Believe me, nobody hopes they find some miraculous answer to this infection more than me," I tell Catherine.

"There you go then. It is possible some answers could be inside you."

"I guess we'll find out, but I can guarantee we won't find anything out tomorrow. They will take some blood samples and send me on my way."

"That's probably true but at least it's a start," Catherine says. "What time shall we set off?"

"We'll have an early lunch and then get on the road. Are you sure you want to come? It'll probably be a lot of waiting around?" I ask.

"You men, honestly. Of course, I am coming with you. Would you send me off alone?"

"No," I reply.

"Well, there you go. I am coming so don't ask again. The kids will be fine for a few hours. Besides, I love driving around Devon."

"So, it's a day out for you then?" I laugh.

"Absolutely!" Catherine smiles.

I take a long tug on my beer and stare into the fire again. The flames have retreated somewhat, and I debate whether to throw another log into the mix.

"Shall we go and join the girls? I'm getting a bit chilly," Catherine asks as if she has read my mind and decided for me.

"Yes," I reply, getting to my feet and holding my hand out to help Catherine up. She stumbles as she rises and I catch her in my arms, pulling her tight into me.

"My knight in shining armour," Catherine says looking up to me.

"You stumbled on purpose, didn't you?" I challenge, grinning at her.

"Who, me?" Catherine smiles, her full lips glistening in the flickering light of the fire.

"Yes, you," I say, moving in to put my lips to hers. I still find it hard to believe that I am actually kissing Catherine after so many years of admiring her beauty from afar. The two of us is the only positive thing I can think of to come out of the last horrific few days. I almost feel guilty for finding something so precious when so much has been lost.

"Something got your attention?" Catherine asks, smiling as our kiss comes to an end.

"I don't know what you mean," I reply, hoping the darkness is hiding my blushes.

"You might get lucky later if you play your cards right," Catherine teases, pulling my hand to take me with her as she heads towards the cottage.

Inside, after putting my empty beer bottle in the bin, I open the fridge to retrieve another beer. Catherine suggests making it the last beer I have tonight, what with my tests at the hospital tomorrow, and I agree. She makes herself a cup of tea and we go through to the living area to sit with Emily and Stacey for a while.

Only the girls' two heads are visible above the duvet they have brought down from the bedroom to snuggle under on the sofa. Stacey's eyes are closed, and the redness of her eyelids tells me that she has been upset again, which I am not surprised by. Emily is leaning on Stacey, and her eyes are open, although droopy and she smiles as I enter the room. I see her legs move under the duvet ready for me to sit down next to her, and so I do without her having to ask. The duvet moves again and her feet, dressed in pink socks, pop out of the side of the duvet to rest on the top of my legs. I pull the duvet over to cover her feet so they don't get cold and Catherine squeezes in next to me.

"You look tired Emily," I say, my hand moving to hold her top foot.

"I am a bit. Can I just watch the end of this?" Emily asks.

"What is it?"

"It's a rom-com," I'm told, and Catherine and I look at each other smiling, surprised by her use of the term *rom-com.*

"How much is left?" I ask.

"Not much, I don't think," Emily replies vaguely.

Not much turns into at least another three-quarters of an hour and it is me who has dozed off by the time the film finishes. A nudge from Catherine wakes me with a start just in time for me to see the film's titles begin to roll.

Emily gets up to get ready for bed with no protests and Stacey wakes as Emily releases herself from the duvet without any subtlety. Stacey decides to follow Emily upstairs to get herself ready for bed. She tells Catherine and me that she is okay before she goes, telling us that she is only tired. Neither Catherine nor I believe her, but we say nothing so as not to upset her any more than she is before bed.

Emily calls for Catherine to come and say goodnight to her when I tuck her in, which I find reassuring. Stacey, in the bed across the room, had her eyes closed before I entered, and she doesn't open them before Catherine and I leave the room. I am fairly sure that she is pretending to be asleep, so I don't push her, and simply wish her goodnight as I leave.

"Shall we go straight to bed too?" Catherine asks me on the landing, just outside our room.

"As tempting as that is, do you mind if we wait until Josh and Alice get back?"

"They're not children, I'm sure they can sort themselves out, Andy," Catherine tells me.

"I know, but old habits die hard. I'd just like to see them when they get back to check they are okay after their first outing. Can we give them half an hour?" I ask. "Maybe we could cosy up on the sofa…" I quickly add embarrassingly, fearing I have blown my chance with my gorgeous woman for the night and feeling like a foolish love-struck teenager.

"Oh Andy, you are a funny one," Catherine smiles. "Okay, but you're not getting past first base."

"We'll see about that," I threaten and chase Catherine down the stairs.

No sooner have I caught her and thrown Catherine onto the sofa, ready to attack and with her squealing with laughter, than an engine sounds outside the cottage and headlights shine through the front window.

"I told you that you wouldn't get past first base. Now off you get, the children are back," Catherine announces victoriously, sniggering.

"I may have lost the battle, but I'll win the war," I counter and kiss her before I quickly get to my feet and

47

straighten myself up before Josh and Alice come through the front door.

"I wouldn't have it any other way." Catherine winks as she moves into a casual sitting position on the sofa.

Josh and Alice are chatting away as the front door closes and they come through to the lounge. As soon as they see us an awkward silence breaks out.

"Not disturbing you are we, Dad?" Josh says with a cheeky smile on his face.

"No, not at all. We've just put Emily to bed," I mumble. "How was the pub?" I ask quickly, changing the subject.

"It was okay, a small country pub, a proper spit and sawdust place. Everyone was talking about the infection though. They have even put an old portable TV on the bar and had the news on the whole time," Josh says.

"Wasn't the night off we were hoping for, to be honest," Alice admits.

"I don't think there's any getting away from it," I volunteer.

"We did get to talk though," Josh tells me.

"Oh yes, what about?" I ask, suspiciously eyeing Josh whose turn it is to look suddenly awkward.

"Well," Josh starts, looking anywhere but at me and looking mostly at the floor. "We've all been through an ordeal, Dad, and I know what you went through to find me and get me to safety. But I can't just sit around here when I'm needed elsewhere…"

"No," I announce, cutting Josh off mid-sentence, knowing exactly what he is going to say. "That isn't happening, no way! Catherine, tell him," I order, my stomach dropping.

"Hold on a minute, Andy, Josh hasn't finished what he was saying. Let's hear him out," Catherine replies, unbelievably not following my lead.

"I don't need to hear him out; I know exactly what he is going to say and it's not happening. Don't play dumb, Catherine, you know where this is going. Wait a minute, have you two talked about this already, behind my back?" I storm, losing my cool.

"No, Josh and I haven't discussed anything behind your back, Andy, and I'll thank you for not talking to me that way. I'm not dumb! Josh has a right to say his piece and you need to listen to him," Catherine fires back at me.

"I'm sorry, I wasn't calling you dumb," I say, regaining some of my cool. "Okay Josh, please continue."

"Not until you calm down, Dad," Josh insists.

"Okay," I say, taking a deep breath before looking at my son, "I'm calm. Close the door though; I don't want your sister overhearing your hare-brained plan."

"You're not calm, Dad," Josh tells me as he closes the lounge door. "Please listen to me. You above all should understand how I'm feeling."

"Should I? I've never seen anything like these things."

"No, but you missed most of my childhood in one country or another, supposedly fighting evil for queen and country. Now I'm not trying to belittle what you did, Dad, you know how proud of you I am and that I've always looked up to you. But evil is actually here in our own country, on our own doorstep, and you expect me to leave it to someone else to fight. That's not the way I was brought up, it's not me. It's my duty to fight this evil wherever I find it, and you would do exactly the same if you were in my position, wouldn't you?"

Silence falls over the room when Josh finishes saying his piece and all I can hear is Dan howling in laughter at me, telling me, *He's got you there, Boss. No doubt about it, he's got you there. Right where it hurts!*

How I miss Dan, I think as I look up at my son. Dan always cut through the bullshit and said it just how it was. I am forced to concede that Dan would have been right, and Josh has got me by the short and curlies.

"So, what's your plan?" I say to Josh with a tear in my eye.

"To report back for duty. Alice and I are going to try and stay together but that's not really up to us."

"Alice, is this really what you want?" I ask, looking at her.

"It is, Andy; I feel the same as Josh. I might be American, but this country is as good as home for me," she tells me without a second to think.

"Well, it sounds like your minds are made up, despite what I think."

"I wonder where Josh gets that from?" Catherine interjects.

"Thank you, Catherine," I reply, slightly irritated.

"Well, I'm not wrong," she pushes, but I let it slide because after all, she is completely right.

"I will speak to Lieutenant Winters, see if he can sort you out with a posting behind the lines. You'd still be doing your duty and helping in the fight, but hopefully not in direct danger," I say to Josh and Alice.

"No, Dad. Thanks, but that's not what we want. We will go where we are ordered, and if that is on the front line, then so be it. We don't want any special treatment," Josh tells me, and Alice nods in agreement.

"But…" I try.

"Dad, no. But you could ask him if he can get Alice and me rolled into the same unit, so that we stay together, but no more, okay?"

I look back at Catherine in the hope that she might back me up on this one. There is no quarter given from her; however, she looks away from me, holding her hand up.

I am fighting a losing battle, that much is clear. That wouldn't stop me fighting, however, if I didn't have sympathy with their arguments and knew deep down that they were committed and probably right.

"Okay," I concede. "I'll phone the Lieutenant in the morning. I just wish there were another way."

"I know Dad; it frightens me to death. But it frightens me more that I'll look back when I'm your age knowing I took the easy way out and didn't do all I could," Josh says, looking me straight in the eye.

"Come here, champ," I say, holding out my arms. Josh gives me a tight hug, which I return and savour. "You two look out for each other," I tell the two youngsters as Josh moves back.

"We will Andy, and thanks," Alice says.

"There isn't anything to thank me for, Alice," I tell her.

"Come on," Catherine says, moving to my side and clinging onto my arm. "Let's get some rest. Tomorrow is going to be a busy day."

"Yes, that's right, you've got your trip to the hospital. What time are you going?" Josh asks.

"After lunch. Get some rest you two, it sounds like you're going to need it."

"I'm going to set up my bed as soon as you lot get out of my bedroom," Josh jokes.

"I'm going up now, I'm beat," Alice says. "I'll see you all in the morning."

Alice leaves the lounge as we say good night to her. She is in the box room upstairs, which is barely longer than she is tall. Josh moves to get his bedding out of the cupboard and both Catherine and I give him a hug goodnight before we leave him to get his bed ready.

"I hope you didn't mind me being honest down there?" Catherine asks as she gets into bed beside me.

"No, I didn't, you were right. I'm sorry for getting upset and saying what I said. I didn't mean it; you know that don't you?"

"Of course, I do. It was a shock for you and understandable," Catherine says as she puts her head on my chest.

"Still, no excuse for talking to you like that. You didn't seem that shocked."

"I had an inkling something was afoot," Catherine replies.

"Oh, how?"

"I saw them talking before the barbecue, and they both looked quite serious."

"Why didn't you mention it?" I ask.

"I wasn't sure. I just got a feeling, but I didn't want to worry you unnecessarily. It could have been nothing."

"It is worrying, and you know how Emily will react."

"I know, but we will deal with it," Catherine reassures me.

"Yes, we will," I agree. "It seems you won the war after all."

"What?" Catherine says, confused.

"I didn't get past first base tonight."

"Never mind, we've plenty of time, and as Alice says, I'm beat."

"Me too," I confess.

Catherine is soon asleep, breathing heavily against my chest. I am quickly discovering that she has no trouble when it comes to sleeping. I wish I could say the same. I slept long and hard when we first arrived at the cottage, drained from events, but that was a one off and I have slept only in fits and starts since. And as I listen to Catherine's breathing, my mind starts to work overtime. Dread begins to fill my belly the more I think about Josh leaving to face the Rabids again. I have to move from under Catherine as my heart rate increases and I begin to overheat. Pushing the duvet off myself at least evaporates the sweat that comes as I run through the different connotations of Josh's and Alice's futures. I have trouble forming any positive scenarios for them, staring at the ominous shadows on the ceiling as the night draws on.

Chapter 5

"Morning all. Something smells good!" I announce when I get downstairs and enter the kitchen. It seems that I am the last up, but I would still bet I got the least amount of sleep last night. I haven't a clue what time it was when my brain finally relented and allowed me to drift off. All I know is that it was in the early hours of the morning and if it wasn't for the smell of bacon and sausages cooking, I'd probably have slept on.

I surprisingly feel quite refreshed and energised this morning despite my troubled night. At some time in the night, I concluded that Josh had made his decision and no matter my reservations, I must support him. His decision has actually made me immensely proud of him. He wants to do his bit to fight the infection and if circumstances were different, I would be mounting up with him, that is for sure, even in my middle age.

Josh stands guarding the grill, cooking tongs in hand, ready to tackle the sizzling sausages and bacon. He is definitely a chip off the old block; no one else dares approach the cooker while he's in command of it.

I lean forward and kiss Emily on the top of her head, and she barely acknowledges me, her eyes fixed in anticipation on the spitting sausages under the grill—she does enjoy a morning fry up.

I am not looking forward to breaking Josh's news to her, not one bit.

"Nice of you to join us," Catherine teases as I lean over to kiss her good morning. "I was about to send up a search party."

"I got fed up with waiting for my breakfast in bed," I respond.

"You'd have been waiting a long time for that," Catherine says and smiles.

"How's my breakfast coming along, Josh? Don't overdo the bacon," I tell him as I go over to him.

"You let me worry about the bacon, old-timer," he snaps at me with an annoyed look.

"I've caught one on my hook," I laugh.

"Very funny! Why don't you sit down and drink your coffee?" Josh says.

"Don't worry, I'm not going to interfere," I tell him, putting my arm around his neck, squeezing it playfully.

"Get off, Dad," Josh insists, pulling away and raising the cooking tongs in a threatening manner.

"Okay, okay," I say, and I take a seat next to Catherine, satisfied that I've wound Josh up like he was a little boy again.

"Morning Alice, did you sleep okay?" I ask, looking at Alice in a chair opposite.

"Morning Andy. I got some sleep, thanks."

"Where's Stacey?" I ask, looking around.

"I looked in on her a few minutes ago and she said she would be down shortly," Catherine tells me.

"Okay, good," I reply.

"You seem in a good mood," Catherine says.

"Yes, I suppose I am. I had a good think about things last night," I say looking at Josh, "and I am feeling more positive about the hospital. It could provide some answers and you never know, they could find something useful for all of us."

"Let's hope," Catherine replies.

"Can't I come with you Dad?" Emily asks again.

"No, you won't enjoy it anyway. There'll be a lot of boring waiting around, so you'll be better off here. We will be back before you know it anyway."

Emily's eyes divert back to Josh and the sausages with a look of defeat and without saying another word. Taking the opportunity, I get my phone out of my pocket to catch up with the latest news on the infection.

The reading isn't good. North London is still a battleground with no indication of who is actually winning the battle. The government are trying to make positive noises about how operations are going. I am not convinced, well aware of how governments tend to try and paint roses out of a pile of shit. And from what I'm reading, this sounds like the latter.

More outbreaks are reported in South London, which has now also been designated a quarantine area. The South Circular Road has joined the North Circular to form a quarantine perimeter to encircle London. The outbreaks are being dealt with more decisively south of the river than when the outbreak happened in North London and are reported to be contained. Overwhelming force is used to contain any hint of an outbreak. Troops line the streets and strategic airstrikes are hitting that part of the city at regular intervals. Bombs are raining down on poor civilians cowering in their homes. They must feel like they have been transported to one of the far-flung under-siege cities that they see on the news or one of the televised Save the Children donation adverts.

Martial law and night-time curfews are enforced throughout the UK, brought in to tackle the riots and looting that was spreading from city to city like wildfire. The softly-softly approach to bring the rioters under control was quickly abandoned and scores of rioters, and/or looters have been shot in almost every large city in the country. The public may have protested at the deadly force, to begin with, but at least the towns and cities outside London are now calm. All, that is, except the towns and villages lining the River Thames, east of London.

Bodies have begun to wash up on the coastline down river from London, lots of bodies and the Thames Flood Barrier has been closed to stop more bodies from washing down river. But it wasn't closed until bloated zombies began to stagger out of the river and into the towns and villages that line the river downstream. The authorities are insisting that no significant outbreaks have been caused by undead wandering up the beaches along the coast. I am not convinced by that claim and neither are the countries that border the North Sea and the English Channel, they are up in arms. Holland has closed all its sea defences, and countries such as Germany, Belgium, France and beyond are all on high alert in case bodies that were washed out to sea make port on their coastlines.

Finally, yesterday, the government froze all prices and wages, effectively putting the UK economy on hold. They also secured an undisclosed but eye-watering large loan from the World Bank, rumoured to be well in excess of two trillion US dollars, a figure I cannot even begin to comprehend.

I must avert my eyes from my phone screen before the entire refreshed and energised feeling I was basking in when I arrived downstairs is extinguished completely.

"Happy days, eh?" Catherine says from beside me as my phone plonks onto the table in front of me.

"Very," I reply, rolling my eyes.

"Don't wallow in it. You were positive when you came down, remember that," she says, taking my hand in hers.

"I'm trying, believe me, I'm trying," I reply with a somewhat forced smile.

Catherine smiles back at me, with a smile that I can only wish, mine was as convincing as.

Josh announces that breakfast is nearly ready, and I look around the table, noticing that Stacey still hasn't come down from her room. I go to get up from the table to go and get her, but I hear a door slam from upstairs and then footsteps crashing down the stairs. The noise takes us all by surprise and in unison, we look towards the kitchen's entrance.

"Andy!" Stacey cries as she bursts into the kitchen, her phone to her ear, looking as though she has seen a ghost. "It's my mum!"

Stacey's words hit me like a thunderbolt. I am flabbergasted, frozen for a second, unable to answer her.

"Andy, she wants to speak to you!" I hear Stacey say as she thrusts the phone across the table towards me.

Quickly pulling myself together, I reach out to take the phone from Stacey's shaking grasp.

"Hello, Karen, is that you?" I ask redundantly as I get up from the table and leave the kitchen, which has fallen into complete silence apart from the sound of sizzling.

"Andy, thank God. Yes, it's me," Karen replies, her voice quiet and croaky.

"Where are you, and *how* are you?" I blurt.

"I'm still at work inside our building, with Jim. We're wiped out but okay; we've been hiding in a storage room, but we don't know what to do now. The zombie creatures seem to have vanished, so we snuck into one of the offices to use the phone. The power is out so our mobiles died, and we couldn't risk moving before. What shall we do? Can you still come and get us?"

"We did come for you in a helicopter, but the building seemed to be overrun," I tell her.

"I think we heard the helicopter flying around the building, but we couldn't risk coming out. It was too risky then."

"I don't know what I can do, Karen; we escaped to Devon." The line goes quiet for a moment, but in the background, I hear Karen becoming upset. "Karen?" I say into the phone.

"Andy, it's Jim. I'm sorry to put pressure on you but can you tell us what to do?"

"Hello, Jim..." is all I can think of to say for a moment.

"Are you there Andy?"

"Yes, sorry Jim, I was thinking. Are the zombies still in the building? Can you get outside?" I ask.

"They're still inside, we can hear them on other floors occasionally."

"Shit," I say out loud before I can stop myself. "So, you're safe where you are for the moment?"

"I think so, we're in a small office and we've got the door barricaded."

"Can I phone you back? I need to think," I ask.

"You won't be able to phone us, it'll just go through to the main switchboard," Jim tells me.

"Okay, let me think."

"Take all the time you need, Andy."

A minute or two passes before I speak again, my mind racing to think of some way to help them, but I come up empty-handed of any plausible suggestions. "Jim, can you phone me back? I need to think this through properly. Say in an hour?"

"Yes Andy, we can do that. Anything you can do to help us; we're desperate to see Stacey again."

"I'll try my best, Jim, you know that."

"Yes, Andy, we do, thank you. We'll phone you back in an hour, yes?"

"Yes, in an hour."

I pull the phone away from my ear, my head spinning. I don't move from the spot, unable to contemplate the barrage of questions that will surely come when I go back into the others. Eventually, I sit down on the sofa that's behind me in the lounge, trying to calm my thinking, staring at the floor.

"Andy?" Stacey says quietly from the door across the room. Her face looks desperately at me for any positive news, news that I don't have for her.

I look up at her and smile. "They are alive, Stacey; they are still inside their work building, but they are alive. That's good news and they are going to phone us back in an hour. That is all I can tell you at the moment; I need to think it over, okay?"

"Please help them, Andy," she begs me, tears rolling down her cheeks.

I get up and go over to her, putting my hands on her shoulders to look her straight in the eyes. "I will do whatever I can, Stacey, I promise you that."

"Thank you," she snivels.

"Come on, let's go and see the others," I say, directing Stacey back to the kitchen.

Thankfully, everybody lets Stacey and me sit down before anyone says a word and Josh even starts to put the breakfast out.

"What's happening Dad?"

Unsurprisingly, it is Emily who is the first to ask a question and I tell her and everyone what I know, not that it satisfies my little girl's curiosity.

"They have to get out and come here with us, don't they, Dad? Stacey is really missing them."

"Yes, I know she is, and we're going to try and figure a way out to help them. But we need to think about it. It isn't going to be easy for them to get out of London, you know that Emily, don't you?"

"No, it won't be easy, but you'll think of something, Dad, you always do," Emily says while she fiddles with her knife and fork.

No pressure then, I think to myself as my young daughter inadvertently applies it. The table goes silent with all eyes on me, waiting for my response to Emily's innocent interrogation.

"I'm trying to think of a way to help them Emily, but it's going to take time. Now let's have breakfast while I think and then after breakfast, Josh, Alice, Catherine, and I will talk about it, okay?" I say looking at Stacey.

Stacey nods her understanding and Emily says, 'okay, Dad,' while Josh brings the plates over.

"Emily, it's a nice day outside, so why don't you and Stacey go and play for half an hour while we clear up the dishes?" I say when breakfast is finished.

"So, you can talk, you mean?" Emily answers.

"Yes Emily, so we can talk while we're clearing up."

"Okay," Emily replies and jumps down from her chair. "Come on Stacey, let's leave the brainboxes to think."

"Stacey, can you leave your phone with me? I'll call you when they phone back," I ask, and she leaves it on the table where she was seated before she takes Emily's hand to go outside.

"The poor girl; I feel so sorry for her," Catherine says as soon as the back door closes.

"We all do," Alice agrees.

"So, any ideas anyone, because I'm struggling?" I confess.

"Let's give Lieutenant Winters a call, see if he can help?" Josh suggests.

"I don't think that's an option," I reply.

"Why? There may be troops in that area who could get them out," Josh points out.

"The area is in quarantine, so even if there are troops there, they won't be going into random buildings to get civilians out," I answer.

"Then we go and get them. Perhaps the Lieutenant can arrange for us to borrow a helicopter?"

"Josh, Winters is only a lieutenant, he won't have that authority. Even if he wanted to help with an escape plan for two people he's never met. When he worked under Colonel Reed, he had more power than he should have had for a lieutenant. Colonel Reed is dead, along with any extra authority Winters had. I don't think we can count on Winters for any help, not this time," I explain.

"No, you're probably right," Josh concedes. "But we've got to do something, for Stacey's sake."

"I'm not sure there is much that can be done, unfortunately," Catherine volunteers.

I don't say anything, but Catherine may be right in this instance, as much as it pains me to admit it. Karen and Jim are stranded; the best they can do is try and hold out until it's over and London is liberated if that is ever going to happen. Stacey will be devastated, but what can we do from our holiday cottage on the coast in Devon?

I am just about to have my say and admit that Catherine is right when Alice says something.

"What about the river?" She says, out of the blue.

"The river?" I ask. "What do you mean?"

"Can we use the river? My father's best friend from his university days lives right on the river with his wife, in Richmond. Their house backs straight onto the Thames. He worked in the diplomatic service for the US government; he was based in London and they never went back to the States when he retired. They have a small river boat, I know, as I've been out on it plenty of times. Stacey's parents' building isn't far from the river, is it?" Alice explains.

"What are you suggesting? That you use his boat to sail into London to mount some kind of rescue mission?" Catherine asks, bewildered.

"It's an idea," Alice replies.

"A damn stupid one!" Catherine states angrily. "Isn't it Andy?"

I don't answer for a moment while I consider Alice's suggestion. The very last thing I want to do is go back into London. I dread even thinking about it. But I asked for ideas and Alice has given me one, which I am forced to consider on its merits.

"Dad?" Josh says.

"Andy, you can't possibly be considering this!" Catherine insists.

"We have to think it through if we want to help Karen and Jim," I explain.

"It's one thing trying to help them and quite another setting off on a suicide mission for them! I know how you feel about Stacey; I feel the same, but this is madness. Think of your daughter," Catherine says exasperatedly.

"I am thinking of her, as well as Stacey. I am not even saying it's possible but let's consider it. Please calm down so that we can talk about it, see if it's viable," I ask her.

"Fine! You're all nuts, anyway. Addicted to the thrill of the danger." Catherine has her last say but then does calm down…some.

"Okay, let's assume we decide to go for it, what would be the obstacles?" I ask.

"Would they let us use the boat?" Josh starts us off.

"I'm sure they would. They are a lovely couple and if they don't, then we will have to insist, but I don't think that will be an issue," Alice assures us.

"The army isn't just going to let you sail up the river like it's the bloody boat race or something. The river will be cordoned off, surely?" Catherine makes a very good point.

"It will definitely be cordoned off by armed forces, but the river will be in use for operations, I'm sure of that. We would have to blag our way through the cordon. I've done it before, on more than one occasion," I offer.

"Oh, I'm sure you have, Mr Superhero!" Catherine hisses sarcastically.

"Thank you, Catherine," I respond gently. "So, say if we get through the cordon, we follow the river until we get as close to their building as possible. That is when it'll get dangerous, but we do have one advantage…"

"Here we go," Catherine interrupts me sarcastically, rolling her eyes, "Andy's superpower!"

"It's not a superpower Catherine, but it is an advantage," I reply.

"Come on Andy, you don't know if it even still works. Just because the infected ignored you on that day doesn't mean they still will. They could be tearing you to bits as soon as they see you, and you'd deserve it!" Catherine's anger builds.

"Excuse me, what did you just say? I'd deserve it?" Now it's my turn to sound angry and hurt.

"I'm sorry. I didn't mean it; you know I didn't," Catherine says, looking at me with a wounded expression. "I just don't want to lose you, any of you," she says, looking up to Josh and Alice.

"I know you didn't mean it," I say, taking her hand. "We are just talking it through, don't forget. We don't know if whatever it was that stopped the Rabids attacking me still works, but it did work. I could walk right past them."

"That was then, this is now."

"Okay, let's assume for the sake of argument that it does still work. I go ashore once we reach our destination, go to the building, enter it, find Karen and Jim, and then bring them back to the boat. Josh and Alice will cover our escape."

"Simple; I don't know what I was worried about!" Catherine says. "If you think it's going to be that easy then you're all completely crazy."

"No one is saying it's going to be that easy; we sure as shit know it won't be. It's just a basic outline. That phone is going to ring any minute and we need to tell them if we have something, or we don't. If we do, we are going to have to form a detailed plan of the mission. So, Josh, Alice, what do you think?"

"I think it's the beginning of a plan and we should look at it closer," Josh offers.

"Me too," Alice agrees.

"It's a barmy plan, if you're interested to know my opinion," Catherine says.

"Okay. I'll tell Karen and Jim that we are looking into a plan, but we need more time to work out the details. I'll tell them to stay put and phone us back in say… two hours?" I suggest.

"Agreed," say both Josh and Alice.

"This is too much," Catherine says, getting up from the table, angrily grabbing my plate from in front of me.

"What do you suggest we do then, Catherine?" I ask.

Josh and Alice look at each other apprehensively; they can feel trouble brewing, just as I can. They quickly make their excuses and leave the kitchen, like rats leaving a sinking ship. Josh gives me a grimace as he goes and mouths good luck as he disappears.

"Please don't be angry Catherine," I say when we are alone. "I just feel like I've got to do something to help Stacey's parents."

Plates crash together in the sink as Catherine turns on the hot tap, but she says nothing. I go up behind her and put my arms around her waist and my head nuzzles into the side of her neck.

"That won't work," Catherine says, pulling her head away from me. "I know you want to help them, but does that have to include putting yourself in so much danger?"

"I can't think of another way. Can you?"

"No, but perhaps that means there isn't a way, and they will have to try and ride it out themselves, like everyone else. And you shouldn't be encouraging your son either, never mind Alice."

"They had already made their decision to report back for duty. They could have been back on the front-line tomorrow and you supported that, remember?" I point out.

"That's different and you know it, Andy!"

"Why's it different? Them going back on duty could have been just as dangerous or even more so."

"That was them going back on duty and not on a foolish rescue mission," Catherine says, unrelenting.

"We are the only chance Karen and Jim have, Catherine."

"And what about your hospital appointment this afternoon?"

"I will have to rearrange it when I get back," I tell her.

"If they'll let you."

"Of course, they will. Listen, I don't want us to fight."

"Neither do I. I'm just afraid," Catherine says and turns to me.

"I know, it's not somewhere I'm in any rush to go back to. But I feel I've got to, for Stacey's sake."

"Promise you'll come back to me," Catherine says, looking into my eyes.

"I promise," I tell her and pull her in close to me.

Chapter 6

After we have talked, Catherine calms down and comes to accept that we are going back to London despite the danger. I made her another promise, that if my apparent invisibility to the Rabids has gone, we will turn the boat around and head straight back. It was an easy promise to make because the whole mission is dependent on my concealment. If we get there and the first Rabid I see attacks, there is no way I will be able to go into the building and we will have failed. There is no way around that, not with just the three of us.

Karen and Jim rang us back and their relief that we were working on a plan to get them out was overwhelming for them. I had to make them understand, however, that we could only try our utmost to reach them but absolutely nothing was guaranteed. They were almost in shock when I asked them to phone us back in two hours and I passed them over to Stacey.

Then came the hard part, speaking to Emily and telling her that Josh, Alice, and I were leaving to help Stacey's parents. She took the news far better than I had expected, she was happy that we were going to get Stacey's parents back. I didn't go into detail with her though, and I certainly didn't tell her of the dangers we would inevitably have to tackle.

"Dad's going to get your mum and dad for you, with Josh and Alice!" Emily exclaims to Stacey when she joins us after finishing on the phone with them.

"Yes, I know. I've got my fingers crossed, Emily," Stacey replies.

"You don't need to cross them; he will get them back. Remember how he got Josh back?" Emily informs Stacey.

No pressure then, I think to myself again, as Emily gets over-excited.

"I know he will try his best, but my mum said it won't be easy," Stacey tells Emily before turning to me. "Thank you, Andy," she says.

"We will do all we can Stacey, but I can't guarantee anything. You know that?" I ask her.

"Yes, I understand," she confirms.

"Come on Emily, you, me and Stacey will have a walk down to the beach and let them get ready," Catherine says, reading my mind.

"That's a good idea isn't it, Emily?" I agree.

"As long as you don't go without saying goodbye," Emily replies.

"Of course, we won't. You'll be back long before then."

A few minutes later, I watch out of the kitchen window as Emily leads them down the beach path towards the sand dunes and the beach beyond. The changeable weather of late proves that Autumn is closing in but it's a nice day outside today. As they disappear, I am more than a bit jealous that I can't join them on their trip to the beach.

"Shall we, Dad?" Josh asks from behind me. "Alice and I have got the equipment in from the shed?"

Reluctantly, I drag my gaze away from the beautiful view of Devon that the kitchen window offers. Josh and Alice are eager to get preparations underway and to get back into the fight. They are young and crave the action. I am definitely not young, and I've seen enough action for two lifetimes. I've had my fill of it. Even the drive back up the M5 to Bristol and then onto the M4 to London fills me with dread. The drive isn't particularly long; we should reach London in about three hours, but London is the last place on earth I want to go back to. I'd much rather nip upstairs, put on some loud swim shorts, grab a towel, and join Catherine and the girls on the beach.

Alice is already hard at work when I follow Josh into the lounge. She is seated on the sofa with her SA80 rifle in pieces on the coffee table in front of her. Her concentration on the weapon is total, so she doesn't give me a second look as I enter the room. My M4 is standing against the arm of the sofa waiting for my attention, with the rest of the kit in the middle of the floor.

I don't know if I can face it, I think when I see my weapon. I need to get my head in the game. I make my excuses, leave the lounge, and head upstairs to take a moment and to use the loo.

I stop suddenly when I enter the bedroom; lying on the bed is something I'd hoped I'd never see again. Set out across the bed is a combat uniform and I am confused about where it has come from. I edge close to it, as if afraid it might bite me. Catherine must have put it out for me, but God knows where she has conjured it up from and below the bed, sitting on the floor, are the boots I arrived in.

Hanging on the end bedpost is my worn combat vest. I thought the vest had been discarded, thrown away after I had stripped it off on the doorstep when we first arrived at the cottage. Perhaps Catherine knew that it was inevitable that I would need to suit up again and she had kept it. She knew that the nightmare hadn't ended, not for any of us.

Deep down, I always knew it too. I don't know why I torture myself with fantasies of spending a day at the beach. This is my uniform, not a pair of overpowering swim shorts and sunglasses. My arms reach to pull off my t-shirt, and quickly I am standing in front of the tall mirror in the corner of the room looking at myself, dressed for combat. The uniform feels as though I've never taken it off and the only thing missing is my sand-coloured beret with the winged dagger insignia of the SAS.

I have no immediate idea where I lost the beret? Is it still in Sir Malcolm's private bathroom at the Orion building, or did I lose it on my trek through London or at the battle of Notting Hill? I didn't have it on at Heathrow Airport before the airport was nuked, my brain thinks through the fog of that day. As I go to use the loo before joining Josh and Alice, I decide the beret must be still on the floor of Sir Malcolm's bathroom.

My back shivers horribly as thoughts of the time I spent in that dreaded bathroom return; it was absolutely hell on earth. Unimaginable pain torturing my body in the darkness, nightmares and psychotic episodes nearly ripping my mind to shreds.

How I survived through that night is a mystery to me, even now. Did my body go through an unexplained metamorphosis in that horrendous time? My appointment at the hospital for tests today was supposed to tell me that. I won't be suffering those tests today. The tests will happen tomorrow, and they won't be carried out by an attentive doctor, but by the first undead Rabid, I encounter.

You're supposed to be getting your shit together, I tell myself as I flush the toilet and turn to wash my hands. I try not to look at myself in the mirror as I stand at the sink; it won't help my state of mind, but it is inevitable.

The jagged remnants of the Rabid scratch marks down the side of my face are unavoidable for me to look upon. The scabbing is almost gone but that barely improves their appearance. The swelling under the skin and their redness persists, no matter what ointments and potions Catherine gives me to dab onto them. Undoubtedly, the best relief for the marks would have been a day at the beach with the sun on my face and salt water on my skin.

Keep dreaming, I think as I switch the bathroom light off and step back into the bedroom. Picking up my trousers from a chair beside the bed, I fish in the pockets for my wallet, phone, and anything else I'll need. I check the wallet to ensure the military ID card is still in it, before I stuff it into the pocket of my combat trousers. Then, leaning down, I slide my hand under the mattress on my side of the bed until it touches cold steel. My hand closes around the grip of the Sig and I pull the gun out of its hiding place with satisfaction. Automatically, I eject the clip and check it before sliding it back home, even though I know the gun is fully loaded.

My trusted Sig is soon nestled in its home in my shoulder holster that I retrieve from the wardrobe. My Gerber combat knife is already secured in the holster; it has been since I put the holster into the wardrobe.

That's it, I think and go to exit the bedroom to go back downstairs, but suddenly I stop at the doorway. I've nearly forgotten one of life's most important pieces of kit, my bloody phone charger, and I turn to go and pull it out of the wall.

"Back in uniform, eh Dad?" Josh says with only an ounce of sympathy when I arrive back in the lounge.

"I wouldn't have it any other way," I lie. "Do you know where it came from?"

"There was quite a bit of kit in the cars that we brought down from London. Lieutenant Winters insisted I offload it on the morning, before he, Dixon and Collins left. He said we'd need it more than they would. I'm not sure he meant for another mission to London, though," Josh informs me.

"I'm sure he didn't," I agree. Although I think it's more than a coincidence that the uniform has a captain's insignia on each shoulder. "How's it going here?" I ask without pushing the subject.

"We've gone through most of the kit and separated out everything we think we will need, which is mostly weapons and ammo. The kit we are taking is over here and the rest is over there," Alice tells me pointing.

"How's the ammo looking?" I ask.

"Put it like this, if we run out, we will have been in one hell of a fight," Josh says joking, but I don't laugh. "Here, we've taken an inventory," he quickly adds, handing me a piece of paper seeing that I am not amused.

"Thanks," I say, taking the piece of paper and studying it in silence while Josh and Alice look on. "No night vision goggles then?" I ask eventually.

"No, I'm afraid not," Alice answers.

"Okay, it looks like a dawn raid then."

"Yes, Boss," Alice replies.

Alice's use of the word *boss* hits me like a ton of bricks. Memories of Dan return, as boss was his word, his term to address me. He used the word that often that I wouldn't have been surprised if he murmured it in his sleep. I can confirm that he didn't though; I've been holed up in enough crusty hotel rooms over the years with him to be sure of that. Even when we were socialising, he couldn't stop himself from calling me boss. When I would protest, he would just grin and laugh and send me to the bar to get the drinks in.

"If you don't mind, Alice, please just call me Andy. I think Dan wore out the word boss," I ask her gently.

"Oh, yes, of course, I'm sorry Andy, I never thought," she replies, blushing, her embarrassment obvious.

"Don't worry; it's not your fault. It's just a bit difficult."

"I should have thought," she says, almost to herself.

"Honestly, don't worry. Now, do we have a decent map of London?" I ask, changing the subject.

"Yes," Josh confirms, turning to look for it.

"Good, spread it out on the coffee table."

With the map spread out, Alice quickly finds Richmond and shows us where the house and boat of her family friend are situated on the river. Then, using the map and internet, we attempt to calculate how long it will take to sail down the river to reach a drop-off area on the riverbank, as close as possible to the Cheesegrater building. Our calculations turn out to be more of an educated guess, as the river twists and turns as it snakes into London, so judging the distance is tricky. We also don't know how fast the boat is and how long the delay getting through any cordon, or possibly *cordons* will be. In the end, we decide to allow at least two-and-a half hours sailing time, which is longer than I thought it would be.

"This is where the river will be cordoned off," I say, pointing to Kew Bridge on the map, a bridge which spans the Thames at the same point as the North and South Circular Roads. "That's the perimeter of the quarantine zone."

"Yes, that'll be the place," Josh agrees.

"Have you thought of a blag to get us through?" Alice questions me.

"I'm still thinking about it, but I'll come up with something," I tell her confidently.

We have less trouble identifying the best-positioned drop-off point from the boat and on to the riverbank. I had assumed that the closest position would be near Tower Bridge next to the dreaded Tower of London. I am more than a little relieved to discover that it isn't. The farther I stay away from that tower and the ghosts it has entombed in its belly, the better.

I will be dropped off at Tower Bridge's neighbour, London Bridge, with the added bonus that London Bridge is situated closer on the river as we travel. Hopping off the boat should be easy enough on that part of the riverbank and steps lead straight up off the bank and onto the bridge. Once on the bridge, it will be about a half klick jaunt up to Karen and Jim's building, hopefully using the main road that leads off the bridge all the way.

"Do you think the bridge will be barricaded?" Alice questions.

"It definitely will be on the south side of the river but hopefully not the north. But we won't know until we arrive," I answer.

"If it were me, I'd have left the north open to create a kill zone on the bridge," Josh offers.

"It's possible. Let's hope so, and let's hope I'm not a target wandering into that zone," I say.

"Surely any sniper will only target the undead?" Alice tries to assure me.

"I'm sure that's true," I reply, even though I am not. There could be some very itchy fingers attached to sleep-deprived squaddies covering the bridge.

"Do you think I should try and phone ahead, tell my parents' friends we are coming?" Alice asks.

I have to think about that one for a moment and I feel my hand go to my chin while I consider. "No," I finally say, "if they decide they are not happy about it, they could throw a very large spanner in the works. Alert the authorities even."

"But what if we travel all that way and they're not there, or if there is a problem with their boat?" Alice presses.

"Then we improvise and find another boat; there must be plenty of them on the river in Richmond," I assume.

"There always was, but who knows now?"

"We'll find one," I say confidently. "Okay, let's check comms and then load up before they get back from the beach."

Josh and Alice move as soon as I've spoken, and I finally reach over to pick up my M4 from its resting place. The weapon feels heavy in my grasp, heavier than I remember and almost alien to me. I press ahead and begin to strip it down and before I know it, my hands are moving over the rifle at speed, exactly like the professional I am.

Josh and Alice load up the gear that we are taking with us into the back of what was once Colonel Reed's black Land Rover Defender. I was surprised when Lieutenant Winters said he was going to travel back in one of the other cars that we had arrived in and leave the Defender with us. Dixon had joked that it suited him more and that he should have the Defender. Winters had none of it though and said the Defender would be more useful where it was. That it suited the countryside landscape of Devon better than any city. Winters may have been right about that, but the four-wheel-drive was about to head back to the city in any case and loaded for action to boot.

The gear that isn't required is taken back to the outside shed, then Josh and Alice disappear upstairs to change into their uniforms. With the house quiet, I take the chance and go into the kitchen and put the kettle on. Once my brew is steaming in its mug, I sit at the kitchen table, splitting my time between looking out of the window for the girls to return and contemplating the mission ahead.

My wandering mind is interrupted by a sudden ringing sound coming from Stacey's phone that is sitting on the table beside me. The word MUM is flashing on the screen and I quickly realise that it has already been two hours since I spoke to Karen and Jim, telling them to ring back. I give the phone a second to ring so that I can gather my thoughts before I pick it up to answer.

"Hello, Karen?"

"Andy, thank God. I thought you weren't going to answer for a moment then," Karen replies.

"I'm here, don't worry. Are you and Jim still secure?"

"Yes, we can still hear noises in the building, but they still seem distant."

"That's good news. You are going to have to hang on until the morning; we will try to get you out then."

"Oh Andy, thank you, you don't know how much this means to us," Karen tells me, snivelling, with Jim's voice in the background saying, *thank God.*

"Okay, listen carefully. I'll tell you what we are planning. Have you got a pen and paper there?"

"Yes," Karen replies.

"Firstly, take down my number." I give them my number. "Use that number from now on if you need to contact me or if anything changes. I have to know if things change there, and I need you two to promise me that you'll tell me straight away if they do. I'm putting myself, Josh and the other person who is coming, Alice at great risk and if things change for the worse it might become impossible for us to try."

"Of course, we promise, Andy. We know how risky this is and we won't put you in any more danger," Karen insists.

"We promise," Jim agrees.

"It's easy to say that, but if things go downhill, you may be tempted not to tell me out of fear and desperation. That wouldn't only put our lives at risk, but Stacey's too. If we don't return from there, there will be no one left to protect your daughter… or my daughter."

"That won't happen, Andy, we swear it. Stacey is the most important thing to us and if we can't protect her, then we need you to do it," Karen says.

"You can rely on it, Andy," Jim states.

"Sorry if I seem harsh, but I am trusting you on this," I tell them and they both assure me again. "Okay, this is what we are planning. We will be setting off to drive back up to London shortly. We are heading for Richmond where a contact we have has a boat. We're going to use that boat to reach central London and we will aim to arrive at just gone dawn, so we have the light. We plan on setting off at 0400 hours and arriving at around 0630 hours. Once we arrive, I will come and get you so be prepared to move at a moment's notice from 0600 onwards. Do you understand?"

"Yes, we understand, will be ready at 6 a.m. Andy," they confirm.

"Good; we are going to have to move quickly, so don't bring anything with you and don't wear anything that will slow you down. I know how you like your high heels Karen," I say, deadpan.

"I'll have flats on and don't worry Andy, I can run," Karen tells me.

"Any running will be on my orders. You will both do exactly as I say at all times, understood?"

"Understood, we are in your hands, Andy," Jim confirms.

"Good, now tell me exactly where you are in the building and the layout as best as you can."

"We're on the tenth floor," Jim begins. "We don't know if the lifts are still working but the power is out so probably not. As you come onto the tenth floor, go right and through the main doors into our company, Cole and Co. That will bring you into the reception area. From there, go right and into the main office area, which is open plan. We are in a small office off that area on the right and it will have the name Phil Matlock on the door. I think that is about all I can tell you, Andy."

The tenth floor is going to be quite a haul, I think. *I suppose it could be worse, that skyscraper must have forty or fifty floors*. I think again, trying to stay positive.

"Okay, can you think of anything Karen, any security doors or any potential hurdles?" I then ask.

"No, nothing like that. I think Jim has told you everything."

"Okay, thank you. Now, I'll want to speak to you again at certain times in the morning, so phone me back at these times. Phone me at 0345, before we set off on the boat to give me an update on your situation, and then at 0600 to do the same, understood?"

"Understood," Karen says.

"But what if the phone goes dead here for some reason, Andy?" Jim asks nervously.

"If I don't receive your calls, we will be forced to proceed as planned. So, in that case, still be ready to move from 0600."

"We will be," Jim says.

"I think that is everything. Are you both clear on the plan? Have you any questions you need to ask?"

"No, everything is clear, Andy. We will phone you at 0345 and at 0600, and be ready to move from 0600, agreed?" Karen says, sounding almost like a military operative. *Perhaps she has missed her vocation*, I think, but then quickly remember the high heels.

"Okay good. Be under no illusions tomorrow, this is not going to be easy. There will definitely be death, blood, and guts on show in that building and in the streets. It will be a miracle if I don't have to fight my way in and we all don't have to fight our way out. Our best bet is to move slow, keep quiet and stay hidden, but that probably won't be possible. So, expect frantic and gunfire, moving at speed with zombies attacking. The important thing is not to panic; even if all seems lost, don't panic. Panic will get you killed or worse, bitten. Be ready to follow my orders, even if you don't agree. There won't be time for discussions or arguments, and I know best, believe me. Agreed?"

"Absolutely Andy, we agree. You are in charge and we will be ready for anything. We just want to see Stacey again," Karen speaks for both.

"So do I and my daughter, and that will be my priority, for me to see them again. I will try my best, but if I don't think I can succeed I will be forced to abandon the mission; there are no guarantees, I'm afraid," I tell them plainly.

"We know that. We are just grateful you are going to try. Please know how grateful we are," Karen tells me.

"I do Karen," I reply. "That's everything then and I need to get final preparations ready here. So, good luck tonight and I'll speak to you in the morning." I finish.

Taking a deep breath, I lay Stacey's phone back down onto the table, my mind straining. I haven't any particular final preparations to do, I just had to get off the phone. I said my piece and now I just want to chill with another brew until the girls return and we say our goodbyes.

"What the hell!" I huff as I get up from the table and Josh hovering in the doorway makes me jump.

"What's wrong?" he asks confused.

"Why are you hovering in the doorway?"

"You were speaking, and I don't want to disturb you. Is everything okay?" Josh asks concerned.

"Yes, sorry. That call put me on edge I suppose. Did you hear it all?"

"No, just the last of it, I think," he tells me. "Are you sure you're okay, Dad?"

"I'm fine, do you want a brew?" I ask.

"You sit, I'll do it," Josh says, moving to the kettle.

"Thanks."

"What's going on Dad, it's not like you to be so jumpy?"

"That call and the thought of going back to London has me on edge," I tell him honestly.

"It's not just you who's on edge. I'm nervous as fuck, so don't beat yourself up."

"You've got the advantage of youth; I'm getting too long in the tooth for all this stress."

"You're not old Dad, well not that old. Don't forget you're still not one hundred percent after your last ordeal in London. Maybe we could delay a day or two?" Josh suggests.

"No, it's now or never. They're at the end of their tether and probably won't last another day or two. They'd get desperate and do something stupid. I'll be okay once I've got another brew inside me."

"I'm with you all the way Dad. I've been thinking, I should come with you to get them, cover your back. Alice can watch the boat," Josh says. God bless him.

"I know you'd come with me son, and if there was anyone I'd want to cover my back, it would be you. This isn't the time though; this only has any chance of succeeding if I can get past the undead without them reacting to my presence. If you came, they'd definitely attack us, and we wouldn't stand a chance. I need you to cover our retreat with Alice, okay?"

"I know it isn't an option, but I just wanted you to know that you're not alone in this," Josh tells me sincerely.

"I already know that champ, and thanks."

"Are you making me one?" Alice asks from behind me.

"If you want one?" Josh replies.

"Of course, I want one. Tea though, please. I may be American but some of your Brit's bad habits are rubbing off on me."

"Take a seat then madam; it'll be right up." Josh smiles.

"Everything good?" Alice asks, obviously having heard at least some of our conversation.

"Yes, Dad and I were just discussing the mission. I wanted to go with him to the building."

"I don't think that's a good idea," Alice says.

"Yes, I know, but I wanted to offer."

"Fair play," Alice responds.

Just as Josh puts Alice's tea in front of her, I see a little head emerging from the path in the sand dunes. Emily dashes out of the dunes and is halfway back to the house by the time Catherine and Stacey appear from in amongst the swaying long grass.

"Here comes trouble," I tell Josh and Alice.

Emily jumps straight onto my lap when she arrives in the kitchen. She doesn't say anything, she just sits hugging me tightly around my middle.

"How was the beach?" I ask eventually, after savouring her hug for a while.

"It was okay. A bit boring without you running around like a madman."

I smile, a smile that widens as Catherine comes into the kitchen, followed by Stacey. Silence ensues for a moment as we all look around the room at each other. All of us probably wondering the same thing. Will we all be here again with each other, in our hideaway on the coast of Devon? I pray that we will, and with any luck, Karen and Jim will have joined us. I try to ignore the shadow that looms in the back of my mind. I struggle incredibly hard not to acknowledge it.

Chapter 7

Major Doctor Stephen Rees's mind races back to the same time and space it always does when he allows his guard to drop. The horrific images are constantly waiting, knocking on the back of his consciousness to present themselves and to torment Rees's sanity. He knows exactly what the diagnosis is and what treatment should be prescribed for his sickness, but he won't allow his PTSD to prevent him from trying to fix the chaos and suffering his negligence has caused.

Once more, as he knows he will for eternity, Rees sees himself desperately pressing his security card against the sensor next to the locked, airtight doors blocking his path. He pants, out of breath, after his panicked scramble from his office two floors above from where Molly is overseeing the loading of equipment in the storage facility.

Not even his top-level security card will override the locking mechanism of the security doors. Not once the facilities computer algorithm has triggered the emergency quarantine procedure. The door remains locked tight, no matter how forcefully he bangs against it. All he can do is stare in terrified panic through the thick glass panel of the airtight door, through to the glass panel in the second airtight door and into the storage facility beyond.

Bright bubbled orange biohazard suits suddenly appear and then disappear from his limited view into the storage facility. Rees feels a glimmer of hope that the situation is being contained, that his trusted Lieutenant and colleague Molly is already following protocol and implementing the facilities decontamination procedures.

On his tiptoes, Rees cranes his neck to try and get a better view through the doors to see what is happening, to see if the protocols are being adhered to. He manages to catch a glimpse of Molly and then all at once, he goes dizzy as dread and terror rip through his entire body. Inexplicably, Molly is outside her biohazard suit and exposed. *What is she thinking,* Rees panics? She is not following procedure; she could be contaminated, and containment could be lost.

A flash of bright light blinds Rees for a second and he ducks in reflex as a thunderous boom explodes from inside the storage facility. The door in front of him shakes, and the building around him shudders from the shocking explosion. Rees's panic escalates as he tries to regather himself, looking again to see what has happened inside.

Smoke billows up to the ceiling and light flickers beyond the glass and on the far side of the storage room. *There's a fire*, Rees's mind screams as he waits for the storage facility's fire suppression system to activate. *Why isn't it kicking in?* he thinks as Molly's panicked face suddenly comes back into his view as she races towards the sanctuary of the decontamination room.

Rees watches dumbfounded in terror as a figure crashes into Molly, knocking her out of view and stopping her from reaching her salvation. Rees only catches a glimpse of the figure as it careers into Molly. Just a fleeting glimpse of the heinous creature's face as it follows Molly down, its evil eyes fixed on her and its mouth gaping. The beast's grotesque features are haunting Rees's mind as they will for the rest of eternity.

"ETA, ten minutes."

The announcement feeds into Rees's ears through the headset that adorns the top of his head. Instantly, the beast's hideous face retreats into the back of his mind, but it doesn't disappear; it lurks in the background somewhere, watching and waiting for its chance to terrorize Rees again.

Replacing the tormenting creature's image is the lush green countryside of Devon, dotted with villages, dissected by grey winding roads. Rees turns his head to try and get a bearing on where they are, the sweat from his day terror dampening the clothes against his skin. The city of Plymouth is close enough for him to see in the near distance; they will soon be leaving the green of the countryside behind.

"Are you feeling alright Major?" a different voice asks through Rees's headset.

"Yes, I'm fine thank you Lieutenant," Rees replies.

Rees fidgets in the seat of the comparatively comfortable helicopter his superiors laid on for this trip. He is far more used to the unforgiving holds of the standard everyday military helicopter transports he travels in. This cabin's interior is far more comfortable, almost executive.

"Are you sure, Sir, you look a bit peaky?" the voice insists.

"I'm sure Lieutenant."

Lieutenant Winters eyes Major Rees opposite him with concern. Despite Rees's insistence to the contrary, he doesn't look well; he is visibly sweating and looks quite pale. Winter's leaves it at that, not questioning the Major any further; perhaps the man suffers from air sickness and it won't be long until they land.

"Give me your impressions of Captain Andy Richards, Lieutenant," Rees questions.

"I don't know him that well, personally, Sir. I only met him for the first time in the run-up to the mission to retrieve the safe from Orion Securities," Winters begins, not being entirely truthful. "With regards to the mission, I found him very capable, even though his hand was forced by Colonel Reed to carry out the mission. As you know, Sir. My guess is that he will take part in the tests and want to get back to his family as soon as possible, Sir."

"Didn't you spend some time with him after the mission was over and he returned to Heathrow Airport?" Rees presses.

"Yes, Sir. After we escaped Heathrow just before the blast hit, me and the Special Forces men found ourselves in a cottage with him in Devon to regroup. I spent a couple of nights at the cottage with the SF guys before we left to report back for duty. All of us were in a bit of shock after the events in London and needed some R and R. Captain Richards spent most of the first night and the next day recovering and then we left the next morning."

"Didn't you have dealings with Richards through Colonel Reed beforehand?"

"No, Sir. Colonel Reed's arrangement with him and Orion Securities was unknown to me, Sir. The two men dealt with each other directly, without my knowledge," Winters tells Rees. This statement is all but true; Winters knew of Orion Securities. He had heard Colonel Reed mention Andy Richards and had heard him talking to him on the phone on occasion, but what those discussions were about, Winters didn't know at the time.

"I see… Did you talk to him much at the cottage?" Major Rees continues, like a dog with a bone.

"Only small talk, Sir, nothing of significance," Winters lies. The two men had had some quite in-depth conversations after the barbeque and over a few beers on the second night. Richards had told Winters of his thoughts to try and ensure the safety of his family. One of those thoughts was to leave the country, possibly to try to get to

America. Those discussions were between the two men, however, and not for sharing.

"Do you think Captain Richards will be a willing subject?"

"To a point, Sir. It depends on what you plan to subject him to," Winters tells Rees, wondering what the Major actually has planned for Richards.

"Good, I'm sure Captain Richards will have no objections to the tests we will be carrying out."

Winters is suddenly very dubious about what is planned at the hospital and wonders how far the military doctor's remit goes concerning Richards. Winters has a nose for smelling deceit and there is a definite aroma rising in the helicopters hold.

Thankfully, Major Rees's interrogation ends there, and Winters sits back in his seat to ponder their conversation. His eyes begin to wander around the hold with a newfound suspicion. Three of the other seats in the six-berth hold are occupied by what Winters had assumed were Major Rees's medical team, but now he looks at the men differently. Winters decides that at least two of the men could be from a team of a different nature entirely, possibly a Special Forces team even. He also begins to eye the single empty seat in the hold, which suddenly seems to have Andy Richards' name written all over it.

Winters peers out of the hold window as he questions the whole trip and why he is on this helicopter. Is he just here as a familiar face to put the military's target, Captain Richards at ease so that they can seize him, or are they are just going to carry out some routine tests? Winters tries to tell himself he is overthinking it and is turning it into a conspiracy, but unfortunately, he knows the military far too well to fully convince himself of that.

The helicopter closes in on a tall slender chimney standing next to a large building that is itself surrounded by other buildings. Winters guesses that the chimney is the outlet for Derriford Hospital's incinerator and pinpoints their destination. He is correct, and the pilot takes them down towards the chimney and Winters soon makes out the exact destination of the helicopter, a helipad, mounted a short distance away from the main building.

Touching down with ease, the pilot kills the engines, and his co-pilot quickly jumps out of the front of the helicopter to open the door for the Major. Winters waits until all the other passengers have retrieved their luggage and exited the cabin before he moves from his seat. Following the other men off the helipad, Winters idly wonders where the actual air ambulance will land if it comes in with a medical emergency.

Winters' idle thoughts are quickly overridden by his brain trying to work out how he is going to play this out. He understood he was on the mission with Major Rees to assist the Major while he carries out his tests on Andy, tests Andy has agreed to. He wouldn't be helping him medically; as far as he is concerned; he is here to iron out any nonmedical issues they run into, that is his speciality after all. But what if the Major's remit does go further than standard and innocent tests, what does he do then? What if Major Rees decides he needs to perform more sinister and invasive tests on an uncooperative patient, or worse, decides that the patient needs to be relocated for the tests to be carried out? After all, Winters knows full well that Andy would not agree to be relocated, certainly not without his family. Andy may agree to extra tests, even invasive ones, but leaving his family, no, that would turn nasty.

Winters follows the 'medical' team in through a side entrance and into the hospital, where they are met by a middle-aged woman, presumably a doctor due to the fact she is wearing a white medical coat. The smell that can only be replicated by other hospitals wafts into Winters's nostrils at which point he makes a decision. He will do all that he can to assist Major Rees, even going as far as helping him convince Andy to undergo whatever tests the Major needs to carry out, within reason.

If, whatever happened to Andy's metabolism after he was scratched can help ease or even eradicate the infection, then perfect. Winters is sure Andy would be the first in line to volunteer and help find a cure, even if it did mean pain and discomfort. But if attempting to find a cure, which might not even be contained inside Andy means unacceptable procedures or experimentation or detaining Andy against his will, then that is where Winters will draw the line. He is not here to help Major Rees iron out those kinds of actions.

"Has Captain Richards checked in yet, Doctor Wilson?" Rees asks their welcoming committee.

"Not as of yet, Sir. Unless he arrived after I left the department but it's probably a bit early," Doctor Wilson answers.

"Good, then we have time to prepare. Please lead the way Doctor," Rees asks.

The doctor turns and heads straight down a long corridor, directly in front of them. Rees notices that Lieutenant Winters has become distant since the conversation they had before landing. He didn't say a word after and has been hanging at the back of their group ever since. He wonders if the conversation has raised Winters suspicions on why they are here.

Raised suspicions or not, if Winters has any qualms or objections to the actions they are going to be forced to take, then he had better stow them away and follow orders; this is no time for pussyfooting around. The information retrieved from Sir Malcolm's safe, whilst promising, has yet to deliver any tangible results. And even with the endless funds and extensive research the authorities are putting into that information, any vaccine or treatment to stop the infection could be years, if not decades away.

London hasn't got weeks, never mind years or decades. Millions of people are still trapped inside the original quarantine zone and now South London is in a similar mess. The infection could escape from that zone at any time or mutate and become airborne or, God forbid, mutate and become impossible to cure. Captain Andy Richards is the only prospect of saving all those people and stopping the virus from spreading outside of London. Should that mean he must be sacrificed, then so be it. Young soldiers are being transported into London on a daily basis; they are no more than sacrifices to try and stem the spread of the virus in the short term. This virus must be halted now, before London is completely lost and the whole country follows or the whole world and humanity itself succumb.

Rees looks over his shoulder at Winters. *He had better get on board*, he thinks. *If he thought that we were just here to take a couple of vials of blood from the Captain, then the Lieutenant is not as clever as he likes to think he is, not by half.*

Winters sees Major Rees eyeing him and decides to make sure that he is stood next to the Major when they all step into an oversized hospital lift.

"Have you visited Plymouth before, Sir?" Winters asks the Major, to make conversation.

"No, not Plymouth specifically, but I have holidayed in Devon. Have you?"

"No, I think I've only been to Devon once. On a training exercise, on Dartmoor."

"Yes, I've been involved in at least one of those on Dartmoor. Beautiful up there, isn't it?" Rees replies.

"Yes Sir, it is, beautiful and wild," Winters agrees, pleased that he has at least taken the edge off any tension between the two men.

Four floors up, they are led down another long corridor and it is obvious that this section of the hospital is closely attached to the military. A good proportion of the staff on the floor, some dressed in medical gear, quickly move out of the Major's way, standing to attention as he passes.

The doctor leading them stops at a set of double doors to press her security pass against a sensor. Above the doors is a sign that simply says, 'Ward X', which Winters finds slightly ominous as the door swings open.

"Leave the doors open," Major Rees instructs the doctor, who complies without question. Obviously, Rees intends to make Andy's entry as normal as possible, making it easier to catch him in his lair.

Directly inside the ward is a deserted waiting area with seats and a reception desk. Major Rees stops just inside to inspect the area where his visitor will arrive, his head turning this way and that.

"Does anybody man the reception desk?" Rees asks the doctor.

"Not normally, Sir. Patients ring the bell in the corridor and are then invited inside," the doctor replies, looking a bit unsure of herself.

"Can you find someone to man it, to greet Captain Richards?" Rees enquires.

"Yes, Sir, of course."

"Thank you, Doctor. Now, I believe you have set up an examination area for us?"

"Yes, Sir, right this way," the doctor replies, turning to lead them into the ward.

Just past the reception area, the doctor takes them into a good-sized room with two beds inside. Each bed has a skirt around it close to the ceiling for the wrap-around hospital-style privacy curtain.

"Very good," Major Rees says as they enter the room that looks like any other hospital patient's room. "You also have a preparation room for us to use?"

"Yes, Sir, it is right next door if you would like to follow me."

Winters watches from the doorway as Major Rees and his men settle into their preparation room after the doctor has left them to arrange somebody to man the reception desk.

Rees opens his doctor's bag and begins to unload his equipment, some onto a desk and some onto a wheeled high table. Winters presumes that the equipment that goes onto the high table will be rolled through to use on Andy when he arrives.

"Lieutenant Winters," Rees says.

"Yes, Sir."

"When Captain Richards arrives, I would like you to go and welcome him with Doctor Wilson and show him to the examination room," Rees instructs.

"Yes, Sir."

"It'll be good for him to see a familiar face. Tell him you decided to tag along for the journey to see that everything went well," Rees says without looking up from the desk in front of him, where he is arranging his equipment.

"Of course, Sir," Winters replies, knowing full well that Major Rees is trying to manipulate him.

"Very good, Lieutenant. Why don't you take a seat until the Captain arrives?"

Winters is sure that Rees thinks he has him right where he wants him, and that's okay. Winters will play along with the Major until he goes too far with Andy and then it will be time to manipulate him back. Winters has played these games many times, with operators more skilled than the Major, and was taught by an expert in manipulation, Colonel Reed. Major Rees is an amateur compared to the Colonel.

Winters takes his seat and is quickly joined by everyone else in the room while they wait for Andy to arrive. Time ticks on and they wait, Major Rees fidgets, looks at his watch and eventually tells one of his men to go and check with Doctor Wilson.

More than an hour passes and there is still no sign of Andy; he is more than half an hour late for his appointment. Winters begins to wonder whether Andy has outmanoeuvred everyone and in particular Major Rees, who grows more impatient with every passing minute.

"Captain Richards must be delayed. Could you phone him to see where he is, Lieutenant?" Major Rees asks, frustrated.

"There's no answer on the number I have for him, Sir," Winters informs the Major after Andy's number rings out.

"Where the hell is he?" Rees demands, his frustration boiling over.

"I don't know, Sir."

"Have you had any communication with him since you left him, Lieutenant?" Rees growls accusingly at Winters.

"No, Sir, I certainly have not!" Winters replies, not liking Rees's insinuation.

"Damn it!" Rees spits out, picking up his phone and stomping towards the door. "I will have to speak to General Cox."

Winters watches Rees storm out of the room, as do the other men waiting for Captain Richards' arrival. Major Rees is beginning to test Winters' patience much like Colonel Reed once tended to before his downfall.

Winters has a phone number for both Andy's son Josh and Catherine Hamilton, both of whom he could attempt to phone to try and find out where Andy is, if he were so inclined. Winters decides not to divulge that information to Rees. Instead, he makes his excuses and follows the Major out of the room.

Winters sees Rees pacing the waiting room beyond the reception desk, his head down and his phone clamped to his ear, deep in discussion with General Cox.

"Can I help you?" a voice says from beside Winters, startling him.

"Can you point me in the direction of a toilet, please?" Winters asks Doctor Wilson, who has appeared from nowhere.

"Straight down, on your left," the doctor says, pointing further into the ward in the opposite direction from Major Rees.

Ideal, Winters thinks, as he sees that there is only one toilet, and he locks the door behind him. He needs privacy for his phone calls. First off, he finds Josh's number and clicks on it, but it rings out with no answer. He then scrolls to find Catherine's.

"Hello," Catherine's well-spoken voice answers.

"Catherine, it's Lieutenant Winters. Can you tell me where Andy is? He's missed his appointment at the hospital?" The line goes quiet for a moment, raising Winters' suspicions. Catherine is obviously working out what to tell him. "Catherine, please tell me where he is. The military command isn't going to let this go. I think you know that, and I can't help if I don't know what is going on."

96

"Do you remember Stacey?" Catherine says, deciding to trust the Lieutenant. After all, if things go badly for them in London, Winters will be her first phone call for help.

"Yes," Winter replies.

"Do you remember her parents were trapped in London?"

"Yes," Winters says with a sinking feeling in his belly. "Please don't tell me Andy is going to try and get them out of London, Catherine. That would be madness. He isn't, is he?"

"Yes... he is."

"Holy shit, what is he thinking? It will be suicide," Winters tells Catherine, not sparing her feelings.

"I tried to stop them, but you know what Andy's like," Catherine tells Winters.

"Them," Winters exclaims. "Who is them?"

"Josh and Alice are with him."

"Oh, my God, Catherine! When did they go? I've got to stop them!"

"They left late this afternoon. I don't think you'll be able to stop them," Catherine confirms.

"How do they plan to get into London? It's blocked off," Winters asks.

"I don't think I should say any more, Lieutenant. They have a plan, and it could work."

"*Could work!* Have you lost your senses? Andy obviously has, taking his son into hell on earth! Tell me where they are Catherine, I can stop them," Winters insists.

"I'm sorry, I can't. Josh and Alice insisted on going and they are confident of the plan."

"You've all gone fucking mad. Tell me, Catherine, for their own good," Winters demands.

"I'm sorry Lieutenant. Now I must go, please keep this to yourself."

"Keep this to…" The line goes dead as Catherine hangs up.

Winters' heart races; he can't believe what he's just heard. *Going into London, what the fuck!* he thinks. He suddenly wishes he had never phoned Catherine. What the hell is he supposed to do with this information, withhold it from Major Rees? How can he? And if he does tell the Major, what will that mean for the three idiots on their way to London?

Winters goes over to the sink, putting his phone down on it and looking at himself in the mirror above it. He turns on the tap and splashes some cold water onto his face. *Sit on the intel, for the time being*, he tells himself. *This information would send the top brass into meltdown and who knows what they'd decide to do.* All he can do is pray that Andy gets out alive and be ready for a call from him if he suddenly decides he needs help.

Winters grabs some paper towels from the wall beside the sink and dries his face. He looks at himself in the mirror again as he throws the wet towels in the bin and tries to compose himself. After taking a few deep breaths, Winters grabs his phone and turns to unlock the door.

Shit, great timing, Winters thinks as he exits the toilet at the exact same time Major Rees appears at the end of the corridor. Rees locks eyes with Winters as he leaves the waiting room and strides in his direction. Winters prays that the Major turns in the direction of the room they have both just left, but he doesn't. He comes straight at him.

"What are you up to, Lieutenant?" Major Rees demands of Winters as he closes in.

"Sir?" Winters asks, trying to look confused about the question.

"What are you doing, it's a simple question, Lieutenant?"

"I was just relieving myself, Sir," Winters replies.

"Are you sure you weren't making contact with Richards?" the Major asks bluntly, his eyes looking to the phone in Winters' hand.

"Sir, no Sir. I can try him again if you wish though, Sir," Winters replies.

"Who have you been talking to on your phone then, Lieutenant?" Rees presses, still eyeballing his phone.

"No one Sir. I was just checking to see if I had any messages, Sir."

"You won't mind if I look at your phone then?" Rees tests.

"Of course not, Sir," Winters replies, his belly tightening as he raises his phone up towards the Major.

Rees's eyes now move away from the phone between them to stare at Winters. Winters' belly tightens further as he calls Major Rees's bluff, but his eyes meet Rees's challenge.

"Follow me, Lieutenant," Rees suddenly orders and turns on the spot.

Winters does as he is ordered, whilst slipping his phone out of sight and back into his pocket, his belly relaxing slightly.

Major Rees now does return to the room where the other men are still slouched in their chairs. Winters follows him in and stands to attention while he waits for the Major's next move and he doesn't have to wait long to find out what that is.

"Where is this cottage that you were at with Richards, Lieutenant?" Rees questions.

"It was near the town of Salcombe, on the South Coast, Sir," Winters replies, already knowing where this conversation is heading.

"And you will be able to find it on a map, I presume, Lieutenant?" Rees asks.

"Yes, Sir."

"Good. Get your gear together men, we are leaving," Major Rees announces to the whole room.

Chapter 8

After a quick chat with Doctor Wilson, Major Rees leads his team rapidly out of the hospital. The team's arrival back on the helipad takes the pilots by surprise. Both the pilot and his co-pilot are caught sleeping on the job, with their heads back in their pilot's seats, mouths wide, catching flies. Rees soon shocks them back to reality and scrambling out of the cockpit.

"Sorry, Sir. We weren't expecting you back so soon," a red-faced pilot apologises.

"Neither was I. We have a new destination. Lieutenant Winters will give you the coordinates," Rees tells the two men before he turns to retake his seat in the cabin.

The two men eye Winters with some confusion as he approaches them to pinpoint on their map where the cottage is. Neither of the men asks Winters why they are being asked to fly to a cottage in the middle of nowhere on the South Devon coast. They simply tell Winters that they have '*got it*' before they climb back into the cockpit to plot their new flight path and Winters slowly joins Major Rees in the helicopter's cabin.

Thankfully, the uncomfortable silence in the cabin is soon broken by the sound of the helicopter's engines starting. Both Winters and Rees stare out of the cabin's window as the helicopter's engines power up and it begins to rise off the helipad. Neither of the men turns away from the window, preferring to watch Derriford Hospital shrink in their view than look at each other.

"ETA, fifteen minutes," the pilot announces into the men's headphones.

Winters is beginning to panic slightly at the thought of Catherine giving away to Major Rees that they have recently spoken on the phone. If she decides to tell the Major that she has told Winters where Andy is, it could end very badly for him. He debates whether he can get away with taking his phone out of his pocket and pretend to be flicking through it innocently whilst actually sending Catherine a warning message. Winters quickly decides against it, as Rees is no fool. He will have to count on Catherine's discretion; she is no fool either and Winters will try and gesture to her somehow to ward her to keep shtum.

The helicopter soon leaves Plymouth behind and the scenery below changes back to countryside and villages. Off in the distance is the sea, which will only get closer as they near Salcombe.

"Do you think Captain Richards will be at the cottage, Lieutenant?" Rees's voice comes through Winters' headset.

"I don't see why not, where else could he be, Sir?" Winters replies innocently.

"I wonder," Rees says. "Richards seems to be a law unto himself, wouldn't you say, Lieutenant?"

"If you say so, Sir."

"Wouldn't you, Lieutenant?" Rees questions.

"He certainly has his own agenda, Sir. Which isn't always in line with ours. His family is his priority, but we would be nowhere without him, Sir. He led the team to get the safe out of the Orion building, after all, Sir," Winters tells Rees.

"I suppose he did, in his own way," Rees concedes.

"Yes, Sir," Winters agrees.

Daylight begins to fade, and the sea almost fills the entire view outside of the cabin window as the pilot begins his descent. Winters cannot see any sign of the cottage from his vantage point in his seat, but he knows that they are closing in on it. Catherine and Andy's daughter Emily are going to wonder what the hell is going on when the helicopter closes in and lands in the grounds next to the cottage. Winters prays once more that Catherine will keep their conversation to herself as the helicopter slows for its descent.

The helicopter manoeuvres around, changing Winters' view, and then he sees it, the cottage just past the sand dunes. He doubted he'd ever see the building again when he left it and yet there it is, growing larger in front of his eyes.

Light suddenly pours out of the cottage's front door as it is swung open for a moment and a single person comes out of the building. Winters focuses on that person and sees it is a woman, her dark hair swirling above her head, caught in the downdraft of the rotors. He is not surprised to see that it is Catherine who has come out to face the unexpected arrival. She waits close to the cottage for them to land, her arms crossed and a stern look etched across her face.

As the helicopter touches down, Winters notices two of the men in the cabin, Major Rees's supposed 'medical assistants', pad the left side of their chests under their windbreaker jackets. Any notion that the two men have any significant medical knowledge is dispelled from Winters' mind. They are here for one reason and one reason only, just as he had suspected.

The engines begin to wind down and just as before, the co-pilot jumps out of the cockpit to open the cabin door to let Major Rees out. Rees doesn't hesitate; he climbs straight out of the cabin and strides across the grass, towards the cottage and the waiting Catherine. This time, Winters doesn't delay, he follows Rees straight out, apologising to the two armed men as he goes, who stall in their seats as Winters beats them to the door.

Following Rees, Winters keeps pace with the Major whilst not crowding him, keen to give Catherine some kind of warning signal. The last thing he or Andy needs now is for him to be up on charges of insubordination and out of the game.

"Catherine Hamilton, I take it?" Major Rees demands as he approaches the woman before him.

"Who are you and what business is it of yours?" Catherine answers, her arms still crossed and appearing unfazed by the Major.

"I'm Major Stephen Rees. I was due to meet Captain Richards for his appointment at the hospital today. He didn't attend his appointment, so I thought I'd drop by to see him, where is he?"

Catherine's head turns slightly to look at Lieutenant Winters as if unsure what to say. The look is obvious, and Rees's head begins to turn to look at Winters also. Winters' bulging eyes and the faint shake of his head evaporate in the instant before Major Rees's eyes fall on him. Winters, his nerves prickling, can only hope that Catherine saw his signal and thinks fast to divert the Major's attention.

"Lieutenant Winters, I didn't think we'd be seeing you again so soon." Catherine's words covering her look perfectly.

"I thought I'd tag along with the Major to see Andy at the hospital and to see how he got on," Winters replies.

"That's nice of you Lieutenant," Catherine plays along.

"He didn't turn up though, where is he?" Winters asks, knowing full well.

"I'm afraid he was called away suddenly on urgent family business. I told him to phone the hospital to tell them he couldn't make the appointment, but it must have slipped his mind."

"What family business?" Rees asks, his attention now back where it should be.

"*Private* family business, Major." Catherine bats Major Rees's question away.

"Ms Hamilton, I demand you tell me where Captain Richards is," Rees snaps.

"It is none of your business, Major. But if you'd like to leave me your number, I will try and get a message to Andy to contact you as soon as he can."

"That is not acceptable Ms Hamilton. I'm here in an official capacity and I need to speak to Captain Richards immediately," Rees barks, edging forwards, losing his cool.

"If you need to speak to Andy urgently then I suggest you try and phone him, Major. Lieutenant Winters has his number," Catherine replies coolly.

"He isn't answering his calls, Ms Hamilton."

"Then I can't help you," Catherine retorts.

"Are you sure he isn't here, inside maybe?" Rees presses.

"He isn't here. If he were, I wouldn't be out here being interrogated. You are welcome to look."

Rees turns and nods sternly at the two men with weapons under their jackets, who immediately step forward, towards the cottage's front door.

"Just one moment, please," Catherine says, stepping back towards the door and blocking the men's path.

The two burly operators come to a sudden stop in their tracks, unsure what to do. They look at each other and then at the Major, foiled by the woman in front of them with the windswept hair.

Catherine leaves the two men where they stand and turns for the front door. "Girls, can you come outside for a minute please?" she shouts as she opens the door. Almost immediately, Emily and Stacey emerge from inside the cottage, both wearing their pyjamas and both obviously listening close by inside.

"Gentlemen," Catherine says, when the girls are by her side, showing the men inside with one hand and an annoyed expression on her face.

The two men accept Catherine's invitation to go in, even if they do so sheepishly.

"Are they looking for Dad?" Emily asks, looking up to Catherine.

"Yes, Emily, they are."

"Well, they won't find him in there, will they?" Emily remarks.

"No, no they won't," Catherine agrees.

"Silly men," Emily says looking back towards the door, her pyjama legs flapping in the breeze.

Winters suppresses the grin that tries to spread across his face as he stands silently waiting. Rees, next to him, turns away from the front door to look at their surroundings, obviously realising that Richards isn't inside the cottage.

"Captain Richards isn't inside, Sir," the men tell Rees as they come out empty-handed.

"If that will be all, Major? I don't want the girls catching a chill," Catherine asks, already edging back towards the cottage.

"When you speak to Captain Richards, please ask him to phone Lieutenant Winters immediately, Ms Hamilton," Rees asks defeated.

"Of course, Major," Catherine replies and goes back inside the cottage, ushering the girls in front of her.

The unannounced visitors are unceremoniously left stranded on the grass in front of the cottage, wondering what to do with themselves now.

"Back on board," Rees orders defeated, for now.

Winters climbs back aboard leaving Rees to give his orders to the pilots. He presumes that Rees must be ordering them to fly them back to base. *What else is there to do?* Winters thinks. It was a close-run thing, but in the end, Rees met with a dead-end at the cottage.

"Are we heading back to base, Sir?" Winters asks Rees when he is back on board and just before he puts his headset back on.

"We are, Lieutenant, we just need to make a quick stop first," the Major replies cryptically before he turns to his two men in windbreakers. "Sergeant, get your gear together. You will be dropped by the edge of town; get any supplies you need and then return to the cottage. Take up a position where you can observe the cottage and report back to me what you see. Richards might not have been inside, but he could be close by. Inform me immediately if he is, understood?"

"Yes, Sir," the older of the two men confirms as the pilot starts the engines.

"Oh, and Sergeant. Don't take Richards for granted, he is well trained and will probably be expecting company. Don't make a move until you have my order."

"Yes, Sir," the Sergeant simply says again before he and his partner reach under their seats. Both men pull out generously sized and tightly packed army issue rucksacks, having come prepared.

Winters curses himself for not anticipating Rees's move, but he doubts it will be of much consequence. He knows Andy is not close by, but the relevance of the men's presence is likely to change as this plays out.

Following Rees's orders, the pilot finds a field near the edge of Salcombe and brings the helicopter in to land. The area is more than enough distance away from the cottage for the helicopters landing to go unnoticed by the occupants of the cottage.

"Keep a low profile, Sergeant," Rees reminds the two men before they grab their gear and pop open the cabin's door.

Chilly air and bits of grass blow into the cabin when the door is opened. The pilot doesn't stop the helicopter's engines while the two men disembark, jumping down onto the grass. The younger man slams the cabin's door shut behind himself, cutting off the attack of wind and then he turns and runs, head down under the powerful, spinning rotors. As soon as the two men are clear, the pilot guns the engines and lifts the helicopter back into the air. Both the two men and the pilot are clearly well trained, as the helicopter was on the ground for no more than a minute.

Winters manages to watch the two men for a moment out of the window as the helicopter lifts off. Neither of them looks back at the helicopter as it leaves. They simply sling their rucksacks over their shoulders and march off in the direction of the town before they disappear into the darkness.

Tongues will be wagging in town, Winters thinks as the pilot flies right over the town centre, in the opposite direction to the cottage. He keeps flying in that direction for a couple of minutes before he brings the helicopter around on a new bearing, a bearing that will take them back to base.

"ETA, please?" Major Rees asks the two pilots.

"Approximately fifty minutes, Sir," the co-pilot replies.

"Patch me through to General Cox, secure line," Rees orders.

'Yes, Sir,' is the last piece of conversation Winters hears through his headset as the secure line is established with General Cox for the Major. After that, Winters' headset goes silent, cut off from the conversation that he can see Rees having with the General, but cannot hear. That doesn't bother Winters; he may not be privy to the conversation, but he can imagine what is being discussed. Winters takes the opportunity to close his eyes and get some rest for the remainder of the flight. He doesn't get any sleep, but his headset cuts out a good proportion of the sound of the helicopter engines and he at least gets the chance to rest his eyes and do some thinking.

Chapter 9

Winters' eyes remain closed until he feels the pilot begin to bring the helicopter down. He isn't sure how long Rees was talking to the General and he is pleased his headset remained silent for the entire journey. The silence gave him time to rest and to think, and it also meant there weren't any probing questions put his way by the Major.

Ignoring Rees and his assistant next to him, who both look at Winters with disdain, Winters instead peers out of the window beside him. The light of the cabin reflecting in the window makes it difficult to see anything in the darkness outside. He leans forward and manages to block some of the cabin's light so that he can get a partial view into the darkness.

Illuminated below are the buildings and roads of Porton Down, the top-secret and controversial, Ministry of Defence research facility. Situated just outside the town of Salisbury, it is probably the most top-secret site in the UK, both before and after the virus outbreak. Known for its chemical weapons research amongst other clandestine activities, the facility has always been a favourite source of material for 'crackpot' conspiracy theorists, peddling their wares on the internet. Nowadays, however, since the outbreak, those theories have moved into the mainstream media. There isn't a day that goes by without Porton Down being mentioned on the news and quite often it is the subject of the headline story, which isn't surprising in the slightest, considering.

Over recent years, Porton Down has tried to sanitise its reputation by expanding its scope and turning itself into a scientific community. Private companies have been encouraged to join the community and set up their own facilities in the immediate vicinity and this has been quite successful. Make no mistake, however, the core, military facility is still engaged in controversial research. The site is still considered top-secret and is treated as such, with all the overbearing security that comes with such a delicate site.

Hanging up his headset, Winters waits patiently for the door to be opened for the Major. Last out of the helicopter, Winters hangs his satchel over his shoulder and waits with the pilots and the other passengers to be invited through security.

In contrast to the swarms of helicopters and other air transport at Heathrow Airport, Porton Down only has a small heliport. There are three other helicopters parked on the ground adjacent to theirs, all of which are also of the executive type.

Somebody at least has learnt a lesson from the compromised Chinook that crash-landed at Heathrow and the catastrophic consequences it had for the airport—the airport eventually incinerated by a tactical nuclear strike. Surrounding the heliport, which has been moved well away from the sensitive main facility, is a freshly constructed tall masonry wall, built to contain any such 'accidents' at Porton Down.

Eyes peer down from the top of the wall behind heavy machine guns. The soldiers are poised, ready to unleash their firepower on any breach in security from incoming passengers. Winters only hopes that the soldiers are well trained and don't have itchy trigger fingers.

There is only one entrance and exit built into the high wall, a heavy door with an enclosed security station standing next to it. All passengers must wait for the station to be staffed and then for a light mounted at the top of the station to turn from red to green before they can approach the exit.

Eventually, the light does flick from red to green and Major Rees leads the five men over to the security station.

"Identification," a tired-looking woman in combat uniform demands from her first customer.

Rees hands over his military identification, placing it into a letterbox-sized hole cut into the thick Perspex fixed to the front of the station.

"Look into the camera," the guard tells the Major without ceremony as she looks down to the counter in front of her to study Rees's ID. Next, she peers at a computer screen mounted next to her on the counter, the screen indicating if the eye scan has been passed or if the person is infected.

"Clear, wait over there," she then tells Rees, who looks none too pleased with her attitude. His disgust escalates when the woman says 'next,' and makes no attempt to hand Rees his ID back. Rees reaches forward to retrieve his ID, swiping it off the counter in anger before he turns away to do as he's told.

All the men pass through security, and the woman does not attempt to touch any of the ID cards placed in front of her and Winters doesn't blame her.

Her task complete, the woman disappears through a door in the back of the security station where it joins onto the wall. A minute or two passes, with the five men standing like lemons until the main door in the wall finally opens.

As Winters expected, waiting on the other side of the wall is their transport to Porton Down's main facilities. The electric shuttle, much like you'd find at a large holiday resort complex to ferry guests around, is empty apart from their driver, the same woman who has just carried out their security check.

Winters doesn't rush to take his seat, rather he waits until he sees where Rees is going to sit before he takes one. He finds himself at the front of the shuttle, right behind the driver, at the opposite end of the shuttle to Rees.

The journey is going to take some time, Winters knows that from the journey out to the helipad. He wobbles in his seat as they get underway, the track they follow wasn't laid for small electric shuttles. Wire mesh, similar to chicken wire, encases the track and reaches up both sides and curls over the top of the track much like a tunnel. Bright lights lead the way, beyond which are grassed open spaces, undisclosed buildings, and darkness.

After trundling along for a good ten minutes, the shuttle stops next to a manned security door in the mesh. A sign attached to the mesh above the door tells the passengers that they have stopped at 'Station 1'. The woman in front of Winters looks around to see if anybody is getting off. Nobody is and so she sets off again, without saying a word.

The two pilots who are sitting right behind Winters, chat quietly until they get off the shuttle at station 3a. There are three more stops until Winters is due to get off, unfortunately; he knows that Major Rees will also be disembarking at the same station. That station is the last on the line and is at the very heart of the MOD facility. There will be further security checks before the shuttle is permitted to move into that area of Porton Down. Winters longs to reach the area, because that is where the Mess Hall is sited and the hall will be his first port of call; he is beyond hungry.

"Final stop, all off," the woman driver finally declares, as she stops at the last station, Porton Down Central.

ID's are checked once again before the men are allowed to exit the wire tunnel and again, Winters is last through, despite his eagerness to get to the Mess Hall.

"With me, Lieutenant Winters," Rees announces as he clears security.

"Sir?" Winters asks, his stomach protesting.

"General Cox is waiting to debrief us," Rees tells him.

"Now, Sir?"

"Yes, immediately. Unless you have another urgent matter to attend to?"

"No, Sir. Very good, Sir," Winters replies, hiding his frustration.

Porton Down Central is busy, *probably with people heading to get their dinner, even though they've all had their fucking lunch,* Winters curses to himself.

Rees, unconcerned by Winters' hunger pains, turns and marches off in the direction of the newish office block that sits on the other side of the square, opposite to the shuttle drop off point they have just come through. Some of the buildings in Porton Down MOD site are modern, especially the ones in the central area where they are now. You don't have to wander far, however, to find the old brick-built buildings, some probably dating back to when the military first began their 'testing' on the site in 1916. Many of these old buildings are still in use and have an ominous feel to them, even if what goes on inside them is mundane.

The real sensitive MOD work goes on in areas of the site that Winters doesn't have access to. He can only imagine what that part of the facility looks like from the ground. What he has seen of it, from the air, it looks nondescript, but flight paths are restricted above that area and so he has only glimpsed it from a very long distance away. Also, from gossip that he has heard, the majority of the sensitive facility is subterranean, but extensive nonetheless.

ID cards are inspected once again before Major Rees, his assistant and Winters are granted access to the building where General Cox's department is housed. Winters is not looking forward to his debriefing by Cox, to the extent that he begins to get his story straight in his head as they travel through the oversized building.

Major Rees is invited into the General's office before Winters, who takes a seat in the waiting area outside. He feels like a schoolboy waiting to be summoned in for a telling off by the school's Headmaster. He eyes the General's PA, another Lieutenant, who sits behind his desk near the entrance to the General's office. The impeccably presented Lieutenant is younger than Winters. He reminds Winters of himself when he was first posted to become Colonel Reed's assistant, which seems as though it was in another lifetime.

He takes the chance to go through his phone while he is waiting, first to see if he has any new messages and second to delete any incriminating evidence that might show that he has been in touch with Andy's family or his associates. Winters realises that the process is futile, his phone records are readily available to his superiors if they decided to request them. It could, however, fool the Major and the General, if this time they call Winters' bluff and order him to show them his phone.

"You can go in now, Lieutenant," Winters is informed after about fifteen minutes of waiting, by the Lieutenant behind the desk.

Winters notices the faint smug look he is given by the smart-looking Lieutenant as he crosses the room to enter the General's office. The young man is probably thinking, 'look at how the mighty have fallen,' which is probably true of Winters to be fair to the young Lieutenant, since Colonel Reed's demise. Winters was once well renowned by his fellow Lieutenants of the British army, almost infamous. Winters wouldn't change what happened to Colonel Reed though, and he brushes the smug look off.

Enjoy the sunlight while you can, Winters thinks in return as he walks past, *because things are going to shit and that comfy chair under your arse won't be there forever.*

"At ease, Lieutenant," General Cox orders Winters from behind her large glass desk as he comes to attention. Rees is seated to Winters's right, in a chair positioned in front of the desk and his assistant is sitting at the back of the large office.

"Not a successful trip then, Lieutenant?" General Cox enquires.

"No, Ma'am," Winters responds, standing with his hands behind his back.

"Did you know Captain Richards would not be attending his appointment at the hospital today?" General Cox asks Winters, her warm smile attempting to disarm Winters.

"No, Ma'am, I had no idea, I expected him to attend. From what I know of Captain Richards, he would be as eager as anyone to get to the bottom of what happened to him. He would also submit to the tests in the hopes that it can assist in stopping the outbreak, Ma'am."

"I see," Cox says, her finger tapping the glass below it. "And what if those tests went further than he was willing to allow? Would you say he would have foreseen that we may have had other plans for him?"

"That is certainly possible, Ma'am. As I said to Major Rees, there is nothing more important to Captain Richards than his family and his loved ones, Ma'am."

"So, you're saying that you didn't speak with him prior to the appointment and that you didn't warn him?" Cox probes, her eyes focusing on Winters.

"Certainly not, Ma'am. I have no idea of the plans for Captain Richards. I got an inkling from my discussions with Major Rees on the flight out, but I wasn't privy to that information before the flight, Ma'am," Winters insists, trying to look slightly offended by the line of questioning.

"Okay, Lieutenant. I have to ask these questions, you understand? Especially given everything that's at stake."

"Of course, Ma'am. I'm happy to answer all of your questions, Ma'am," Winters lies.

"Good," Cox says, giving Winters another one of her smiles. "So, what about after Captain Richards missed his appointment, I understand you couldn't reach him on his phone?"

"Yes, Ma'am, that is correct, there was no answer, Ma'am," Winters lies again.

"And what about his family and friends, did you speak to any of them?"

"No, Ma'am, I did not," Winters replies bluntly.

"Have you tried to phone Captain Richards again?" Cox enquires.

"No, Ma'am. Major Rees hasn't asked me to, and I wasn't sure if he'd want me to. I can certainly try to phone him again, Ma'am. Would you like me to try now?" Winter volunteers.

"No, thank you, Lieutenant, that won't be necessary," the General says, looking away from Winters. "Major, have you anything to add?"

"No, Ma'am," Rees replies.

"Thank you for your help, Lieutenant. Take a seat in the waiting room. Dismissed," General Cox orders.

Winters stands to attention and salutes the General before turning sharply to leave and retake his seat in the waiting room.

"Thoughts?" General Cox asks Rees once Winters shuts the door behind himself.

"Lieutenant Winters is a highly intelligent soldier, Ma'am, probably too clever for his own good. He has an affiliation to Richards, and I think that he's holding something back."

"You are probably right in that respect, Major. We must remember that he learnt from one of the best in Colonel Reed, the lecherous old manipulator. Even the thought of Reed still makes me shiver in disgust," General Cox says, feigning a shiver in her chair. "I think it's best if we keep him in play, at least for now. He may be useful when we acquire Richards."

"Ma'am," Rees responds wondering what history General Cox had with Colonel Reed. *No doubt it was sordid if Reed was involved and judging by Cox's reaction,* he thinks.

"Winters will come with us to the Zero station tomorrow, agreed?" Cox asks.

"Yes, Ma'am. But we need to keep a close eye on him, Ma'am," Rees replies.

"Indeed, Major. Give Winters your orders on the way out, and I'll see you at 0500."

"Yes, Ma'am," Rees replies, getting up from his chair.

Winters stands to attention as Rees emerges from General Cox's office and heads straight for him.

"Sir," Winters says.

"You are dismissed for the evening, Lieutenant. Tomorrow, you will be at the shuttle pickup point at 0500 and bring your kit with you, Lieutenant," Rees orders.

"Sir, can I ask where we are going, and for how long?"

"I cannot disclose our destination at this time, Lieutenant, but bring everything you will need for an undetermined time, understood?"

"Yes, Sir. 0500, Sir."

"Dismissed," Major Rees orders before turning to speak to his assistant.

Winters turns on the spot and walks away from Rees, heading to exit the building. His confusion about Major's orders overriding his hunger, at least for the moment.

Chapter 10

My feet sink little by little further down into the cold sand. Every tiny wave of the tide sweeping over the top of my feet washes more grains of sand out from under them. Soon the sand will cover the tops completely and begin to edge up towards my ankles. My feet sinking doesn't bother me at all. No, the sound of the surf is too relaxing, its resonance soothes my mind and the warm, low sun on my face heals my troubled soul.

Yellow and pink printed flowers entwined into my shorts flap in the breeze that rolls off the endless expanse of the sea spread out before me. Any second now, I will take the plunge and dive forward to let the saltwater wash over me entirely. The water's salt and minerals will soak into my skin, bringing their goodness to bear on the scars cut into the side of my face. Any malignancy still festering under the scars' red skin will be healed by the minerals, dissolved by the salt, and washed away completely. I long to emerge from the sea's healing powers and let the scars dry out in the sun, where they will dissipate and become almost invisible.

I build the courage to jump, to take my dive, preparing myself for the shock of the cold water. *Better to get the shock over quickly*, I tell myself, *rather than torturing yourself by wading in slowly, one wave at a time*. My legs tense up and I am ready to sacrifice myself to the healing waters of the cold sea.

A voice in the distance, carried on the sea breeze stops me before I can jump. It calls my name. *Emily… why is she calling me by my name, why isn't she calling me Dad?*

Daddy, the voice calls again, *good Emily*, I think, *I'm Daddy, not Andy to you.* I turn to look for her, to watch her running down the beach to jump into my arms, but the beach is empty. I look back, farther up the beach, towards the sand dunes to find my little girl, but again I don't see her.

Has she fallen over, I panic, *is she hurt or lost in the dunes?*

My right leg pulls to release my sunken foot from the flooded sand. My muscles strain but my foot is stuck, sucked into the heavy sand that now reaches over my ankles. I pull my leg again as Emily cries out and as my left foot sinks deeper into the quicksand, my right foot suddenly pops free. I lose my balance from the unexpected jolt and fall backwards onto the damp sand behind me, my left food still trapped.

Twisting onto my front as far as I can without breaking my leg, my fingers dig into the hard, damp sand and I pull with all my strength. I feel the sand move around my foot as my fingers and arms pull, and as I strain, my foot slides slowly free of the unforgiving sand.

Free from the trap, I scramble across the sand until I am upright and on my feet. *Daddy!* cries out across the beach and I run towards the cry, towards the dunes that loom like demons over the back of the beach. Darkness is falling impossibly fast, and Emily is scared and possibly hurt, she needs me. I aim for the path that disappears into the foreboding dunes that are completely in shadow, putting my trepidation to enter them aside.

Long stems of beach grass wave at me, inviting me to enter the mounds of sand, and I do enter, ploughing straight into them. Darkness encompasses me, the dying rays of the sun completely cut off by the tall hills of sand and grass that tower over me. I feel the hardness of the path beneath my feet, and I call out for Emily, but she doesn't answer. The only sound that answers my call is the sound of the breeze wisping through the tall rough grass and the vibrations of disturbed sand.

Where is she? I panic, my eyes widening to search the black shadows of the hills surrounding me. Edging forward, deeper into the darkness, my head turns this way and that, searching for any sign of my lost daughter, but I can see nothing.

My eyes adjust to the darkness, showing me shadows of swaying grass moving all around, threatening to slice into my skin if I venture too close. I peer ahead, hoping to see Emily somewhere on the path but there is nothing, only a dim light that thankfully shows me the way out of this black maze.

I step towards the light, carefully treading to stay on the path and away from the sharpness of the threatening prongs of grass. A shadow breaks the light ahead on the path, a shadow of a small person. *'Emily'*, I shout and move quickly to follow her as she runs out of the dunes and towards the yellow lights shining from the windows of the cottage.

Free of the dunes, I see the cottage's door swing open, spilling light out into the darkness. The light shows me Emily rushing inside, only for the door to swing immediately shut. Figures move behind the cottage's bright windows, I see Catherine, Josh, Stacey, and Alice. My heart skips when I see them. *I am coming*, I say, *don't forget me. I'll be inside with you all, in only a few moments.*

I race up the path towards the cottage, to join my family inside. My legs push me forward but no matter how hard they run, the cottage remains in the distance, the light from the windows comes no closer. My desperation to reach them escalates and I run faster to catch up to the light, until my lungs burst, and my legs give way.

"Catherine, I'm here," I cry out as I stumble to my knees, the cottage still out of reach.

Gradually, I push myself back upright, ready to try again. I look ahead to see my destination, my family still there in the yellow light, behind the cottage's glass. A black figure drifts across the front of the cottage, breaking the light. Fear tightens my stomach as another ominous figure moves across the light, and then another.

The breeze around me suddenly ceases and every sound of the beach it carried vanishes. The darkness around me closes in to bring a new chilling sound to my ears. A low vibrating screech comes from the direction of the cottage, from the black figures that are growing in number to block the light from the windows completely.

Undead Rabids have come to haunt me, to cut me off from my family. They move towards me, coming down the shortening path from the cottage. Fear forces me to step backwards, the dunes now offering my only salvation from the creatures of death stalking me. *My family*, I think desperately, *they won't be safe inside that cottage, the beasts will find their way inside, I do not doubt that.*

I take another step back, too scared to do anything else, too frightened to try and help my loved ones. I bang into something on the path behind me and I freeze, terror paralysing me instantly. My eyes wide, strain to the side to see what I already know is there, I can feel its presence, hear its grunting throat.

A hand touches my shoulder, fingers winding around it, gripping me to the bone. Dead eyes appear to the side of me, the glint of teeth as the Rabid's gaping mouth closes in on my neck and I scream, I scream for my family…

"Dad, Dad!" a voice shouts.

I wake up suddenly, darkness intersected by streaking lights fill my vision. A face looms close by, blinking in and out of focus. My brain rushes to remember where I am, my body shivering in a cold sweat.

"Andy, are you alright? I think you were dreaming," Alice's voice sounds in front of me, from the front seat of the Defender where she has turned in her seat.

"Where are we?" I ask as reality bites back.

"We're on the M4, but we'll be coming off shortly. You've been asleep for quite a while. Are you okay?" Alice asks.

"Yes, I'm fine thanks. Just my normal sleep pattern I'm afraid."

Alice is right, I have been asleep for a long time. The last thing I remember was leaving Exeter behind when there was still daylight, now it's all but fully dark. Josh had insisted on driving, he said I needed the rest before our task ahead, and he wasn't wrong.

Straightening myself up in the back seat of the Defender, I take a deep breath and look out of the window, my nightmare still fresh in my mind. I don't have to ponder long about what the visions meant to me, it's obvious. They tally almost perfectly with me leaving Catherine and Emily to go on another foolhardy mission. I try not to dwell on the nightmare and take action to take my mind off it.

"How long do you think, until we arrive?" I ask my pilots.

"About half an hour, I think," Josh informs me.

"Yes, won't be much longer than that," Alice agrees.

"Has there been much traffic?" I ask.

"No, the roads are quiet. I don't expect many people would choose to be travelling at the moment," Josh guesses.

"No, they wouldn't… especially towards London," I agree. "Any police around?"

"Not that we've seen. I've been checking my speed just in case though," Josh tells me.

"Good thinking," I tell him.

"Lieutenant Winters tried to phone me, but I didn't answer it," Josh tells me.

"He was probably phoning to see why I missed my appointment at the hospital," I reply, while I quickly retrieve my phone.

"That's what I thought," Josh says.

My phone tells me I to have a missed call from Winters too, along with several others from two numbers my phone doesn't recognise. One of the numbers is a landline number, with a Plymouth dialling code. I would guess that call has a good chance of being the hospital, trying to see where I am and the other, a mobile number was probably doing the same.

My absence from the hospital has obviously not gone unnoticed, as I knew it wouldn't. The pretence that the tests were for my benefit didn't fool me for one minute. I know full well that the authorities are desperate to find out what has happened to my body since it was infected. I understand the reasons why they are desperate, and I am willing to let them run their tests, just as soon as I have the time...

I debate for a moment on whether to phone Lieutenant Winters back and tell him I am delayed, and that I will phone him again as soon as I can attend to make a new appointment. But I decide against it, he would have numerous questions on why I've missed my appointment and they are questions I don't want to answer right now.

"I have missed calls too, from Lieutenant Winters and two other numbers," I tell Josh and Alice. "I think it's best if we ignore the calls until we are finished."

"It must be nice to be so popular," Josh jokes after he and Alice agree about the phone calls.

"Always popular me," I reply sarcastically.

"Are you hungry?" Alice asks, after a minute. "I have your sandwiches here."

"Yes, I am. I'd better eat them before we arrive. Thanks."

Alice rustles through a bag and hands me the sandwiches back over the seat together with a packet of crisps and a bottle of water. By the time I've finished my snack, Josh has turned off the motorway and we are driving through the side roads to reach Richmond.

"We're not far now. We will be in Richmond on the other side of this bridge," Alice tells us as we drive over the river Thames. "And they're just around the corner."

"What are their names?" I ask.

"Bill and Lillian."

"Very American," Josh jokes.

"Take a right here," Alice says, ignoring Josh's quip.

Josh does as he's told, without any further witty remarks and after several more instructions, Alice tells him to slow down.

"This is their house," Alice confirms as Josh comes to a stop outside a large and affluent looking house.

"It looks dead," Josh says, referring to the fact that the house is in complete darkness.

"Yes, it does," Alice agrees. "It's usually lit up like a Christmas tree."

"Perhaps they have left the house due to Richmond being close to London or they could be laying low inside," Josh guesses.

"I'm not sure where they would go if they have left? They've no family here or back home in the States. This house was their life," Alice tells us.

"Well, there's only one way to find out if anyone's home," I announce and pop open the Defender's back door.

Josh and Alice follow me out of the four-wheel drive. Josh and I then let Alice lead us up to the front door and climbs up a flight of stone steps that lead up to the house with some confidence, but she then looks quite nervous when it comes to the knocking part. She looks back over her shoulder before she knocks, and I give her a nod of encouragement for her to go ahead. The first knock goes unanswered, as does the second knock, but on the third one a dim light switches on inside the house.

I don't know about the other two, but I feel relieved when I see the light come on. The last thing we wanted to do after we arrived was to have to start trawling the riverbank looking for a boat to 'borrow'. Somebody being home is our best bet for getting a boat and getting some rest before we set off.

"Who is it?" an old-sounding, male voice, with an American accent asks nervously from behind the large wooden door.

"Uncle Bill, is that you? It's Alice, Alice ward."

"Alice?" the voice asks surprised.

"Yes, it's Alice. Can you open the door please?" Alice requests.

A few seconds of hushed voices talking from the other side of the door is followed by the sound of a lock turning and then finally the door opening up, but only a sliver. In the gap, the side of an elderly gentleman's face appears to look upon his visitor.

"Alice?" the man says once more.

"Yes, Uncle Bill, it's me."

"What are you doing here my dear?"

"My friends and I need to ask you and Lillian a favour, can we come in please?" Alice asks, convincingly.

The face disappears back behind the door, which is pushed to again for a moment. More hushed voices talk feverishly until the door begins to open again. This time the door opens wide, and the man ushers us into the house urgently.

"Thank you, Uncle Bill, Aunty Lillian," Alice says, looking at the shocked elderly couple, who are standing in their hallway in their nightclothes and dressing gowns.

"I didn't recognise you in your uniform Alice. We have been worried about you, haven't we Lillian?" Bill says.

"We certainly have dear," Lillian confirms. "Who are your friends?"

"This is Captain Richards and his son Josh. We need your help, if you're willing."

"Oh, well you know we will help you if we can, but let's not stand in the hallway. Let's go through to the kitchen and you can tell us all about it," Bill suggests.

Bill leads us all down the extensive hallway and through a door leading into a large kitchen and dining room at the back of the house. He then insists on making us all a hot drink before he will hear anything about why we have disturbed their night.

While Bill makes the drinks, I wander over to the large windows and patio doors on the far side of the room. I then proceed to peer out of the glass at the dark back garden and then farther to the river beyond, as if I were just being curious.

Alice wasn't exaggerating when she told us that the house backed straight onto the Thames. Flowing water is clearly visible at the end of the garden, shimmering in the moonlight. The problem, however, is that there is no boat to be seen, no matter how much I squint my eyes to concentrate my vision. I can see a small pontoon jutting out into the water, but there isn't a boat moored up against it.

"Captain Richards," Bill's voice calls me over when my drink is ready. I debate whether to tell him that I am in fact, no longer a Captain but decide against it. It will serve our purpose better for him to believe that I am a Captain in the British Army.

"Now Alice, why don't you tell us what this all about and how we can possibly help you?" Lillian says.

"If I may?" I interject.

"Of course, Captain," Lillian replies.

"I'll get straight to the point if you don't mind. We are in need of a boat and Alice tells me that you have one that we could borrow?" I tell the couple, who look at each other confused after I have spoken.

"Is there a problem?" Alice asks.

"Well," Bill says. "If you're talking about our old boat, I'm afraid we sold it some years back. We were too old for taking it out on the river, it was never used and so we decided to sell it. It's been many years since you came to visit, and we took the boat out Alice."

Shit, I think to myself, *it looks like we are going to be trawling the riverbank after all.*

Alice looks terribly embarrassed by this turn of events, but how could she have known. She did suggest phoning ahead, just in case of such a situation, so she can't be blamed.

"Oh dear, I can see you're disappointed. Have you come far to borrow it?" Lillian asks.

"Well, we were kind of counting on it," Alice replies.

"Oh, what a shame. You could have borrowed it if we still had it. Couldn't they Bill? Lillian says.

"Yes of course," Bill agrees.

"What we gonna do now Dad?" Josh asks, but I don't answer him while I am thinking.

"Do any of your neighbours have a boat nearby?" I ask.

"Only the Kennedys have one that I know of, our neighbours," Bill answers.

"Good, can you take me round to see them?" I ask.

"They aren't there. They left when the trouble started, I'm afraid," Bill tells me.

"Is their boat still there?" I ask.

"Yes, it's still there. It's undercover, on their pontoon."

"Well, we will have to borrow that one," I announce.

"How can you borrow it if they're not there?" Lillian asks innocently.

"I'm sure they won't mind," I say. "If it's for military business. We will return it tomorrow in any case."

"But you haven't got the keys?" Lillian insists.

"That won't be a problem, Lillian. I've had training for exactly this kind of situation." I smile at her.

"What do you think Bill?"

"I think I'd better show the Captain where the Kennedys boat is, Lillian. Don't you?" Bill tells his wife.

As soon as Bill opens the porch doors that lead onto his garden the sound of the river washes across me. He leads us down his garden until he is close to the riverbank and then he turns right. The fences that separate the gardens stop well short of the riverbank so there is a clear path into the neighbour's garden. As soon as we turn, I see the boat on the river, hidden under its soft covering and moored up against its pontoon.

"Normally the boat would have been taken off the river about this time of the year," Bill tells me. "You're lucky it's still there. If it wasn't for the trouble, it could well have been taken for storage, until next season."

"That is lucky then," I reply. "And thanks for showing us."

"Can we get anything for you while you work?" Bill asks me.

"We could do with a good meal if that's not too much trouble?" I reply.

"No, not at all Captain. Lillian and I will rustle something up."

"That's kind of you, Bill. We shouldn't be more than half an hour or so. We just need to load our gear into the boat and make sure it starts."

"We'll get it ready for you in an hour then, how does that sound?" Bill suggests.

"Perfect Bill, thanks. Also, would you mind if we rested up in the house before we go? We will be gone by half three in the morning."

"Anything we can do to help. I'll leave you to it, Captain," Bill says, turns and does just that.

"Come on, let's get the cover off and see what we've got," I tell Josh and Alice.

The Kennedys boat will be ideal for our purpose, it is a small launch of around twenty feet. The fifteen-horsepower outboard motor will propel us along at a steady speed and there is plenty of room to store our gear. I can see why the Kennedys have this boat; it would be perfect for frolicking around on the river when the sun is out.

I tell Josh and Alice to go and get the gear from the Defender so that we can get most of it stowed away, ready for the off in the early hours. While they do that, I go about bypassing the ignition on the motor, which is a fairly easy job and within ten minutes the engine is fired up. As an added bonus, there is already a full can of fuel stored on the boat, so we won't have to worry about running out.

As I expected, our preparation of the boat takes thirty minutes, more or less. We soon have the boat recovered and are heading back to the house to see what Bill and Lillian have prepared for our meal.

Bill offers us all a beer when we get back inside which we all eagerly accept. He joins us in one while he helps Lillian finish off the food, which I'm overjoyed to learn is steak, mashed potato, and veg.

While we eat, Bill and Lillian sit with us and their questions lead us into telling them why we have gate-crashed their home. We are all set to go so there is no harm in telling them. They are amazed by our story and wish us all the best in finding our friends and getting them out safely.

After we've eaten, we all help with the clearing up while we share some more beers. We are offered beds upstairs in their spare rooms, but we kindly refuse their offer, instead asking them if we can bed down on the kitchen floor, if they don't mind, which they don't. We don't refuse the offer of some pillows though; however, we might not want to get too comfortable but there's no point in being uncomfortable.

We thank Bill and Lillian for their hospitality as they hand us the pillows and we tell them we will let ourselves out in the morning. They then leave us to rest up and they go upstairs to bed. Nobody mentions if we will see them tomorrow, we will cross that bridge when we come to it.

I step outside to give Catherine a call, to see how they all are. I don't spend too long on the phone and I don't mention my phone call from Lieutenant Winters. Alarms are set and then the three of us settle down on the dining area floor with our pillows. Little sleep will be had tonight, if any, our brains, and nerves will be working overtime, but we must get whatever rest we can

Chapter 11

"Oh, I'm sorry," Lillian squawks as I jump out of my skin coming out of the downstairs toilet in the hallway.

"I'm sorry, did I wake you," I ask, quickly regaining my composure.

"No, not at all. I don't sleep well, so I thought I'd come down and make you all some breakfast before you go," she tells me as she shuffles towards the kitchen in her dressing gown and slippers.

"Thank you, Lillian, but that wasn't necessary," I reply.

"Don't be silly. You can't set off on your journey on an empty stomach," I'm told.

I smile to myself as I follow her into the kitchen, where she proceeds to switch the lights straight on. Josh and Alice groan as the lights blind them, but that's okay, they need to wake themselves up now anyway. We will be setting off in just over an hour.

"Bacon sandwiches everyone?" Lillian asks loudly as she shuffles over to the fridge. There are no groans to that question but muffled 'yes pleases'.

While Lillian begins to retrieve food from the fridge, I once again get my phone out of my pocket to see if there has been anything from Karen and Jim. There's still nothing, not that any communication is expected yet unless their situation has changed.

I managed to resist checking my phone through the night, even though I don't think I managed to get one wink of sleep. I did manage to relax, some, but it was tough not to keep playing the hours to come over and over in my mind. I tried to take the advice that Catherine had given me when I spoke to her last night, which was to concentrate on something else. I chose to concentrate on her, and it did work for a time, but the mission ahead kept seeping into my thoughts, until it took over completely once more.

"Mushrooms and tomato?" Lillian asks.

"Yes please," I reply as I check the weather forecast for the day ahead.

According to the forecast, the weather isn't going to be an issue today. It's telling me that it will be overcast in London today, with sunny intervals. The news hasn't changed much from yesterday, I see when I click off the weather. There is no good news, but at least it hasn't got any worse. Although it is probably too early in the morning for the website to have updated with today's latest horrors.

"Come on you two, look lively," I say to Alice and Josh as I put my phone away.

"I'm up," Josh tells me as he rises like the creature from the black lagoon.

"How are you feeling?" I ask.

"I'm okay. Wish I'd got a bit of sleep though."

"You did," I tell him. "Your snoring kept me awake."

"Did I?" Josh asks surprised.

"Yes, you did," I tell him.

"I don't snore," Josh protests. "Are you sure it wasn't Alice?"

"Hey, you cheeky sod," Alice bites.

"Only joking," Josh quickly says.

"You'd better be," Alice tells him as she picks up her travel bag and heads off to freshen up.

"Excuse me," Bill says as he meets Alice at the doorway and lets her by.

"Ah, Bill, you can get the kettle on," Lillian tells him, before he has had a chance to say good morning.

The bacon sandwiches come off the production line and they are gratefully received and consumed. Bill keeps the brews coming and before we know it, we are approaching the off.

Both Lillian and Bill sit on stools in the kitchen, cradling cups of tea and watch us in astonishment as we do our final weapons checks and load up with ammo. Their looks of astonishment turn to concern as we clip grenades to our bodies, throwing them between us like candy, to share them out.

I've got to hand it to the elderly couple, they have taken our arrival in their stride, and treated us kindly. I am sure the last thing they expected to happen last night was to have three soldiers arming up in their kitchen with assault rifles and grenades in the early hours of the morning.

Just as I am about to go over and thank them for looking after us, my phone starts to vibrate in my pocket. *It must be Karen and Jim*, I think, as my hand goes to my pocket.

I am already heading to the patio doors to take the call outside when I see that it is Catherine calling.

"Good morning Captain," she says in a husky voice as I put the phone to my ear.

"Good morning, I wasn't expecting you to call me so early in the morning."

"I can phone my man whenever I want, can't I?" Catherine teases.

"Yes, you certainly can, I just thought you'd be asleep."

"Did you get any sleep?" she asks me.

"No, afraid not," I reply.

"Well, neither did I. I've been waiting to phone you. I wanted to wish you luck and remind you what's waiting for you when you get back," Catherine teases.

"It's good to hear your voice. I can't wait to see you again?"

"And why's that?"

Her question confuses me for a second, but there can be only one answer. "Because I love you, Catherine."

"That's good because I love you too, so come back to me, Andy. And remember the promise you made me; do you understand?"

"I do, I will turn straight around if it's changed. I'll phone you as soon as I'm back on the boat, okay?" I explain.

"You'd better. I'll be waiting for your call," Catherine replies. She still resists the temptation to tell him about the events of yesterday. The phone call from Lieutenant Winters and then the helicopter landing next to the cottage. He has enough to think about without adding to his troubles.

"Okay, please try not to worry too much. Speak later, my love."

She will be worried to death, I think as I take the phone away from my ear and look inside to see Alice speaking to Bill and Lillian. Before I have a chance to go back inside the phone vibrates again. This time, it's not a number stored in my phone, it must be Karen and Jim.

I only speak to Jim, who sounds very groggy, like he hasn't slept in days, which he probably hasn't. He tells me that nothing has changed, they are still holed up in the same office. I tell him that we are all set to go and that they should try and conserve their energy and eat whatever they can. He tells me that they will, but they are running extremely low on food and water. We confirm that they will phone me back at the agreed time and we then say our goodbyes and good lucks.

This is it, I tell myself as I put my phone away and head back inside to collect my gear. Everyone turns to me as I enter to see what I say.

"Let's get moving," I announce as I get inside, my M4 slung across my back.

Josh and Alice's faces immediately change, and they move to get their gear, as do I. Alice gives Bill and Lillian a kiss goodbye and Josh and I shake their hands thanking them for their hospitality.

Bill closes the door behind us, and he watches from behind the glass with Lillian as we march down his garden and leave them behind.

Not much is said in the darkness as we uncover the boat and get on board. The gear is double-checked under torchlight and once that is done, I move to the back of the boat, where the motor is mounted. Again, under torchlight, I show Josh and Alice the procedure for starting the outboard motor and then let Alice try to start it.

The motor roars into life as if it were a jet engine in the silent darkness of the early morning, at Alice's first attempt to start it. Josh casts off and a quick explanation on how to control the motor is all that is needed for Alice to reverse us away from the pontoon and into the flow of the river.

We can see Bill and Lillian's shadowy figures are still at the windows watching, as we reverse out. Alice gives them a quick wave before she adjusts the motor and brings us about to point the boat downriver.

We will be travelling downriver on the journey into London, and the river rather than the motor will do most of the work to get us there. The river Thames isn't particularly full after the fairly dry summer that we have had and so the currents aren't too difficult to navigate.

The overbearing noise of the motor dissipates as we become used to it and it is kept in low revs in the water as the river does most of the work. Josh and I show Alice the way with our torches and we make her aware if we see any obstacles that we need to avoid.

Daybreak is already underway and the sky in the distant east is beginning to brighten, it won't be long until Josh and I can store away the torches. The town of Richmond is an affluent one, with large gardens, ample parks, golf courses and general greenery. In dawn's dim light, the majority of manmade structures on the riverbank are hidden behind the greenery or lost in the darkness. Even the sound of any traffic that may be on the adjacent roads is subdued by the trees or drowned out by the boat's motor. In the darkness, with the motor chugging away, I could easily be transported back to my numerous missions and training exercises that I have taken part in, on dark rivers around the world. I could easily be fooled into thinking I was in the jungles of Borneo, on route for a dawn raid on rebels hiding out in the deep jungle.

A car speeding across an upcoming bridge we are approaching soon bursts my illusions and my mind returns to the here and now.

"How are you feeling today?" Josh asks from beside me.

"I'm good thanks. Sorry about yesterday, I was a bit down because I was leaving the girls again and it got a bit on top of me," I explain.

"That's okay, I understand. I count myself lucky that I haven't got your responsibilities in these unbelievable times."

"You say that, but I need to ask you something." I look at Josh.

"I know what you're going to say but go on," Josh says.

"If anything happens to me, I need you to go back and take on that responsibility. Promise me you'll do that and there won't be any going back to your unit, your sister will be your priority."

"Of course, Emily would be my priority, Dad. But don't think like that, she needs you back, not her big brother," Josh tells me.

"I would disagree with you there; she needs both of us. I know you've got to tread your own path, but you'd have to put that aside if anything happens."

"Yes Dad, I know, and it wouldn't be a sacrifice to look after Emily," Josh says earnestly.

"I know Son, you're a good lad."

"Turn it in Dad," Josh smiles.

Alice begins to navigate her way down the river without us having to direct her as often when the sun begins to win its fight with the darkness. The riverbank takes on a completely different character in the daylight. It becomes obvious that we aren't on any deserted Borneo jungle river, this is the Thames, and it is flowing into London.

Cars begin to appear at regular intervals on roads that join the riverbank before they turn and disappear again. We even see some brave souls out walking their dogs or cycling in the early morning light, probably before they head off to work. We get some strange looks from the riverbank, and not just from the dog walkers. We keep our weapons hidden, but people wonder nevertheless where we could be going in our small boat so early in the morning.

Our nice, quiet boat ride comes to an end quicker than expected. We make good progress and as the daylight increases, it shows us Kew Bridge directly ahead.

"Pass me the binoculars," I tell Josh.

I was right, even from a distance away and in the dim light, I can see that the bridge isn't as it should be. The wide three arches of the low slung, stone bridge are blocked, but I can't see by what from this distance, but there is barely any light coming from under the bridge. Scaffolding bars are visible, however, jutting up in a disorderly fashion above the bridge's side and the roadway.

My biggest concern though, is the sudden movement of figures I see through the binoculars as our little boat floats closer. On each side of the riverbank, soldiers are moving into what I know will be defensive positions, as they are on the roadway spanning the river above.

A bright light suddenly bursts across the river, twinkling in the rippling water. The light is coming from a spotlight mounted on top of the wheelhouse of a military patrol boat. Smoke drifting into the air tells me that the engine has just come to life and the boat will be heading our way at any moment.

"Pass me that bag," I tell Josh.

He swings the bag to me by its strap and I quickly unzip it to retrieve its contents.

"Where did you get that?" Josh asks me.

"Bill kindly lent it to me," I tell him, taking the old fashioned long lensed camera out of the bag and hanging it around my neck.

"Doing a bit of sightseeing on the way?" he asks confused.

"In the army, we call it reconnaissance," I tell him sarcastically. "And in the Special Forces, we call it mind your own bloody business. You catch my drift?"

"Yes, Sir," Josh replies but looking unsure.

"Just follow my lead," I tell him grinning.

The small patrol boat is soon making waves to our position, its wake telling me it is motoring at speed. As it approaches, I stand up in the boat ready to greet them, the camera hanging down across my chest as if I am off on a trip to the zoo.

As the patrol boat closes in, its nose sinks back into the water as its engines are powered down. There are four personnel aboard, all of them, apart from the pilot are pointing assault rifles directly at us and their aim focuses as the boat pulls up alongside ours.

"This is a restricted area, turn the boat around and leave or you will be fired upon," a man shouts from behind his rifle.

"Who's in command of your craft?" I shout back.

"I am. Sergeant Jennings. You have been warned, turn your boat around."

"Sergeant Jennings, you will address me as Sir, and you will escort us through that cordon. That is an order," I bark back.

"Identify yourself, Sir."

"Captain Richards."

"And what is your business, Sir?"

"We are on a reconnaissance mission for Military Intelligence. That is all I am at liberty to say. Now, you have your orders Sergeant," I insist.

"Sir, only authorised personnel are to be let through the cordon," Jennings replies.

"As you say, Sergeant. I am authorising you to escort us through."

"Please show me your papers, Sir," Jennings requests.

I retrieve my Military ID card and hand it to Josh. Alice gives the motor a burst to take us closer so that Josh can stretch out and hand over my card. The Sergeant takes the card from one of his crew to inspect, before handing it back.

"This is very irregular, Sir," the Sergeant says as Josh reaches to get the card back.

"Nevertheless, you have your orders, Sergeant," I tell him.

"Very well, Sir."

"Thank you, Sergeant. Oh, and Sergeant, we will be two or three hours gaining out intel, from our boat. Please inform your men to watch for our return."

"Yes, Sir," Jennings agrees.

The men on the patrol boat pull in their weapons as the boat turns to lead us towards to bridge. Alice opens up the throttle on the small motor and she just about manages to keep pace with the boat in front.

As we close in on the bridge, the patrol boat peels away to the side slightly and I tell Alice to keep going, straight ahead. I can see, now that we are closer, that the bridge is covered with a thick meshed material, hung over the scaffolding. The mesh makes perfect sense, I suppose, it will let the rivers waters flow through whilst forming a barrier to any 'unauthorised' river traffic.

Alice keeps the boat going in a forward trajectory and we all pray that the thick black mesh will begin to open to allow us through. As we get nearer the point of no return Alice throttles back slightly, but as we glide past the patrol boat, the mesh begins to raise. With the mesh opening, Alice applies the throttle back to full so that we can pass through the cordon before any of the personnel guarding the bridge can change their minds.

Young looking squaddies look down on us from on top of the bridge as we float through the opening and into the darkness of the underbelly of the bridge. *I only hope we can blag our way back through, on our return*, I think as we emerge from beneath the bridge and into London's quarantine zone.

"That was butt-clenching," Alice says from the back of the boat as we emerge.

"All in a day's work," I say playing it cool.

"Dad's an expert in the art of the blag," Josh tells Alice. "How do you think he used to make me eat my vegetables when I was a kid and he came back off tour."

"You used to be an easy mark," I say laughing.

Josh and Alice laugh along with me. Jokes somehow seem funnier after a stressful event.

"Stay away from the riverbank," I tell Alice. "We're in bandit country now."

"You got it, Andy," she replies.

Kew Bridge marks a change in the scenery on the riverbank. The greenery begins to give way to brick and concrete as the buildings become more substantial and tightly packed. We find ourselves passing under bridges on a more regular basis, but none of them has traffic, or pedestrians passing over them. Josh and I point our rifles up towards the roadways as we approach each bridge and we have swivelled to cover the rear as we emerge from the other side. Rabids could be waiting to pounce on any of the bridges in the quarantine zone and we know all too well that they wouldn't think twice about jumping off to attack.

Alice works the motor behind her to eat up the long winding river. The Thames meanders around to the left in a large semi-circle and then decides to roll right in another large semi-circle before the river has barely had a chance to straighten. Progress is slow, but the waters are calm and apart from some tension when we pass under a bridge, I find the journey quite relaxing. The three of us chat intermittently, keeping the conversation light-hearted. We don't try and tackle the glaringly obvious bigger issues that could ruin our chilled morning boat ride. Those issues will get their chance to be discussed, but for the moment, we all resist their growing pull.

We realise that we have reached the outskirts of London proper when the river widens out considerably and when we pass a towering football stadium perched on the riverbank. Fulham Football Club's stadium is only small by comparison to some stadiums in London, but in our small boat on the wide river, it appears overbearing.

"Contact, directly ahead," Alice announces, professionally and without panic.

My attention is quickly drawn away from the changing scenery and I curse myself for letting my concentration wander.

"I see it," I confirm, my concentration back to where it should be.

Ahead, coming into view from around another long bend in the river, another boat is heading upriver and towards us. The boat is larger than ours and is moving quicker, but not by much. I pick up the binoculars to get a better look and am soon focused on the front of the boat.

"What can you see?" Josh asks.

"It's hard to make out with the lights shining on it, but it looks like a medical relief boat or something. It looks like there is a red cross on the side of its hull," I reply.

As the boat draws nearer, the red cross becomes clearer until there is no doubt of the boat's purpose. Refocusing the binoculars, I see that the craft has a pilot in the wheel room and there are shadowy figures in an open area at the stern of the boat. The people back there seem to be blurred though, as if I was looking at them through glass smeared with dirt.

"Give them a wide berth," I tell Alice, suddenly worried that there might be infected on the boat.

Alice does as I ask and steers us away from the path of the oncoming boat—there is ample room on the river to do that. We all watch in silence as the boat draws level with our position on the river and we can see more clearly its layout.

Behind the wheelhouse, there appears to be a large Perspex screen retrofitted to the craft. The screen is obviously there to separate the pilot from his passengers and there is only one logical reason for that. None of the passengers in the stern, of which I only count three, pay any attention to us. The shadowy figures keep their heads down as if they have seen enough of the world for a whole lifetime.

With the boat behind us, Alice adjusts her course again and takes up a more central position on the river.

"That was strange," Josh finally says, breaking the silence.

"It looks like they were being evacuated." I guess.

"They didn't look in good shape," Alice adds from the rear.

"And there wasn't many of them, especially considering how many troops have been drafted into London," Josh says.

"No there wasn't, was there," Alice agrees.

"Let's not second guess it. They could have been on a specific mission," I tell them.

"What, like us?" Josh says with a hint of sarcasm.

"Something like that," I reply, not wanting to delve any deeper. "Let's concentrate on our task, instead of guessing what's what with them."

Josh and Alice go quiet, and we all let the motor at the back of our boat do the talking for a while.

Following each bend in the river, London grows taller on both sides of the river and the Thames becomes more congested. The congestion isn't in the form of other river traffic, but rather pontoons jutting out into the river from the bank, most of which are packed with idle flat barges, river taxis and large sightseeing boats, all of which would normally be plying their trade up and down London's main artery. More long and wide barges, some of which are piled high with stagnating refuse are anchored off the riverbank in various positions in the waterway. None of the obstacles poses Alice a problem, the river is amply wide enough for her to give them plenty of room.

None of us can bring ourselves to speak as we begin to drift past the prime waterfront developments that tower over us on each side of the river. While it may be incredibly early in the morning, residents of the once much sought-after apartments, with views over the river, are visible in their windows or on their balconies. The people watch us, from a distance, go past their part of the river. Their haunting looks or upsetting cries of desperation that carry across to our boat are chilling, especially from the north riverbank.

"There are so many people trapped, it's heartbreaking," Alice finally says.

"It's terrible, you don't realise how many there are," Josh agrees. "What is going to happen to them?"

"God knows, but if something isn't done soon, they will probably starve or be forced to try and escape," Alice says.

"They'd have no chance if they are forced to try and escape," Josh points out.

"Desperate people do desperate things," Alice replies.

"The best they can hope for is that the army takes back control or at least begins to turn the tide," I tell them.

"There doesn't seem to be any sign of that happening any time soon," Josh says.

"Things can change very quickly in the field," I tell him, even though I am not sure I believe that is possible in the current circumstances myself.

Chapter 12

We motor under Chelsea Bridge and close in on an uninviting low dark tunnel ahead. Our rifles are trained on the railway bridge, its wide expanse cutting off the light and making it appear extremely low in the water. My eyes stare into the dim light searching for any threats that might be lurking underneath its steel ribbed arches. Josh's rifle suddenly explodes into life beside me, making my head jolt in search of what he is shooting at, shock tearing through me. A body tumbles down from the edge of the bridge just as the boat begins to pass under it. I see the drop late and before my rifle's muzzle gets anywhere near a shooting position, a body slams into the water beside the boat.

My rifle trains on the water where the body hit, but the body disappears into the murk and a crescendo of frothing bubbles. The froth follows us under the bridge, carried by the tide, only the boats motor pulling us away from it. Every small sound echoes back at us under the low bridge and our rifles dart in every direction pointing into the darkness aimlessly.

I am sure I hear a low gargling moan vibrate into the tunnel, above the boat's motor as we approach the light at the exit. "Cover the exit," I snap at Josh as I turn back to where I think the sound emanated behind the boat. My move is a mistake, Josh's rifle immediately bursts into action again as the front of the boat emerges from under the bridge. My rifle's muzzle cuts through the air to find the targets Josh is firing at. The body in the water isn't a threat and I was foolish to go looking for it. My finger squeezes the M4's trigger as a silhouette jumps over the side of the bridge, its form black against the sky, its screech chilling. My bullets thud into the silhouette and send it into a spin as it drops through the air to splashes into the water, just missing the boat.

We gain distance from the low-slung bridge and we ceasefire, despite two more Rabids slinging themselves off the bridge as we move away.

"How many did you count?" I gasp at Josh.

"I saw five, you?" he answers.

"I don't know, about the same," I reply.

"I think seven hit the water," Alice offers breathlessly, and she was in the best position to tell.

I am angry at myself for my poor display. First, I got transfixed by the darkness under the bridge instead of concentrating my focus on the bigger threat from the top of the bridge. Then, to make matters worse I went looking for ghosts in the water, when again the threat was from above.

Josh's reactions put mine to shame, he embarrassed me, but I don't mention it to him or Alice. They will soon be dropping me off on the riverbank and I don't want to sow any seeds of doubt in my ability, which so far has not been convincing.

Silence ensues for a minute as Battersea Power Station, the famous behemoth of a building, travels past on our righthand side, its four towering white chimney stacks surrounded by cranes. The building's transformation into a residential and business development brought to an abrupt halt by the outbreak.

I wonder what Josh and Alice are thinking to themselves as we pass it by. Did they recognise my shortcomings or are they just regathering themselves after the sudden call to action? One thing's for sure, if I continue in this vein, our odds of reaching the drop-off point are slim. There must be ten or so bridges we still need to pass under before we arrive, never mind me actually succeeding in extracting Karen and Jim.

"You okay, Dad?" Josh asks.

"Yes, thanks. Well done back there, you did well," I tell Josh.

"Oh, it was nothing," he replies smiling.

"No, credit, where credit's due."

"Your dad's right, Josh," Alice agrees.

"Thanks, but we've still got a long way to go." Josh points out.

"Very true," I agree, telling myself that, *I'd better up my game*, at the same time.

We pass the newly built, cube-shaped American Embassy and the sights of London become more and more familiar as we travel farther down the Thames. We see ominous-looking figures moving on the north riverbank. Some of the creatures take a passing interest in our small boat but most just seem to stumble around aimlessly. I am not fooled by the subdued creatures, who only need a whiff of human flesh to re-energise. I keep my concentration focused, however, ignoring the sights on the riverbank, not wanting to be caught wanting in my performance again.

The next bridge comes upon us quickly, as Alice takes us around yet another bend in the river, another low bridge, which is all we can expect from here on out.

"God, I don't like the look of this one," Josh says, referring to the appearance of the bridge, rather than anything else. Mounted on the red and yellow painted sides of the bridge, statues of people hang, who they are meant to portray, we have no idea. The haunting stone figures give us the chills, whoever they are, and the smoke in the air does little to dispel that feeling as we close in on the bridge.

"It's Vauxhall Bridge," I inform Josh, just as a figure dashes across the bridge from left to right.

Looking like it is getting into position to launch itself at us when the boat draws near, the creature stops right above our path. The figure at least shows us that the side barriers next to the roadway are low, giving us good visibility onto the bridge. Both Josh and I have the figure in our sights when a shot rings out from the right side of the bridge, taking us both by surprise.

"A sniper shot," I announce as the threatening figure drops backwards and out of our sight.

"Yes, it looks like the army has this bridge covered, let's hope it isn't the only one they have covered," Josh replies.

"Hopefully, I would have thought they would all be covered. Perhaps somebody was sleeping on the job at the last one?" I question.

"Just our luck," Alice says.

I don't allow myself to get distracted as we motor under the bridge and out of the other side, without further incident. I don't even afford the statues that peer down at us a second look.

A smoke haze begins to hang heavily over the water on the other side of Vauxhall Bridge. London is certainly still smouldering, at least, after the heavy rainfall the city has had since large parts of it went up in flames.

I resist rubbing my eyes as the smoke is beginning to sting, knowing it will only make the irritation worse. Instead, I look ahead to our next challenge, Lambeth Bridge, another road bridge and one that will cross us into Westminster. The bridge has wrought iron panels next to the roadway, which again affords us a decent view, and it looks clear.

"This is going to be tough to see, I should think," I say as we come out of the other side of the bridge.

"What do you mean?" Josh asks.

"That," I say pointing through the dense smoke that is getting trickier to see through.

"Oh God, yes," Josh coughs after a moment of staring.

We are fast approaching the Houses of Parliament, on the left side of the Thames and the source of much of the smoke that is irritating our eyes and clogging our lungs. The Palace of Westminster has been burning for days, unchecked, save for the rain that dampened its flames for a while. Thick, acrid smoke is still billowing from different sections of the long old building, built along the riverbank, and the fire has done horrific damage to the already delicate structure. A large section of the ornate side of the building has crumbled and fallen into the river, the resulting hole leaving the building's innards exposed showing no window that hasn't cracked and disintegrated from the intense heat.

We gawp at the damaged building, that was until very recently the seat of government, in silenced astonishment. Through the collapsed side, we can see into its obliterated interior to some extent, through the thick smoke. The view is only made possible by the disappeared roof of the building, allowing extra light in. All we see inside is non-descript black charred remains and rubble, the inferno has destroyed everything.

"Fucking hell, where's Big Ben!" Alice says in disbelief from behind me.

I was so shocked by the damage to the building I hadn't even considered Big Ben and my eyes dart to find the massive clock tower. It has vanished, there is nothing but sky and smoke where it once stood tall. The shocking loss churns my stomach. I look again, craning my neck, it can't have disappeared into thin air and then I see, as the boat moves along, the mighty clock tower has toppled over and is now a pile of rubble, heaped across the adjacent road to it and the bridge we are about to float under.

There is no time to mourn the loss of the iconic landmark, however, my rifle quickly reverts to scanning Westminster Bridge as we approach it, as does Josh's. Any hope that Big Ben's rubble will have blocked any access to the bridge disappears, Rabids scramble over the rubble and onto the bridge towards us.

I quickly open fire, aiming for anything that moves and Josh's rifle erupts almost in unison to mine. We fire at multiple targets, as creatures scurry and crawl over the rubble and burst onto the bridge. Desperately, I take aim and shoot, trying to hold back the wave of Rabids before they can get into position on top of the bridge ready to launch themselves at us when we get closer to it. I am aware of the sound of gunshots coming from the right side of the bridge but I daren't pause my firing to steal a glance to try and see who is assisting us.

A Rabid, that neither of us has seen, launches itself into the air as we come upon the bridge and both Josh and I open fire on it. One, or both of us, I don't know or care which, hit the creature and it falls into the river in front of the boat.

Alice swerves the boat urgently, and thankfully, takes us under the shelter of the bridge. The lull in the attack doesn't last, by the time Josh and I have changed out the magazines in our rifles, the front of the boat becomes exposed again.

A Rabid, attacks too soon, miss timing its jump and flops into the water in front of the boat, it is ignored.

Shadows fly at us from the top of the bridge and this time, Josh is the first to open fire by a split second. Alice maxes out the boats motor to try and get us away from the danger zone next to the bridge, while Josh and I take out our targets. There is no time to aim for headshots, all we can do is shoot at heinous targets as they present themselves, hoping the force of the bullets will direct the Rabids into the water.

A body falls through our hail of bullets, hitting the deck of the boat. It pounces up onto its feet in a flash, baring its teeth as it goes to attack Josh. In reflex Josh recoils from the attack and stumbles backwards, losing his balance and teetering on the edge of the boat, about to go overboard.

The creature's brains are suddenly ejected from its head, splattering across the front of the boat and into the river. I barge the Rabids body sideways as it falls, and I go to grab hold of Josh before he topples backwards into the river. As I pull Josh back from the edge, the beast's body takes Josh's place and plops into the river with a whimpering splash.

Josh secure, I spin around raising my rifle again ready to shoot, but the boat has travelled clear of the danger zone. I look to Alice to check she's okay and she stands at the back of the boat with the throttle for the motor in one hand and her pistol in the other. She was the one who relieved the Rabid of its brains, all the while she was getting us away from the bridge.

"Good shooting," I tell Alice and she gives me a nod as she calmly slips her gun back into its holster.

"Thanks, Alice," Josh says breathlessly, still shaken up.

"You'd better reload, there's another one coming up," Alice says, looking straight ahead.

"It's never-ending," Josh says.

"We knew it wouldn't be easy," I tell him.

"I can't wait for the journey back," Josh jokes, making me and Alice laugh ominously.

Josh and I do as Alice says and reload as the London Eye Ferris wheel reaches above us on the right of the boat. Thankfully, the next bridge, which carries the rail lines into Charing Cross Station passes without incident and we are quickly closing in on Waterloo Bridge.

We can see figures on the bridge as we approach, but then, just as Josh and I get into position to fire, a heavy machine gun erupts from our right. By the time the firing stops, nothing moves on the bridge, but we still stay alert as we go under.

"Somebody must be watching out for us," Josh says, referring to the machine gun.

"Yes, that's more like it," I reply as we come out of the other side, our rifles at the ready but not needed.

The next two bridges come in quick succession, the first a road bridge with low slung sides, is again cleared for our passing by a heavy machine gun from the right. The second is a strange-looking one with a roof of some description, no machine gun sounds before we go under it but to our relief no Rabids attack either.

"Somebody has definitely got the message we're coming," I tell Josh and Alice.

"About bloody time," Alice responds. "Let's hope it continues."

"We're nearly at the drop off point," Josh says, and he is right. The City of London and all its skyscrapers are beginning to fill our view away to our left. The Cheesegrater building, the one Karen and Jim are trapped in, reaches up to the sky in the middle of the cluster. We have been able to see it for some time, but it was only a silhouette before. Now that we are closer, added to the fact that the Sun is higher in the sky it is becoming more than just a shadow. Even through the swirling smoke haze, we can see the buildings glass walls starting to reflect the sunlight and an image of Karen and Jim trapped inside the building pops into my mind.

"Yes," I agree, knowing my feet will be on solid ground soon. "But let's stay on point," I tell Josh as we approach the ultra-modern Millennium footbridge, that has unwanted figures making use of it.

Once again, heavy machine-gun fire rips the Rabids on the bridge to pieces. This time we see the location where the tracer rounds are being fired from. The munitions are flashing down from the roof of the Tate Modern Art building that is adjacent to the footbridge. Alice even gives a quick wave of thanks to the soldiers that we see up there, in the distance.

An unknown party really has taken it upon themselves to help us and clear our path, and I wonder who? More than likely, as we have ventured farther downstream, the word has gone down the line that a boat is coming through and so we have become expected. *Perhaps we should have called ahead then things wouldn't have got so frantic at the earlier bridges*, I joke to myself.

Our estimate on the timing has turned out to be more accurate than we could have hoped for, I see, as I glance at my watch. We have two more bridges to go under and then we'll reach London Bridge, more or less on time to receive Karen and Jim's final phone call to check-in. I am suddenly conscious of my phone in my pocket, against my thigh. I hope that they do phone, so I know they are still there and ready to move. The plan is for me to go even if I don't receive their call, in case the buildings phone system has failed. I would much rather speak to them before though and know my trip into the city isn't for a lost cause.

The final two bridges pass by in a blur as my nervous anticipation builds. Machine gun fire sounds as we approach both and we pass them with ease. And then there it is, London Bridge sitting in front of us, with London's tallest building, The Shard guarding its right flank.

My nerves instantly turn to fear. Sailing into London is one thing but getting off the relatively secure boat and going into the city on foot is quite another. The sight of Tower Bridge in the distance, behind London Bridge, does little to dispel my trepidations, I didn't think I would be back here, not yet, not ever. Catherine's voice echoes in my head, questioning if I will still go unseen past the undead, as I did before? Will my camouflage still work, or will my flesh be as inviting to the Rabids as everyone else's again?

Forcing my fears and concerns down inside me, I try to concentrate on the task at hand. The first task is to locate the best drop off point available in the vicinity of the bridge.

London Bridge is probably the most mundane and nondescript bridge we have seen on our trip down the Thames. There is no red paint or mounted statues here, just bland grey concrete and steel. Nevertheless, it is the one that fills me with the most dread, a dread that escalates as I see HMS Belfast through its arches and my eyes are drawn left, left to the Tower of London.

The Tower is only just visible under the bridge, but I can't help but try and look for it. My stomach churns as I see parts of its distinctive embankment and ancient brickwork. I can't stop horrific images of the Towers blood-soaked innards and piled up bodies, that I found inside its entombed walls, flashing through my mind. My legs go weak, and I'm forced to sit down as my head becomes faint.

My hand goes to my pocket to retrieve my phone as I try to mask my sudden collapse from Josh and Alice. *I'm simply sitting to look at my phone*, I tell them in my head, but I can feel their eyes on me.

"Dad, what's wrong?" Josh asks concerned.

"Nothing, I'm fine," I tell him, my voice sounding distant to me.

"No, you're not, Dad. Your face has gone white," Josh insists.

"I'll be okay, just give me a minute."

"It's being back here and seeing the Tower of London, isn't it? I felt it too," Josh tells me.

"Yes, I didn't expect it to hit me so hard. It's passing, don't worry."

"Take your time, Dad," Josh says, giving Alice a concerned look.

Time isn't afforded to me; my phone begins to vibrate in my hand. I take a deep breath and look at the screen, it displays the same number Karen and Jim have been using.

"Hello," I answer.

"Andy, thank God. It's Jim, are you here?"

"We've just arrived on the river, what's the latest situation there?"

"Nothing's changed Andy; I promise you that. We are ready as soon as you get here." Jim's voice is desperate.

"Okay, hold tight. We are just finding somewhere to land and then I'll be on my way. I'll be as quick as I can."

"Thank you, Andy, thank you. We'll be ready," Jim confirms.

"Good, see you soon," I tell him and lower the phone. "We are a go," I tell Josh and Alice, looking up to them.

"Dad, are you sure you're up for this? We can turn around now and go back, there's no shame in that," Josh insists.

"I'm fine Josh, it's passed. I'm good to go."

"You don't look fine Andy. Don't rush it, if you're still going," Alice says, concerned.

"Thanks, Alice. Honestly, I'll be okay, I just went faint for a second there," I tell her. "Have you any suggestions on where to drop me off?"

Alice, who has stopped the boat, looks over to the riverbank as the boats motor ticks over in reverse, against the tide to keep us more or less stationary.

"There is only one option on this side of the bridge, that I can see. Those steps up from the beach, there," she says, pointing. "We could see if there is a better option on the other side of the bridge?"

"No, let's stay this side, those will have to do," I tell her a bit too quickly.

"But there aren't any steps up onto the bridge this side? You'd have to go under the bridge and use the ones that side," Josh points out.

"There's an adjacent road to the bridge there, it will take me around," I say pointing to the left of the bridge.

"How are we going to cover your retreat down that side road?" Josh asks.

"I don't think it's a good idea for you to get off the boat, to be honest, Josh. We will come to you, it's the only way." I look at him and immediately see his face change.

"That wasn't the plan, you're going to need cover," Josh says, frustrated.

"And you will cover us, from the boat. You won't know when we're coming and you hanging around up there is a recipe for disaster."

Josh looks to Alice for help, but none is forthcoming. "He's right Josh," Alice tells him, "us being up there is not a good idea."

"Josh." I stand, putting my hand on his shoulder. "Those steps down are going to be the pinch point and you can cover us just as well from the boat as you can from up there."

"Fuck's sake. Okay, okay," Josh says, pulling away from my hand whilst raising his in surrender.

"We've got company," Alice says, looking up towards the embankment.

Near the top of the steps, a Rabid has appeared from out of nowhere. The creature's long black hair tells us it is female as it stumbles forward, not stopping. It doesn't seem to realise there is a drop of about three meters right in front of it, down from the embankment and onto the small beach below. All three of us watch as it steps out into fresh air and falls head over heels onto the beach. She would have been swept out to sea if the river were up, but now she slams into the sand, her body almost parallel to it, hitting face down.

"Ouch, that's gotta hurt," Josh cringes.

"Has it," Alice questions, "It's moving."

Alice is right, no sooner has the beast hit the ground, it is moving to get back to its feet. I take it as a small reminder of how formidable these creatures are, and I also see an opportunity.

"Take me in Alice, drop me on the beach," I tell her urgently.

"Are you sure?" she replies.

"Yes, there's only one sure way to find out if these creatures are still going to ignore me," I tell her as I quickly gather my gear. I am not taking much with me, just a small rucksack with a few provisions and my M4 of course.

As Alice manoeuvres the boat to get it aimed at the beach, I reach into my combat vest. Stealth will be the name of the game from here on out and I twist my silencer onto the muzzle of my weapon.

"Give me a new mag," I ask Josh as we approach the beach, suddenly wanting to keep all the ammo I've got on me.

"Dad," Josh says, once the mag is in place and I look up to him. "Good luck and if it isn't on, retreat. Remember, if the streets are packed with Rabids up there you've got no chance of getting Karen and Jim through."

"I know, Champ. I'll be back, try not to worry and be ready for when we arrive."

"You can count on it," Josh says and pulls me in for a man hug.

"Good luck Andy, we'll be waiting," Alice says.

"Thanks, I know you will," I reply, and I sweep my hand through the air to clasp hands with her.

Chapter 13

Alice approaches the beach nice and slowly, aiming a few meters to the left of the Rabid that is still struggling to right itself on the sand. As soon as she feels the bottom of the boat scrape against the riverbed, she cuts the engine.

I immediately launch myself off the front of the boat, my feet thrusting forwards. Luckily, the boat has got close enough to the beach to let me land on the sand instead of in the water, which is a bonus. *At least I'll be dry, if I get my face eaten off*, I joke to myself as I turn to see Alice reversing the boat away.

Alice doesn't venture far, in case the Rabid does attack me and this part of the mission is over before it's begun. Josh is down low in the boat, his rifle resting on its side and aimed directly at the Rabid.

My boots crunch against the sand as I take my first steps forward, low and behind my M4. I step straight towards my waiting experiment, which has just about managed to get back to its feet. I doubt that even if it does attack me, it will be much of a threat, the creature barely looks like it knows up from down, but I still approach with caution.

I can't see the face of the female Rabid, it is hidden by its long black hair, hanging down the side of its face. I am not even sure if the thing is aware that I'm here and I don't want to get too much closer to it, I am only about three meters away now.

"Hey, you," I call, trying to get its attention, but I get no response. "Excuse me, do you know the way to Buckingham Palace?" I try again, saying the first sentence that comes to mind, but still nothing.

With no alternative, I ease myself closer to the creature that is simply standing on the sand with its head down, unmoving, like a sick version of an Anthony Gormley art installation. I move closer and once again call, "Hey," and when I still get no response, I lean forward and with the silencer on the end of my rifle, I poke the creature in the shoulder.

Now I do get some reaction. Slowly the Rabids head begins to come up and turn in my direction. My heart is pounding hard and fast as the creature's face is revealed as it looks at me.

Dead black eyes stare into mine. I know the woman must be quite young by the way she is dressed. Her face has turned old and decrepit though, her skin is greyish yellow, and her lips are blistered and almost black, to match her lifeless eyes. A low vibration begins in the creature's throat, a horrible, inhuman sound and the volume increases as the blistered lips begin to part. The mouth opens and the jaw moves as if the creature is trying to communicate with me. The low screech changing tone, with the movement of the black mouth.

My fear and disgust subside at the display by the unfortunate creature, and I begin to feel nothing but sorry for the poor beast. It has made no attempt to move towards me, never mind attacking and I lower my M4 in case it's that which is stopping the creature from doing so. I must know for sure if it sees me as prey or not, I won't get a better chance than this.

Lowering my rifle causes no change in the creature's behaviour. Eventually, the hideous and yet pitiful noise subsides. Slowly the creature's mouth inches shut, and it just stands there, its head turned looking at me, it is then that I have no doubt that the Rabid definitely doesn't see me as prey and I have my answer. I raise my rifle again and squeeze the trigger, shooting the poor woman through her forehead.

I watch the body fall to the ground and can do nothing but stare at it in pity for a moment, as dark red blood from its head soaks into the sand. I couldn't let it continue to exist in that state of torment. I also couldn't let it live and be washed away by the river when it rises. Who knows where it could have ended up?

Gathering myself, I turn away from the morbid scene at my feet and look out towards Josh and Alice in the boat. Josh is now standing along with Alice and they both stare back at me with looks of shock and pity, the same as mine. I give them a thumbs up and turn for the steps that lead up and off the beach.

Gunshots ring out suddenly and I drop down low, my rifle scanning for danger, but I can't see any. The gunshots came from the boat behind me, that has floated a bit farther out from the beach, to a safer distance. Unable to see any threat ahead, I glance quickly back at the boat. Josh's rifle is pointing at a steep angle, high up at the bridge and I follow his aim.

I am a good distance closer to the bridge and can see only its underbelly and a tight angle on its sides. Whatever Josh is shooting at is out of my field of view. He has seen Rabids on the bridge above, no doubt and if he is keeping them occupied, I can use it as a distraction to move.

Keeping low, my legs move in quick time down the narrow beach and to the steps, which have seen better days. Metal poles that shorten as they bring the steps down, are buried into the riverbed holding the steps aloft against the wall of the embankment. The end of the steps is submerged into the shallows of the river at their lowest point, and I will have to climb up onto them if I want to stay dry, which I do.

I slow, and approach with caution as I get close, the area under the steps doesn't look inviting. Plastic bags and other rubbish are entangled in the supports and the cross members holding the steps up, the litter bobbing around in the water. Anything could be caught up with the litter and my imagination runs riot, fooling my eyes into thinking they see a bloated hand or a foot.

Nothing is lurking within the litter I eventually decide, and I move to the water's edge, pushing my rifle around to my back. In one swift motion, I grab hold of one of the steps and swing my feet over the water, pulling myself up at the same time. The motion isn't graceful, but it gets me onto the steps without touching the water. I stay low while I bring my rifle back around, gripping it in both hands.

Treading carefully up each step, I move up until the M4 and the top of my head rises just above the embankment wall. There I pause and scan the area around the top of the steps, the M4's silencer leading the way.

An old, but smart looking stone building with columns sits on the wharf adjacent to the top of the steps. Next to that is a small office block that has another larger office block next to it. The road I am planning to use runs between the two office blocks, and I check behind me before my legs push to take me up onto the wharf's footpath.

At the top, I make for cover, a tree with low hanging branches in front of the smaller office block. I scan the area again, but nothing moves so I swivel and turn to take my aim onto the bridge behind me. My height on the wharf has changed my angle and I can get a good look at the bridge, although I still can't see onto the roadway. The bridge looks clear, and my head turns to see if Josh is still aiming up to it, since the gunshots have stopped. He is still aiming up, but his rifle moves back and forth across the bridge suggesting that he has no targets.

Bringing my rifle back down and around, I scan my area again before deciding it's time to move into the city. The road that will take me away from the river runs between the two office blocks, it is narrow with the two buildings reaching up each side of it, robbing it of most of its light. Add to that the smoke haze that looks like it is going to get thicker as I move away from the open expanse of the river, means visibility on the road is poor.

Breaking cover and staying low behind the M4, I cross the wharf and move between the two office blocks. Two parked cars are next to the kerb on the righthand side of the road. I keep my distance from them and steadily begin to stalk down the road. My rifle constantly sweeps through the air between checking the way ahead, checking my six and clearing blind spots. My breathing is calm and steady despite the smoke irritating my chest, I don't want to cough because if I do, I might not stop.

Almost at the end of the short road, a shadow appears from the right. I come to a quick stop, as does the shadow, the Rabid has seen me. My heart rate increase as the beast in front turns its body towards me as if it might fancy a stroll down to the river. Before it can decide, my M4 swiftly pulls back into my shoulder as my head lowers down to its sights. The male Rabid still looks undecided as I squeeze the trigger and the silenced M4 spits a bullet into the creature's head. As soon as the Rabid has dropped into a pile, I lower the rifle and continue to the end of the road.

Taking cover against the side of the larger office block, on my left at the junction at the end of the road, I suddenly notice the top few floors of the Cheesegrater building jutting over the top of smaller buildings ahead. *Not too far*, I think as I stick my head out to look around. In front of me is a wide through road with multiple lanes. An overpass on the right, carries the road onto London Bridge. I was hoping that I could get onto that road from here, but I will have to carry straight on and hope that the next junction will meet up with it. The street ahead is another narrow road between office blocks on the left and a building site on the right. The site has a perimeter of blue boards, covered in the obligatory Health and Safety signage.

Something catches my eye, dark figures moving under the overpass, the tunnel dark and foreboding. I lift my rifle to get a better look through its sights. Three beasts are sheltering under the overpass, moving slowly in no particular direction, but their heads are turned towards me and they stare. Have I just slaughtered one of their pack, is it the body heaped in the road that they stare at or is it me?

It makes no difference if it is me or the body that has caught their attention, I am planning to come back this way, to get back onto the boat, with Karen and Jim. Whilst I might be able to slip past the creatures, one whiff of their flesh will prove irresistible to the undead, I am sure of that. The Rabids will have to be dealt with.

The underpass is too far away for me to take out all three creatures effectively from my position. I have two choices, I can either move closer or make them come to me. I choose the first option and push myself off the building behind me.

My movement stirs up the three Rabids. They make no sudden threat to rush forward and attack, but they do begin to mill faster around under the concrete underpass, as if they were agitated. Chilling grunts and squawks echo out from the tunnel and bounce off the surrounding buildings up to me, the noises suggesting that the beasts are trying to communicate between themselves, if that is even possible? Perhaps, they are trying to determine who this newcomer is stalking towards them, or perhaps I give them too much credit.

I use whatever cover is available as I move down the front of the smaller office block. The cover is limited, however and the creatures watch me come, but they still seem unwilling to come out into the open. At the end of the office block, I decide I am close enough and take a knee, my rifle up with my elbow resting on my knee to steady my aim.

Smoke drifts across the M4's sights and the creatures have come to a standstill, watching me. I take the opportunity and quickly calculate the best shooting order. I take aim at the Rabid furthest away from me, behind the other two, in the hopes that shooting that one first may go unnoticed. I squeeze the trigger and hit a headshot, my rifle rapidly repositions and as soon as the second Rabid's head is in my crosshairs, I squeeze again. The contents of the third creatures head are splattering onto the road only seconds after the first and in quick time all the Rabids are down.

Pulling my rifle in, I quickly swivel to check the rear, in case the killings has alerted any other creatures. It hasn't, nothing moves, and I push myself back up onto my feet. Turning, I make my way back up the road towards the blue boards of the building site, crossing the multiple lanes as I go.

Cautiously, my right shoulder brushing the boards, my rifle's silencer leads around the corner and onto the street opposite the one I took up from the wharf. Around the corner, a gate into the building site hangs open where another modern office block stands half constructed. I move out from the side, giving the opening a wide berth, in case anything is waiting to jump out on me.

Nothing moves inside the gate, it is deserted, scattered tools in the mud of the site suggests that the area was deserted rapidly. I slide past wondering where all the workers went, there are no bodies in the mud with the tools, in fact, there is a distinct lack of bodies anywhere in the streets, so far. Has everyone been turned into the undead from this part of the city, or did they manage to escape to safety? I know which one my money would be on.

Ahead, the street splits into two, I'd planned to go right but it is blocked by more blue boards, so I am forced to carry straight on. My pace slows as the way forward narrows into a slim footpath between the buildings on each side. This is not what I had planned, a claustrophobic alleyway with no other escape routes, other than the entry and the exit. A rustic, but trendy wine bar runs up the left side of the alley, a perfect establishment for the cities bankers that would have swarmed around this area before the outbreak hit and the undead arrived. I am more of a pub man myself, but the thought of a drink right now, wine or beer, may have been too tempting to pass up. *A pity the bar is locked up, dark and deserted*, I joke to myself as I inch past it, my rifle poised.

On my right side, is yet another nondescript grey walled office block that has a CCTV camera pointing down in my direction. I wonder, in passing, if any of the countless cameras that cover London are still operational and if anybody is monitoring them. My guess would be that they are working, and somebody is in front of a screen watching and recording.

Ahead, I can see that the terrain opens out, but not before I need to pass another bar and more office blocks. One of the buildings has a clock reaching out from its frontage and over the alleyway. I notice that the clocks gold hands are showing 0620, assuming that the clock is still accurate I am running behind schedule. Despite the odds that I have turned up around the same time, if the clock has stopped being slim, I can't help but glance at my watch to confirm. A stopped clock might be right twice a day, but my watch tells me that this clock hasn't stopped, and I am behind schedule.

I put any time constraints out of my head, this is not the time to start rushing as it leads to mistakes and Karen and Jim are not going anywhere. I must be sure of our escape route to stand any chance of us reaching the boat safely.

Smoke drifting past the end of the alleyway as I approach its end is a tell-tale sign that I am about to leave the relative normality that I have seen so far since I entered the city. The smoke isn't the only giveaway, glinting shards of glass on the roadside also tell their story.

I take cover in the doorway of a takeaway restaurant as I arrive at the expansive road at the end of the alleyway. Safety glass crunches under my boots as I step into the doorway to use it as cover and I scan my new surroundings. The road is in a state of chaos, even though nothing moves apart from the drifting smoke. At street level, there is barely a window that is not shattered, and bullet holes riddle the retail outlets that line each side of the road. Masonry is pitted, steel is pierced, and wood is splintered. My experience tells me that some of the bullet holes are from small arms fire, but the overwhelming majority of the destruction is caused by heavy calibre bullets.

Debris covers the entire area, pavement, and road, and in amongst the debris are bodies, dozens of bodies. I am sure dust from the destruction would be spiralling through the air with the smoke, if it wasn't for the fact that much of it has congealed into the dried, dark blood that stains the street. Not even the rain has managed to wash the slaughter away.

The carnage is sickening, high-velocity ordnance has ripped bodies to shreds, and I am struggling in my shock to find one that isn't torn to pieces in amongst the mangled flesh and guts.

Any relief that I felt in leaving the alleyway behind is squashed instantly as I scan the way ahead and see nothing but endless destruction and slaughter. My experience, unfortunately, makes it self-evident what transpired in this part of the city. I easily visualise the force that the military laid down here in their attempts to exterminate the enemy, and not just from the ground. Deep pit marks in the road assure me that the hailstorm of bullets thundered down from the sky to do their damage.

The sickness that threatens to push its way into my throat must be forced back down and I must move my eyes away from the carnage. Instead, I look ahead, trying to keep the death in my peripheral vision as I find my route on towards my destination.

Leaving the cover of the doorway, I step out into the road to press ahead. Bodies litter the road and the pavement alike, and I have no option but to allow the images of mangled bodies back into my head as I look to pick my way around them. I don't move far until I find corpses that haven't completely succumbed to their horrific injuries. My presence triggers a reaction from the undead corpses, just as it has with my previous encounters. The difference now though, is that they don't reach out, or bare their teeth as I close in on them. Eyes and heads turn in my direction, as if I were a curiosity. Tattered bodies twist and move to get a better look at the stranger stepping near, or do they intend to rise and join me in the hopes they might find fresh flesh. None do rise; however, their broken bodies don't allow it, despite their hunger.

Occasionally, I discover a Rabid that could pose a threat on the return journey with my passengers. These creatures must be dealt with and my M4 does so, quickly and mercifully.

Carefully, I choose my route in case any of the creatures do decide to try and taste the only meat on offer to them. I continue as quickly as I dare farther down the sickening road, towards a pile of burnt-out cars at the junction ahead.

The carnage is endless, as I fully expect it will be from here on out. I still remember vividly my conversation with Jim when the outbreak first happened, and his description of the chaos in and around Lloyds of London. That building is still ahead of me and there is no way this ruin will improve on my journey there.

At least six cars are melded together at the junction, the ferocity of the fire melting everything except their metal components. The smell of burnt rubber, plastic and human flesh is strong as I near the remnants. I keep my distance from the clump, but that doesn't prevent my eyes from falling on charred heads and torsos through the broken windows. As I circle around, a car at the back of the collision has escaped the worst of the fire and some of its blue paint still clings onto its metal shell. The driver's body isn't as totally charred as the others and I can't help but stare at the poor sods burnt face, that stares back at me, its body held back in its seat by the seatbelt. Suddenly, the driver's body jerks and convulses, shocking me backwards and away from it, my rifle pointing at it aimlessly. Its singed mouth begins to prize open and then its crisp eyelids pull apart, their skin tearing. I pull my trigger before the bloodshot eyeballs have a chance to swivel in their sockets in my direction, my fear forcing me to stop the beast from looking at me.

I stumble away, my heart racing, unable to catch my breath. My head spins, and for a second and I think I am going to pass out. Gulping down smoke-laden air does little to stabilise my wobbling body and I must take a knee before I keel over and risk injuring myself. My vision blurs and I have no choice but to lower my head to get blood and the oxygen it contains back into my brain. The position leaves me defenceless, but there is no other choice than to hold it until I can feel my senses begin to return and my oxygen levels even off.

I've seen worse than this, I tell myself, and I have, not only in the Tower of London, but in the killing fields of Iraq and Afghanistan. *Get your shit together and stop being such a wuss!*

Deriding myself, but determined, I push, not willing for a few burned bodies to defeat me. As soon as my legs straighten, however, I know I have made a huge mistake, I've risen too soon and too quickly. The thick taste of smoke in the back of my throat sticks in my mind as my eyes glaze over and I feel myself falling.

Chapter 14

Something prods me sharply in my ribs, my mind searching for where the hell I am. Another prod stirs me further, this time it is aimed at my leg. *What the fuck is that?* I ask myself, *am I dreaming?*

The caustic taste of smoke in my mouth suddenly brings reality flooding back, and with it comes fear. I passed out, all at once. I remember my eyes glazing over and the awful feeling of falling onto the road, near to the pile of incinerated cars and the torrid black charred bodies. How long I have been unconscious for I couldn't say. I hear a scraping noise close by, near my head, and I know I must open my eyes and overcome the dread in the pit of my stomach. My fear of what horrors opening my eyes will reveal, is stifling.

Forcing my eyes open, light floods back into them and it takes a second for them to focus. I am lying on my side, almost in the foetal position. The first thing I see is my M4 lying next to me, discarded in the road. A shadow moves next to it, and then another, and my terror of what is casting the shadows is paralysing. A leg clad in indigo blue jean moves into my field of vision and then I know for sure that the shadows are not random. Someone, or something is next to me, blocking the feeble sun.

A low grunting noise comes from behind me, and it is closely followed by another prod, in the middle of my back. The grunting is Rabid, that's for sure, and it and the prod didn't come from the owner of the leg in front of me. There is more than one creature standing over me, I suddenly realise.

I can't play dead in the middle of the road forever; I've got to continue on to find Karen and Jim. *Turn over*, I tell myself, *if the Rabids were going to make a meal out of you, they already would have*. My muscles tighten as I build myself up to take the plunge and turn over, I even find myself doing a childish countdown in my head, promising myself that I will go on zero.

I roll over, my muscles miraculously relaxing as I turn from my side and onto my back as if they have surrendered to my fate. My eyes blink and I find myself looking up to the sky through the smoke haze, with a circle of creatures standing over me.

Time stands still for a moment as I lay there in a standoff with the ghouls hanging over me, except I am the only one not standing. I risk circling my eyes around and count five pairs of legs but no faces, the Rabids are obviously not that interested in me. Next to my right shoulder, one of the legs move, pushing a foot to stab my shoulder and it is accompanied by another impatient grunt. My eyes move to focus on the owner of the leg, but all I can see is that it belongs to a tall, wide-bodied creature.

My confusion lifts and the realisation of what is going on hits me. The Rabid is attempting to wake me and to get me back onto my feet, but why? Does it want to befriend me in some twisted way? The possibility stuns me. Could the Rabids, or at least the ones surrounding me be not just mindless beasts—is there at least some semblance of consciousness contained behind their dead eyes? Even the most solitary and ferocious of wild animals needs companionship at some point, even if it is only to breed. Is that what I am dealing with here, a pack of ferocious wild Rabids, who are inviting me to join the pack?

These creatures may not need to breed, but they do need to hunt and perhaps it is more efficient if they hunt in groups. It is the only explanation I can think of, while I am flat on my back in the middle of the road, and I decide to play along, at least for now.

My shoulder is hit again by the same creature, and this time I react to the blow and I begin to move to sit up. I take it slowly, taking in my surroundings as I go, my hand poised, ready to pull my Sig out of its holster at the first sign of aggression. There is no aggression and I find that my head is clear, my dizzy spell has passed as I sit in the road. My confidence building, I decide to continue and to get to my feet.

My M4 scrapes across the roadside, its tether, the other end of which is attached to my combat vest, pulls it. I do not attempt to grab hold of it yet, I let the tether bring the rifle up with me. The last thing I want is to act like a human by taking hold of the gun and spook my new friends.

Standing in the middle of the pack, I can now see their abhorrent faces and the evil behind their eyes as they size the newcomer up. There are five Rabids in the pack that I find myself a candidate to join. Three of them were once women and the other two were male. Each face is terrifying in its own unique way, but what they all have in common is they are all grotesquely disfigured and all of them carry injuries. One has a dark red mush where its left eye once sat in its socket, while another's face has shredded skin from what I am sure was the result of an explosion it suffered. The beast probably got too close to an exploding grenade.

Only one of the Rabids has not looked directly at me, the tallest and widest of the pack, the one with the insistent prodding foot. This creature is the leader, the Alpha of the group, I am confident of that.

Tensions build as I stand with my new brethren, unsure of my next move. The pack mill around but none venture far, they are waiting for something, they are waiting for direction and that will only come from one source, the Alpha. I am too afraid to look at the leader directly myself, terrified that the fearsome creature will have a change of heart and decide that I don't fit into his pack and instead decide to launch an attack on me and rip me to shreds. Something needs to happen to snap it out of the daze that it seems to have fallen into, *I haven't got all day!*

Gradually, I bring my head up and straighten my back, my eyes moving to look at the chief beast, that is stood no more than a meter away from me. Wispy strands of matted black hair clinging to the side of the creature's face, its grey skin almost translucent. A wide gash, that shows no signs of healing, festers across its cheek and across the bridge of its nose, a nose that twitches as if it is thinking and building up to something.

No sooner than my eyes fix on the Alpha Rabid, the tension builds again and fear courses through me as the Alpha's head begins to turn in my direction. Every fibre in my body screams for me to take evasive action, grab my Sig, or simply run, run as fast as I can away from this monstrous beast. I am surrounded by creatures almost as terrifying as the leader, however, and I could be cut down as soon as my back was turned if I tried to flee.

I attempt to calm myself; the pack has had plenty of opportunities to taste my flesh, I know something more is going on here and I must front it out. The Alpha's head squares up to mine and it stares straight at me, sizing me up making its decision, and all I can do is wait for its judgement to seal my fate.

Alpha's face suddenly changes, it scrunches up, its decision is made, that much I know. Its mouth snaps open and an almighty, high pitched roar slams straight into me. My ears are pounded by the onslaught, about to burst as the terrifying sound reverberates out of its cavernous black mouth. Spittle from the disgusting hole sprays across me, the infected bile splashing onto my face. I resist raising my arms to wipe the virus away and without a second thought my mouth opens and I scream as hard as I can back at my tormentor in defiance.

My lungs give out rapidly, I cannot compete with Alpha's fearsome display and completely involuntarily my mouth snaps shut and my head bows down in submission to my superior, my pitiful display over.

With my head down, I stand in obedience waiting to discover if I will be shown mercy. I am almost trembling in fear as my eyes reach up, straining in their sockets as far as possible to try and catch a glimpse of Alpha's next move. My arms tense, poised to reach for my weapon if needed.

Gradually, Alpha's roar tapers out and its body relaxes. To my relief, I see its stance turn an inch or two away from me and it is then that I know I have passed my initiation. Alpha has accepted me. My head comes up slowly to see the other four Rabids have been watching the display, their eyes fixed on me and Alpha.

Their eyes move to Alpha alone as the creature turns away from us and without warning springs forward. As soon as Alpha moves, the rest of the pack surge forward after him and I quickly take my cue and launch after them. In unison, I take the chance to take hold of my M4 that is dangling beside me and I'm off after them.

I am in awe of the pack as it manoeuvres at speed through the city. The way they dart between obstacles and fly into the air to jump over bodies and over other hurdles is impressive. The pack is so efficient that I cannot stay with it and in no time, I am rapidly falling behind.

Just as I start to think that my time in the pack will be over before it has begun, Alpha suddenly comes to a stop ahead of me. The beast turns back, to see where I am and I realise that, unbelievably, the fucker is waiting for me.

By the time I reach them, my legs are moving at no more than a jogging pace. My feet are hitting the ground hard, and my lungs are heaving, surely Alpha will decide that I am a waste of time and put me out of my misery? When I come to a stop next to the pack, Alpha just stands there watching though. *Is it giving me a chance to get my strength back before we continue?* I wonder. Whatever the reason, I take the opportunity to recover and mimic the pack, I stand motionless, whilst trying not to sweat too much.

The excursion has built up a deep thirst inside me and the incessant smoke has left a thick film in my mouth, but as tempting as it is, I don't reach for my canister of water. I think that would be taking the piss out of my new friends. Instead, I tentatively look around to get my bearings.

The pack has moved me closer to my destination, I see as my eyes move in their sockets. We are on a wide, devastated road that is directly in line with London Bridge. I can't be sure exactly how close Karen and Jim's building is because I cannot see it above the surrounding buildings, even though they are relatively low. I know that the building is close, however, it must be, I am smack bang in the middle of the financial district. Right in front of me is another skyscraper under construction that I think is next door to theirs.

I bide my time, getting my breath back, trusting that Karen and Jim are waiting, if not patiently. I am going to have to see where Alpha leads us next, if the creature takes us in the wrong direction, I will have to slip away when we move. That might be easier said than done though, Alpha seems to be keeping an awfully close watch on me.

As my breath returns, I am itching to get moving again, but I don't want to push my luck. Instead, I try to show

Alpha that I am ready to go, I start to shuffle around, again mimicking the other members of the pack.

Alpha eyes me and my ploy works because the creature moves off. This time, thankfully, it doesn't sprint away, it slopes off slowly, perhaps it has some sympathy that I am struggling to keep up when they move at speed. Or perhaps there is another reason for the change in speed.

A large open junction is ahead but Alpha stays close to the building on the right side of the road. As we approach the junction, he begins to turn right, sticking close to the buildings. We join on to the next road and I wonder if this beast has a destination in mind or is it just a random path it is leading us on?

As we join the junction, my heart skips a beat when I suddenly see the tall, sloped side of the Cheesegrater skyscraper reaching up into the smoke. I am finally almost in touching distance of Karen and Jim's building. I even begin to imagine them stuck inside that office on the tenth floor.

I almost trip over a body part on the pavement, my neck craned up to look at the building and I quickly bring my concentration back onto the world around me rather than letting my imagination distract me.

The path ahead makes me wish I had remained in my imaginary state. Twisted dead bodies and gruesome body parts litter the road ahead, their number unbelievably sickening. This time, I do not curse myself for my weak stomach, the scene is one of shocking slaughter and devastation, dark red blood and body matter coat everything in sight.

Jim had described the mayhem in the streets from his vantage point in his office when I spoke to him and Karen on the first day of the outbreak. He told me the military was opening fire on the people below, that the undead was swarming through the streets. His description did not convey this devastation, how could it have?

Cars are also strewn all around, smashed into buildings and many of them burnt out. Bodies lay on top of them and squashed beneath them, their heads and bones crushed. The slaughter does not discriminate between men and women, both are torn to ribbons by the high-velocity rounds that have obliterated the area ahead, the gunfire emanating from the road behind me. The one and only solace I can find is that I don't see any children in amongst the carnage in this business district of the city.

I pick my way around the carnage as much as possible, in a half-baked stupor, knowing I must regain my composure, and fast. The tower's overhanging canopy and my destination is coming into view and soon it will be the building's foyer I am adjacent to.

My mind begins to calculate how best to make my escape from the pack of Rabids I find myself entwined with. I look ahead to try and see where they might be heading, in the hopes I can see a potential opportunity to escape. The strange, inside-out designed, Lloyds of London building is opposite to the front of the skyscraper that I am aiming for, and the thought crosses my mind that could be where Alpha is leading us? Jim had also described a car smashing through the side of the Lloyds building, although that might have nothing to do with Alpha's plans.

As if he is reading my mind, the fearsome creature's head turns to look behind, its eyes falling on me, then turns away. Not daring to think it until the beast's head has turned back to the front again and away from me, but *is the beast checking on his new recruit,* I wonder?

The front entry to the Cheesegrater comes into view from behind the adjacent older and nondescript buildings, it is set back from on the side of the road. Tall steel cross members reach up at the front of the building, holding up the front sloping face of the tower. Escalators reach up behind the cross members and into the building. I see that my entry into the building will not be an issue, the shards of shattered glass sprinkled across its entrance confirms that.

Alpha leads us level with the building, but the creature doesn't stop to take in the view, it keeps on going and begins to head right. The beast is leading us towards the Lloyds building, where smashed through the railings that surround the building, is a car. The car must be the same one that Jim had described to me in the chaos he saw. Only the rear of the car is visible, the rest of its body is inside the building. Somehow, it miraculously managed to miss the predominant concrete that makes up the street level of the building and found a softer spot to hit.

I debate whether to make a break for it as we begin to move past the Cheesegrater. I see the perfect route to get inside, through the shattered glass and bodies, and on to the stalled escalators that lead up and inside the building, but I bottle it. Alpha's head keeps swiping back in my direction and the rest of the pack is too close for comfort, no matter how much I try to 'unintentionally' hang back.

Instead, I keep on following, I will just have to continue searching for an opportunity to disappear from the pack. I casually glance at my watch, I am now more than half an hour late, I can only imagine Karen and Jim's state of mind right now. They will be going through turmoil and I am surprised that my phone hasn't been ringing off the hook, or has it? Have I missed the device vibrating in my pocket, more than likely I have? I am prone to miss calls under normal circumstances, never mind when I am running with a zombie horde.

Watching Alpha casually, my hand enters my pocket and slides out my phone. I keep the phone down by my side, so as not to draw attention and turn it slightly up to try and get a look at the screen. My thumb presses the power button on the phone's side when it is in position and the screen illuminates as I glance down. I do have missed calls, I can't see how many or who they are from, but it doesn't take much guessing who has been trying to reach me.

A grunt startles me while my head is down peering at my phone, and I almost whip my head straight up to see what Alpha is grunting for. I must stop myself though and instead, I keep my head down and flop it from side to side while my thumb calmly presses the power button again to cut the screen off. I am not sure how good my impression of a mindless undead beast is, but it can't be that bad because I am not attacked and torn to pieces. Instead, I am grunted at again and this time I bring my head up slowly as if I've only registered the second grunt in my undead head.

By the time my head has come up level, Alpha's concentration has shifted. The creature is looking forwards and looking at a flight of stairs that leads up and into the Lloyds building. My suspicions were right, that is where Alpha is leading his pack, into Lloyds, a building that I saw for myself from the air was ablaze on the day Dan and I found Josh. Why is Alpha leading us there, is the building the pack's lair, where they exist when not out on the streets hunting? If it is, why choose the burnt Lloyds building, why not pick one of the countless other buildings there are to choose from, ones that haven't been on fire?

Perhaps, before Alpha was turned into its current undead state, he was one of the toffs that worked inside the building and so it brings with it familiarity? Was Alpha inside when Rabids swarmed in and was that where his metamorphosis took place? Are the rest of his pack former work colleagues, was he their boss and now they find themselves under his command even as undead zombies?

As usual, I must remind myself that I am overthinking. I will never know if any of the pack actually worked inside the Lloyds building, none of them are going to offer me an explanation any time soon, so it's academic. The only thing I need to worry about is leaving these Rabids behind and getting on with finding Karen and Jim. Get them, get back on the boat and get the fuck out of here, nothing else matters.

My phone is slipped back into my pocket, my other hand gripping my rifle tightly. I have reached my destination so why not pull the M4 up and spray the beasts with bullets. I'm confident that I could deal with the five Rabids effectively, even Alpha's bulk would be no match for the M4's firepower. His head would split just as easily as the others.

No, I tell myself, bide your time and slip away quietly, do not draw any more unwanted attention. There is no way to know what other creatures are in the area, other packs of Rabids could be sizing us up right now. And who is to say that these five Rabids are the only members of Alpha's pack? His lair is upon us and untold numbers could be poised inside, ready to steam out of the Lloyds building at the first sign of trouble.

My hand loosens slightly on the grip of the M4 as I decide to continue to play along. Alpha's leg is already reaching for the first of the steps that leads up to the open doors of the building and I get ready to follow his lead and mount the steps myself.

Chapter 15

The smell of the now extinguished fire is almost overpowering as I reach the final few steps and then pass through the entrance and into the Lloyds building. As I enter the lobby, I am transported back to my childhood, to when my family and I returned home from a weekend away to find our house had caught fire in our absence. The difference here is that the smoke hasn't cleared, it hangs in the air like a fog, clinging to everything.

Alpha doesn't pause in the lobby, he aims for a jammed open door at the back of it, the smoke spiralling around his wide shoulders as he moves. I can only hope that wherever the door leads, the smoke will have dissipated, because my eyes are beginning to water, and my lungs are rasping.

The whole building opens out into a cavernous open space beyond the door. In front of me, sitting on an expansive white marble floor is a tall wooden pergola like structure with a clock mounted at its peak. Each side of the marble floor are rows and rows of workstations and desks, an open-plan office, and a trading floor the size of which I have never seen. Zigzagging up in the centre of the space are five sets of escalators and above them is nothing but a vast expanse... and smoke. The interior of the building is completely open, all the way up to its glass atrium roof that must be fourteen or fifteen floors above.

Thankfully, the smoke haze isn't as dense in here, but it is there none the less. I cannot see any evidence of the fire that has burnt somewhere in the building, perhaps it took hold in another wing or on higher floors. Unfortunately, the thin layer of smoke does nothing to hide the carnage that ripped through the trading floor. Below my feet, the once pristine white marble is stricken with contrasting dark red bloodstains, from small splattering's to large, congealed pools of body matter. A stomach-churning smell of rotting corpses is drawn into my lungs together with the smoke, a hideous cocktail that forces an uncontrollable retch out of my throat that I fail to hold down.

I quickly turn away from the pack, afraid that my watering eyes and red face, together with the sound of my retching will draw close scrutiny. They will finally see straight through my charade. I can barely see through the tears as my sickness grows deep inside me, and I take to breathing through my mouth to try and lessen the stink, desperately trying to regain control of my bodily functions.

I concentrate on controlling my stomach and gradually my nausea subsides, and my eyes begin to clear. The loud retch doesn't seem to have riled the pack, and I remember the retching creature I had a close encounter with inside the Tower of London. Perhaps, stomach-churning retches are not unusual for these beasts.

My clearing vision brings into focus a petrified dead face opposite from me on the trading floor with massive bruising around its forehead. The body of the well-tailored corpse is spread across the floor on its back, its blood-stained shirt in tatters and its belly and guts missing, eaten away. My vision moves away from the torrid scene and out over the trading floor in front of me. Corpses are strewn in every direction, on the floor, across desks, some are weirdly still sat slumped in their office chairs. Not all the flesh has been feasted upon, not yet. The Lloyds building is a veritable larder of meat for the undead and now I understand why Alpha's pack use it for their lair.

A screech rises, echoing into the cavernous space. The sound reverberates around me, reaching up to the atrium, before bouncing back down, until the call is suddenly cut off. In trepidation, I turn around to see Alpha bringing its head down and shutting its gaping mouth.

My confusion at what the call was for is short-lived. The area around the base of the escalators in the middle of the space begins to move, dark shadowy figures move out from around the bottom of the escalator and come towards Alpha. The Alpha creature's pack is more than only five beasts, there are more, many more and they are coming my way.

I have my answer, this is where the undead are concentrated, at least in this part of the city. I would gamble that just like a pride of lions, Alpha and the other four undead creatures were out patrolling their part of the savannah when they came across me unconscious in the road. There will definitely be other Rabids wanting to feed when I get Karen and Jim and head back to the boat, loaners or smaller packs, but there is a good chance that this is the main concentration.

So, what do I do, my mind races as the Rabid horde gets closer? Do I back off and slip away? Get out of the building while Alpha's concentration is diverted, as he stares at the oncoming mass of figures. That will only delay the inevitable when we hit the streets to get back to the boat. *No*, I tell myself, you need to disrupt the horde here and now to give us any chance.

Even now as I am debating this with myself, I am visualising my route out of the Lloyds building, to run across the street and get into Karen and Jim's building. I take a step backwards from the pack and reach up to my combat vest where my grenades are secured. Gently releasing the M4 onto its tether, I pick off three grenades, my fingers curling around them, my nausea replaced by tension. I lower my hands holding the explosive balls to my front and proceed to carefully pull out the safety pins. Not allowing the pins to drop to the floor to clatter against the marble, they hang off my little finger as I prepare myself.

Alpha's head begins to turn in my direction as I drop the first grenade out of my left hand. *Does the creature sense my fear or is it my malice?* I think as my foot kicks out slightly to cushion the grenades drop and to direct it forward into the middle of my five new acquaintances. My questions about Alpha's perceptions are instantly overridden when my right hand swoops up to throw the second two grenades across the wide-open space. I aim for the glut of dark figures coming from behind the escalators, hoping for them to land in the centre of the Rabid horde.

As I spin to make my break for the entrance, I see the change in Alpha's features to anger and hatred, and possibly betrayal. I have no time for Alpha's feelings, my ten seconds until the first grenade goes off is already nearly up. I race for the entrance, the M4 gripped in my right hand, not looking back.

My time is up, I know it and I dive for the jammed open door. The first, explosion hits while I'm in mid-flight, careering through the door. Searing heat and shrapnel rush through the door as I hit the ground just inside the lobby. Only for a second do I pause, spread-eagled on the floor searching my lower half to feel if I am injured. No pain travels up to my brain and so my knees jerk up as my arms push me off the ground and I'm quickly kneeling and taking hold of the M4 in both hands.

As dust falls on me the M4 is pointing back through the door, ready to fire. I have no recollection of the second two grenades exploding but judging by the amount of debris billowing in the air beyond the door they certainly did. I can't see anything moving and nothing rushes at me through the clouds of smoke and so I pull the M4 in and push myself to my feet.

I quickly move across the lobby and take cover next to the top of the steps down to the street to check my rear. Still nothing moves from beyond the door, so I change my stance and point the M4 down the steps, which are also clear.

Filling my lungs with the relatively fresh air of the outside as I descend the flight of steps, I again take cover when I reach the bottom, but I see no threats and move again. Pushing myself off, I sprint the short distance across the street aiming directly for the shattered glass and steel girders that leads the way into the Cheesegrater tower.

My heart is pounding by the time I reach the nearest towering girder and take cover behind it. I scan my new surroundings which are a chaos of shards of shattered glass and grotesquely mutilated bodies, none of which move, however, so using the grey girder as a shield to hide behind, I edge round to see if any of the undead has followed me out of the Lloyds building.

The only thing that has followed me out is yet more dust and smoke, the street is clear. I pull the M4 in and whilst resting my back against the girder, I catch my breath and get my heart rate down before I move out and into the next building.

"Dad, come in, over," Josh's voice squawks over the radio attached to my chest.

"Receiving, over," I reply, my left hand pointing the radio towards my mouth.

"Report, did we hear explosions, over?" Josh demands.

"Nothing to report. I have just reached their building and am going inside now. Will report in when leaving, out."

"Copy," Josh replies.

There is no point in trying to go into the ins and outs of the mission so far over the radio. That would only make him worry more and there'll be plenty of time for that later, hopefully...

Across from my position, two sets of escalators seem to be the way into the building, one reaches higher than the other and that is the one I decide to use, even though the other is closer. But just as I prepare to move, my phone vibrates in my pocket. *Fuck's sake*, I think, *what is this, twenty questions?*

"I'm just about to enter the building, hold tight," I say immediately, not waiting for the 'hello.'

I just about hear Jim's voice say 'okay,' before the phone is stuffed back into my pocket.

Glass crunches under my boots as I finally leave the steel girder behind, my heart rate now under control. I stay low behind my M4 as I move slowly across the front of the building, in between the bullet filled corpses. Light diminishes somewhat as the glass canopy above, which only has a few plates of glass remaining, is replaced by the dark underbelly of the building.

I reach the bottom of the taller set of escalators, that probably stopped their travels as soon as the electricity to the tower was cut and take one last scan behind me. Thankfully, there is one flight of steel stairs that is corpse free, and I step onto it. It seems that practice makes perfect, I climb the escalator without issue. I seem to have to climb escalators more than they carry me of late and I can't see that changing any time soon.

The area at the top of the escalator reminds me of a tube station, it is basic with a row of low-slung walk-through barriers. All the barriers glass doors are wide open, so I simply walk through them rather than having to climb over.

I follow the unfamiliar layout that I presume leads to the stairwells and the lifts, the smell of death concentrates the farther I go from the opening at the top of the escalators, but it is manageable.

Banks of lifts are at the back of the building, on the vertical side of the tower. I walk past the touchpad screens sitting on poles outside each stainless steel sliding door to look for the stairs leading up. Even if I was so inclined to use the lifts, I see from the black touchpad screens that they are not operational.

Past all the stainless steel doors is another door that I see leads to the stairs as I peer through the door's glass panel. The area on the other side of the door is clear and I push my shoulder against it, a whooshing sound accompanies the door opening as the air equalises and the air that flows out to greet me is stagnant and rancid with the smell of death. Once more I must concentrate to hold my stomach down, but I do it while I move, confused why my stomach has become so weak.

Luckily, the stairs have windows bringing in light from the outside, and I hope that the tower's design keeps those windows, at least until the tenth floor. Reluctantly, I remove my foot that is holding the door open, and allowing some fresh air in, and let the door close. Another whooshing sound accompanies the door swinging back into its frame leaving me with only stagnant air to fill my lungs. I try not to dwell on the fact that I am breathing in death and instead try to concentrate on the route ahead.

With my M4 pointed up the first flight of steps I begin my climb. Sticking to the outer perimeter of the enclosed space gives me the best angle to bring the M4 around onto the next flight and check for threats. The first corner rounded; I see the door to the next floor at the top of the second flight.

I reach the first door, which has a number 2 sign mounted on the wall next to it, which will save any confusion about what floor I am on. I don't feel foolish about needing the signs, with the way the entrance is designed, I've already come up one escalator and there was another one next to it going to a different floor. Either of the floors the escalators met with could have been considered the first floor, or the ground floor for that matter? Even with my suspect mathematics, I am confident in my calculations that tell me I've got a total of eighteen flights of stairs to climb to reach the tenth floor, with two of those already behind me.

The glass panel in the door to floor two shows me nothing of interest. I can just about see the edge of one of the touchscreen panels for the lifts but not much else. Under different circumstances and if I had a team of operatives with me, I would have the area outside the door cleared before we continued, but it's just me and I'm running late, so I leave the door alone, and shut.

Floors three and four are passed without incident, but as I approach floor five a sound begins to burrow its way into my ears. The low rasping sound is becoming well known to me by now. At least one Rabid is in the stairwell with me and I would be incredibly surprised if it is just one. Nothing appears as I reach floor five, but there is blood on the floor next to the lifts as I look out of floor five's door panel. The blood is smeared in a hectic pattern across the floor, and I'm pretty sure that there was a struggle in that area to create such a pattern. No matter how much I strain to see through the glass panel I can't see anything else, no body and no Rabid.

Having no other option other than to continue without disturbing the door, I turn and begin to climb up to floor six. My approach to door six is clear but as soon as I arrive, I see a pool of dark red blood at the bottom of the steps up, opposite the door.

Cautiously, I inch around to get a view of the stairs above, my M4 leading the way. As the steps come into view, I see blood staining each of them, the blood has flowed down the flight from its source like a ghastly waterfall. As I inch around, the source presents itself to me, the torrid horror sickening.

On the top step of the next flight, a head hangs down, almost resting onto the step below it. A man's face stares upside down at me from above, his eyes wide and filled with terror, a terror that has stayed with him even in death. The doomed soul's mouth is gaping open in a silent scream, frozen in time. Hair hangs down from the top of the corpse's head, the strands matted and clumped together like straw, the remaining blood in his hair, congealed and dried before it had the chance to flow down the stairs with the rest of it.

The poor bugger must have cracked his head open, I think as I approach the stairs. But I quickly think again, as I come to a sudden stop and duck down out of sight of the top step. With my focus caught on the dead upside-down face, I missed the squelching sound that now seems so clear. But it is not until I see the movement above, and beyond the head that I realise that the man's body is being fed upon.

Suddenly the rasping sound returns and a Rabid rises off the body below it, its head floating up as if by magic from behind the petrified dead face. The back half of the creature's navy-blue blazer is still almost in pristine condition, in complete contrast to the double-breasted front, which is doused in thick red blood.

Oblivious to me crouched down near the bottom of the flight of stairs, watching the scene in horror, the creature continues to stare down at its meal below. The beasts lower face, in profile to me, glistens with its meal's red liquid, the light reflecting off its jaw as it chews on its mouthful of flesh.

With my sudden fright passing, if not my horror, I begin to stand and as I do the Rabid finally notices me. The creature turns its head in my direction, its jaw working overtime to chew up its meat. The beast gives me a cursory look before jerking its head back to allow its mouth full of flesh to slide down its throat. As soon as its mouth is empty, it turns away from me, its back bending to let it carry on with its feast.

My M4 spits a bullet straight through the Rabids temple just before its mouth reaches its goal. Instantly, the creature's back releases its head, to flop straight down and into the gorged-out hole in the petrified man's torso, where it sinks in and comes to a stop.

I stumble up the remaining steps to reach the halfway point to the next floor, where the gruesome scene is frozen in time. I try to be careful not to tread in any of the blood that is seeping down the steps or that is pooled around the dead Rabid and its meal. I am fairly sure that the petrified man is dead, but I fire a bullet through the bottom of his chin to be certain, his brain matter ejected, only adding to the slip hazard on the stairs. I think that my first instinct that he hit his head is right, because if he hadn't, he would have turned into a Rabid himself.

In my over-eagerness to leave the torrid scene behind me, I turn for the remaining steps up to floor seven. I am out of position; however, my rifle is not leading the way and my eyes linger too long on the blood and guts below.

A Rabid launches itself at me from the steps above, stunning me. How long it had been watching me? I don't know, for *long enough*, is all I can think as my camouflage from the undead slips and the baying creature hits me across the shoulders. Only the wall behind stops me from going down and hitting the ground. The blow knocks the wind out of me, nevertheless. In reflex, my hand releases the M4, which is useless down by my side and my arms push up to try and stop the Rabid's frenzied attack.

I lock eyes with the terrifying Rabid's, and only rage and hate stare back at me. The creature's teeth snap at my face, desperate to gorge on my flesh. Hands grip tightly onto my shoulders and I strain to keep the teeth away from me. The female's long blond hair waves in the air as its rage increases and its head jerks back, ready to strike again.

A chilling screech echoes out from the floors above as our fight continues and it is instantly followed by a clattering sound. Other Rabids have heard our struggle and even now are descending the stairwell, rushing to join in the feeding frenzy.

Gathering all my strength, I push my arms up further, lifting the slender body of the female Rabid with them, my hands now gripping tightly under her armpits. The motion sends the Rabid to an even higher state of rage as its mouth moves away from its target and the flesh it craves.

In one swift motion, I step forward, with the Rabid held in the air and push my arms out with all the force I can muster. At my maximum extension, I release my grip and throw the creature over the side of the stairwell, and with a whimpering screech, the Rabid plummets down through the air and smashes into the hard floor outside door six. The Rabids stocking-clad legs hit the ground first with a sickening crunch as its bones crumble beneath it, the force of the fall carrying it into the corner next to the door.

Shriek's blast of out the Rabid's mouth, whether from pain or anger at the loss of its meal, I couldn't say and don't have time to ponder. The next attack is upon me and I reach down to retrieve the M4 from my side, quickly whipping it up to meet the threat.

The first Rabid careers around the corner, its speed slamming into the wall opposite the stairwell's handrail. The blow doesn't faze the creature and it quickly scrambles to carry on its descent, its eyes fixed on me.

I step to the side bringing the M4 to bear, the back of my foot kicking into the Rabid hunched over with its head sunk into the guts of the torn open belly of the petrified man. My aim is true and the M4 spits out a bullet at the Rabid above, the bullet hits home straight into the face of the Rabid as it is about to launch itself at me. Blood and brains splatter onto the wall and the Rabid tumbles down the flight of stairs, head over heels.

Next to me, my kick has overbalanced the Rabid behind me and it topples sideways with a squelching sound, as its head pulls out of the soggy belly. I barely notice as that body bowls down the stairs towards the female Rabid at the bottom, still screaming.

The Rabid that I have just shot lands at my feet just as another creature rounds the corner from above. This one rounds the corner with ease and speed, its left hand taking hold of the handrail to pull itself around efficiently. The speed of the creature takes it flying into the air before I have fixed it in my sights. I adjust my stance rapidly to get a shot away as the creature swoops down the stairs at me. My bullet misses its headshot, but my aim is low to ensure I hit something and the bullet blasts into the creature's throat. The creature's body goes instantly limp, the bullet ripping through its spine, its control lost, and arms paralysed, the Rabid smashes headfirst into the wall behind me with a hideous thud, killing it on impact.

My aim reverts back up to the top of the flight of stairs in a flash, and as the M4's muzzle arrives into position, another target presents itself and I squeeze the trigger again. This shot is easy compared to the others, the Rabid arrives in confusion and hesitates at the top. My shot hits home, spraying the wall with yet more brain matter and the Rabid simply flops down, falling onto the top step, from where it slides and bumps down towards me, its body turning over as it comes.

My aim stays fixed above as I wait for the next beast to arrive. The Rabid below with the crushed legs, wailing away incessantly, the piercing noise drills into my head, penetrating my brain. After less than a minute, I can take the noise no more and pull my M4 back, turn the rifle, aim, and shoot the beast through the forehead, cutting the sound dead.

Within a couple of seconds, the M4 is aimed back up above, but nothing arrives to force me to put it to use. I quickly decide that the onslaught has abated, at least for now and I move to extract myself from the bodies I am surrounded by.

This time, I ensure that I am in the correct stance, with the M4 leading the way before my boot reaches for the first step.

Spots of blood have sprinkled every step on the way up to floor seven, they are impossible to avoid treading in so, I ignore them. The same blood covers the walls, along with body matter. Near the summit, whilst I take the wide way around, I make sure that I don't brush my back against any of the walls.

After checking door seven, I continue up slowly and cautiously, the M4's muzzle floating to follow the movement of my eyes exactly. Arriving at floor eight, I immediately see the difference in the light through the glass panel in the door, it is in shadow. I edge closer, whilst keeping my distance to try and get a view through the panel. Something suddenly moves on the other side of the panel and I gasp to myself when a pair of eyes appear. The eyes don't move for a moment but then they draw closer to the panel, until a grotesque Rabid fills the glass panel cut into the door.

The face stares at me inquisitively, debating its next move. I freeze, hoping the beast will lose interest and wander off, even though I know it must be dealt with. The weight of the Rabid against the door begins to unintentionally push it open slightly, any moment now it will come through and into the stairwell if it meant to or not. The door moves again, forcing my hand and I take aim at the creature's face.

The bullet pierces the glass with a crack, leaving only a small round hole before it enters the Rabids head. Light instantly streams through the glass panel as the creature falls from view, and I turn to take on the last few flights of stairs.

At floor nine, which is clear, I quickly have a discussion with myself as to whether I should climb higher than floor ten? Should I check the floors above to see if they are clear before I leave the stairwell on Karen and Jim's floor? The last thing I will need with two passengers in tow is to be pounced upon again and have to go back into battle.

In the end, I decide against it, if there are any mobile Rabids still in the stairwell, surely, they would have joined in with the last onslaught. Besides which, this is a very tall tower with many floors, and I am not climbing to the top, that's for sure.

I come to a compromise when I reach the last flight of steps before reaching floor ten. After taking a look up to my goal, I step back and position myself at the bottom of the flight, resting my rifle on top of the bannisters, aiming up.

Firstly, I listen intently for any tell-tale sounds of Rabids from above, but I hear nothing. Next, I bang the palm of my hand against the steel handrail where my M4 is resting. I hit it solidly three times and then listen again. Once the echo of the blows has bounced up and down the stairwell and faded, my ears prick to listen again. No noises respond to my call, so I lift the rifle and climb the last flight before I arrive on floor ten.

My look through door ten's panel reveals nothing but debris on the floor beyond and possibly a smattering of blood. My tension rises as my hand goes to reach for the door handle and I suddenly find myself short of breath. I roll away from the door, taking cover on the wall next to it. With my back leaning against the wall and the butt of my M4 resting in my right arm, I take a minute to try and gather myself.

Visions of the large beast crouched over a body that we saw in this building from the helicopter after we had found Josh, return to haunt my thoughts. The chilling creature was fearsome and looked so powerful as it guarded its prey. My fear that the beast is still in this building is stifling and I must remind myself that the helicopter was a lot higher than floor ten when we witnessed its display.

I put the disturbing thoughts aside, taking comfort in the firepower that I have in my grip. My back pushes me off the wall and after taking another quick look through the glass panel, my hand reaches for the door handle again.

Chapter 16

Pulling the door slightly open, until there is a six-inch or so gap, I listen, my hopes that fresh clean air would burst through the gap to refresh my lungs is short-lived. The air is cooler and definitely an improvement on the stagnant dross I have been filling my lungs inside the stairwell, but not by much. More odours of death waft through the gap in the door, the buildings ventilation system having given up the ghost along with the tower's lifts.

No significant sounds can be heard from my position and so my foot pushes the door open wider so that I can ease the M4 through. I step away from the door and immediately take a knee while it shuts behind me and I listen again.

At first, I think that the debris on the floor are just pieces of shredded paper, and indeed there is paper strewn around, but on closer inspection, however, I see slithers of material in amongst the paper, many of them stained by the blood that also dots the dark coloured hard floor. Whatever leaked the blood is nowhere to be seen, which can only mean one thing, that the culprit or culprits are somewhere else on this floor.

I push myself up to head out and find the office Karen and Jim are holed up in. *Phil Matlock*, I remind myself of the name I am looking for on the office door that they are hiding behind, as I begin to stalk forward.

I turn left and into a short corridor that I assume can only lead towards the offices on this floor. A sign is mounted on the wall ahead that confirms my assumption, the brightly coloured sign reads Cole & Co, with an arrow pointing right. Next to it is another, more business-like sign that points in the opposite direction for a company named, Brooks Limited. The signage suggests that the tenth floor of the building is split between two companies, one on the left side of the tower and one on the right.

At the end of the corridor, opposite the signs, my M4 pokes out into the shared foyer of the two companies, my head then inches out, until I can get a view of the foyer and I quickly see that the area is empty. Either side of the signs is a door, one for the Gents and one for the Ladies. Both doors are firmly shut, as are both doors that lead into each company and I pause for a moment to consider my options.

I am going through into Cole & Co to find Karen and Jim, but I don't want any nasty surprises when we come out. I peer around again to see if there is any way to secure the doors of Brooks Limited, so that nothing can emerge from there when we arrive back in the foyer.

The company has black double doors at its entry and each door has a long stainless steel handle, next to each other, in the centre. I could use the M4's tether to wrap around the handles, but I'd rather it stays where it is. The tether has proven its value multiple times already since my boots hit the sand when I jumped off the boat.

I look around the foyer to see if it can offer up anything to use to secure the doors. The only things in the foyer are potted trees in two of the corners, to give the open space a bit of character. *They certainly aren't there to improve the air quality, you can bet your bottom dollar the trees are plastic*, I think to myself, my nose still tackling the stink of death.

The word plastic gives me an idea. I carefully move towards the closest tree, next to the entry to Brooks Limited, my hand reaching for the Gerber combat knife, in my holster.

One chop and two or three slices cuts clean through the flimsy plastic at the base of the tree, the three-inch diameter trunk is no match for the long, razor-sharp blade of the Gerber. Carefully, I carry the tree over to the double door, where I gently push the thick end of the plastic trunk through the handles, I then thread the thinner top end back through the handles and swiftly pull it through until it tightens against the handles. A rasping sound accompanies the pull, as the delicate branches collapse and fold back on themselves. The small noise is worth the risk to keep hold of my tether.

The doors are secure, in a fashion, even though the plastic will not hold a heavy barrage. I turn for the entry into Cole & Co, my tension rising again.

In complete contrast to the professionally mundane blackness of the doors behind me, Karen and Jim's entrance make my eyes hurt. The colour chosen for these doors is a shocking lime green colour, accompanied by one red and one blue door handle. Cole & Co is a quirky advertising agency, I know this because Karen and Jim have raved about the company enough times to me and looking at the doors only confirms everything that they have told me. I am sure that on occasion, they were angling for business from Orion Securities, despite me always telling them that marketing for Orion was not my department.

If I ever had pressed their case to Sir Malcolm and he had come here for a business meeting, I doubt he would have walked through these garish doors. Funky and over the top was not in his style, apart from the red and yellow stripes of his beloved MCC cricket club of course.

As I close in on the bright doors, a sudden rattling sounding behind me stops me in my tracks. I turn instantly, back to the tied-up doors, the M4 poised and my heart racing. Plastic leaves sway on the branches of the tree for a moment, even as the rattling of the doors ceases. I stand rooted to the spot, waiting to see if the noise starts up again.

A minute or so passes and the sound isn't repeated. Whoever, or whatever tried the doors must have lost interest, at least for now. Wishing that Josh or Alice was here to cover the doors is pointless and I turn my back, ready to finally find Karen and Jim.

My left hand closes around the red handle and I carefully pull the door ajar, just enough for me to peak through so that I can listen. I see nothing and all is quiet, so I continue to pull the door open. I release the door handle as soon as my right foot and leg can take charge, to allow me to get both hands back on the M4.

Inside the main entrance, is the reception area just as described, the bright and funky colour scheme is embellished to make my eyes hurt even more. The lime green is transferred to the carpet, whilst the red and blue is transferred to the furniture. More bright colours are added to the collection, with pink and yellow seeming to be another favourite of the wacky designer. *I wish I'd bought a pair of sunglasses with me*, I joke to myself, as I look for targets in the reception.

There are no targets in amongst the upside-down furniture and other debris scattered around the reception. Splattering's of blood break up the lime green carpet, matching the layout almost perfectly, blood also pooled on the carpet around the reception desk to raise my guard even further, not that it needed it.

I step inside Cole & Co's reception; the sprung door closes slowly behind me. The carpet beneath my boots cushions my move forward, towards the opening beside the reception desk, that I'm sure leads into the main offices. A low Rabid gargling sound travels to me as I near the reception desk and the M4 eases over the top of it to check behind it.

My shock is instant as my eyes fall on the ripped apart remains of the woman, whose responsibility must have been the reception area. The woman's torso, who appears to be little more than a girl, has all but disappeared. Her flesh is eaten away, down to the rack of bones that make up her ribcage. Below that, grotesque horror, her stomach and the innards that were once housed there has also been fed upon, only tattered flesh from her body organs remains around the sides of the carnage. The gluttony went so deep that a quivering spine glistens with blood at the bottom of the torrid scene.

My focus moves away, it has to, and I look at the face of the girl, whose once pretty face, which is now ragged and horrific, stares straight at me. I wonder if the sorry look she is giving me would change instantly if I were anyone else, if I were a 'normal' human being. I am sure that it would be a look of feverish hate and hunger and she would go into a feeding frenzy, even though there are no stomach muscles to lift her up and no body organs to welcome the flesh.

A new dose of blood and brains decorates the lime green carpet when, with a heavy heart, I put a bullet through the receptionist's head to put her out of her eternal misery.

I pull my M4 back from over the desk in sadness, but with new vigour, a vigour to get the fuck out of here as quickly as possible, and get back to my girls, Catherine, and Emily.

The opening into the main office stands over me and I step towards it, ready for the fight that surely waits inside.

There will be no hiding I see as my head peeks around the opening and into the large open-plan office, even the forest of desks and computer screens will offer little cover for me to make my retreat with Karen and Jim. *Couldn't the designer at least have had the subtlety to end the garish colour scheme at the reception,* I think as I scan the colourful room? *Perhaps I should give them a break,* I then think, *perhaps I am not their target audience.*

The main office is abundant with desks, grouped together in islands, that are dotted here and there with no symmetry that I can see. Some of the islands have been broken up, their desks and chairs smashed into and scattered, their computer screens toppled or on the floor. It doesn't take much imagination to figure out the chaos that took place in this office, if nothing else, the blood on the floor tells me it was catastrophic.

There is a line of enclosed 'normal' offices away to the right, each door decorated in a different colour. One of those offices is where Karen and Jim are hiding, and I strain to read the nameplates mounted on the front of the doors. I can't read them from my distance away, though, my eyes aren't as good as they once were. My M4 moves away from the row of offices and I see another sister row of offices away to the left. At the back of the room, past the islands of desks is a glass-walled meeting room, complete with obligatory funky furniture.

Where are the Rabids? I ask myself; I know creatures are in here, I can feel it. Then, I see a possibility, in the very corner, over at the back, on the left is a dark opening. There must be another area behind the back wall, I decide, and it must be cleared before I liberate Karen and Jim.

Once again, I take a breath and step forward to accept the challenge, the latest on a long list, that shows no sign of ending. I go left, to stay this side of the oversized office, I don't want to begin my approach to the dark opening until I can do so head-on. With any luck, that will give me a view of what's beyond the opening and what horrors wait for me inside whatever is back there.

As I skirt around an impressive looking printer/photocopier, positioned against the wall, I scan across the office, taking in as much of the layout as possible. The task isn't easy with so many turned over desks and chairs, together with computer screens and other equipment littering walkways.

I come to a stop directly opposite the opening, which thankfully has a relatively clear path all the way down to it, past the row of offices on the left. Stepping forward, I take a covering position, low down behind the nearest desk, on the right and in front of me. My M4 points over the top, directly at the opening ahead, which doesn't look quite so dark from my new angle. A thought pops into my mind as I lower my head down to the rifle's sights. I wonder if Karen and Jim know that I am only a few meters away from them, or do they suspect something is about to happen?

The thought is only fleeting though, all my concentration is quickly taken up with the darkness at the other end of the office. Contrary to my first impression, I see that there is light inside the room. The light is dim, but it is enough to show me the racks lining the walls of the interior, the shelves hold files and other boring stationery that are far too mundane for the 'cool' office environment on show here.

Now I have a decision to make. Rabids have taken refuge inside the storage room, I am certain of it. Dark and dingy is their favourite environment, unless there is human flesh on offer, of course. I need to decide the best course of action to deal with the creatures. Do I draw them out and cut them down as they emerge, or do I go inside to see what I have to deal with?

A third option, which I have discounted before the thought has chance to materialise, is to throw my last few grenades through the doorway and blow the fuckers to pieces. Much as I would prefer that method of clearing the room, it would only alert every other creature in the entire building of our presence, no thanks.

In the end, I decide on option one, draw them out. I could probably walk straight into the room, without a batted eye from the Rabids inside, but have seen how quickly their demeanour towards me changes, however, once I start putting bullets in their heads.

I pull the M4 back from on top of the desk to move closer to the kill zone. I don't want to get too close, but just close enough to make hitting a head shot that bit easier. Clearing my blind spots as I move past the first island of desks, I draw level with the first office in the row of four to my left when I realise something. I haven't considered if any of the other offices are occupied, apart from Phil Matlock's. For all I know each one of them could have employees cowering inside, praying for salvation, or worse, each one could house the undead, hungry for flesh.

Stepping right, off the path forward, I go to take cover again behind the closest desk to reconsider my plan. As I go to duck down, I see a foot sticking out from under an adjacent desk. Surprise automatically makes me reverse my motion down, my legs pushing me up and to the side, my rifle prone. Above the foot, a leg is revealed, and I carry on moving to follow the leg up and under the desk.

In the shade of the underside of the desk, a battered and hunched over body is slumped. I can't tell if the man is alive or dead, or if what I am actually looking at is a Rabid, the head is down with only the top of it visible. My finger brushes the trigger of the M4 with the temptation to take the guesswork out of the situation completely and fire a bullet into the thick brown hair, crowning the head.

The struggle to get my finger under control is real, the temptation to just pull the trigger and have done with it is strong. Finally, my finger obeys me, and my better judgement, and it falls away from the trigger, but not too far away. My foot kicks timidly out at the one poking out from the desk before quickly retreating as if the foot might bite back, which I honestly would not be surprised in if it did. The kick gets no reaction and so I kick again, this time with force, and this time there is a reaction.

The leg shakes and the all too familiar grunt of a Rabid reverberates from under the desk. My finger instantly returns to the M4's trigger in victory and as the Rabid's thick hair begins to move as if the head might rise, my finger's victory is complete. The bullet disappears into the brown locks with a quiet thud, where it must travel through the man's brain and end its journey embedded into his neck somewhere. There is no tell-tale splatter of blood to indicate an exit wound.

Immediately, the man's body goes completely limp, and I move back to the side to take cover, where a nagging doubt begins inside me. Was it a Rabid I have just killed, or was it just a man? How could I be so sure and shoot a bullet from just one quiet grunt? Supposing the man was gravely wounded, he might have only been able to manage a grunt and doesn't one grunt sound much like another? *No*, I tell myself, *one grunt doesn't sound just like another, that was a Rabid grunt, no doubt,* I try to convince myself.

I must put my misgivings about my actions to one side. The bullet is in and the man is dead, Rabid, or not, and I must press forward. Firstly, do I continue with option one and draw the creatures out or do I change my tactics? If there are people inside the offices, they are surely bound to come out, however, I decide to proceed, then if Rabids are behind any of the doors, I assume that they are trapped behind them.

Continue with option one it is, and I break cover, to move to find the optimal firing position.

Three-quarters of the way across the room, a desk is toppled over on its side, with its top facing the opening. The top is almost perfectly aligned between me and the opening and I take a knee behind the makeshift firing position, the M4 pointing over it.

"Jim!" I say loudly. "If you can hear me stay inside the office until I come to you."

I have no idea if Jim will be able to hear my words from behind the office door and can only imagine his and Karen's surprise at my sudden outburst if they do. The outburst is for their benefit, but also to alert the Rabids to my presence.

My aim is high and to the right, just inside the doorway, from where I expect the creatures to appear from. My heart is racing as I wait to see what will happen, my finger poised, brushing the M4's trigger.

"Jim, Karen, stay inside the office!" the words fall out of my mouth as a desperate shout, my patience wearing thin as nothing emerges and I begin to wonder if anything is inside the storage room.

Do I hear a muffled shout of 'okay Andy', from behind me? Suddenly, a shadow moves ahead, breaking the dim light inside the storage room? I am not sure, but I am sure that I hear the groans and grunts of the undead.

A hand suddenly appears, it grabs the doorframe to pull itself out of the storage room, the fingers caked with dried blood. My aim is steady as I wait for the creature to emerge and show itself, I won't fire though, not until it is completely out.

A chilling screech from my right shocks me to my core, my head whipping in the direction of the noise that has not come from the storage room. A silhouette flashes along the floor to ceiling windows on my right, the Rabid appearing out of nowhere.

I am being flanked by the undead, I panic as the owner of the blood-caked hand stumbles out of the storage room, its blood-soaked white shirt hanging out. Adrenaline pumps through my veins as I tap the M4's trigger twice, firing at the Rabid emerging from the storage room already in my sights. I cannot afford the time to home in on the creature's head, the bullets instead slam into its chest, knocking it flying backwards into the storage room.

Instantly, I twist my body, cutting the muzzle of the M4 through the air to try and get a shot at the Rabid flanking me. The creature is lightning fast though, it darts to the left and jumps onto the top of a desk where it launches into the air, directly at me. The M4 spits bullets up and into the air at the flying Rabid, its hate-filled eyes fixed on me as it closes in.

Unbelievably, the creature evades the volley of bullets that the M4 fires in quick succession, and I am forced to take evasive action as it descends, about to crash straight into me. I duck and roll underneath the flying Rabid, travelling until my legs are beneath me again, my knees plant on the floor and in one swift motion the M4 comes up and around until it is nestled back into my shoulder.

Crashing into the floor, the Rabid also goes into a roll but an uncontrolled roll that doesn't end until it bangs into the tall windows at the outskirts of the office. The creature ends up in a pile with its back jammed against the glass, its head coming straight up intent on searching for its prey.

A short burst from the M4 fills the Rabids face with bullets that erupt out of the back of its head to smash into the massive pane of glass behind, which explodes outwards with an almighty, ear-splitting crash, shattering into a million pieces. With the support behind the Rabids back suddenly disintegrated, the Rabid immediately falls backwards toppling out of the building, disappearing from my sight in an instant.

If Karen and Jim didn't know I was here before, they do now, my mind races as my right leg juts up from underneath me. The leg pushes me up to my feet and I am firing, shooting at the head of another Rabid emerging from inside the storeroom. My aim is true and bullets slam into the

Rabid's head, sending it flying backwards off its feet to crash on top of the Rabid that took a volley in the chest only moments before.

With my element of surprise gone to shit, I instead press home my advantage and close in on the storeroom. I fire again as the next Rabid presents itself to me, this one takes two bullets to the head before it has even turned towards the door, yet still, I press forward.

Another figure moves, this one still behind a rack positioned on the closest wall opposite me, the beast partially hidden by the boxes the rack holds. With no headshot, I drill the creature's torso with bullets, a deathly scream blasts out through the opening as the creature is catapulted back against the rack on the back wall and it begins to slide down to the floor. As it comes down, its head comes into view and the M4 spits two more bullets out to kill the creature.

I am now at the opening to the storage room, its door frame above me. A creature rushes at me from the hidden depths inside, my trigger finger reacts in reflex before I have registered the attack, bullet's rip into the Rabid, spiralling up from the M4. One hits it in the chest; the next rips into its neck and the third cracks through the bone of its forehead, killing it instantly. The body falls onto the pile just inside the door, where the bottom beast is still fighting to release itself.

Ignoring the creature's protests, I step past the pile of bodies, my M4 trained right to aim down into the storeroom. The length of the narrow room is no more than five meters, and at the end, one more figure stands, with its head down.

The female Rabid stands almost motionless, dressed in beige slacks and a dark brown frilly blouse. Deep red blood stains the crotch and thigh area of the beige trousers, blood that I assume also soaks the dark brown blouse but is hidden by the blouse's colour. Not wanting the desperate creature to reveal their torrid features to me, I take aim and fire a single bullet. Blood and brain are ejected out of the back of the Rabids head, and the creature falls to the floor in a heap.

Something touches my ankle and I look down to see the hand of the Rabid at the bottom of the pile of bullet-ridden creatures trying to reach for my leg. As much as it tries to stretch to take hold of me, only its fingertips manage to brush the material covering my ankle. With the storage room cleared, I turn and look at the face of the forlorn beast, its head jutting out from the bottom of the stack of bodies.

Weary, I relax my arms, letting the M4 swing down to my side. I look down at the Rabid, its irate anger scrunching up its features, transforming its face into a ball of quivering skin. I wonder if anything other than a hunger for human flesh and blood is going through its mind as my arm tenses to swing the M4 up, to point it directly at the beast's forehead. *Probably not*, I tell myself as I squeeze the M4's trigger.

Chapter 17

Stepping back across the now motionless pile of Rabid bodies, I know that the M4 should be up and at the ready, and I might regret letting my guard down as I leave the storage room behind. My tiredness as the adrenaline seeps out of my bloodstream is overpowering though, and I take the risk.

Casually, I step across the lime green carpet that has a new sparkle added to it from the shattered glass that sprinkled down inside the building to nestle into the fabric. I am completely aware of my surroundings, I haven't taken complete leave of my senses, my arm is ready to lift the M4 at a moment's notice.

Wind blows air through the new opening in the Cheesegrater tower, and I go to meet it. The air cools my overheating body, evaporating the sweat that has formed over my skin, and I hardly notice the smoke contained in the refreshing air and welcome it washing over me.

After I have taken one last look around the large office space, I step up to the edge of the floor before it drops down ten or so storeys to the ground below. I am still not entirely sure how many storeys I am up from the ground because of the confusing entrance, despite this one being classed as floor ten.

My left hand takes hold of the vertical runner that held the glass in place before my bullets shattered it and I look over the edge. I don't think that I am even one-third of the way up this tower, but the ground is still a long way down. A crumpled body seeps blood onto the surrounding concrete directly below me, surrounded by shards of shattered glass.

My head suddenly goes dizzy, and I sway dangerously forward. Thankfully, the runner in my left hand stops me tipping beyond the point of no return to add to the splattered blood below, and I quickly step back from the edge.

I don't move away from the precipice completely though, but I don't continue to look down. Instead, I look across London, which brings balance back to my inner ear, the depressing sight does little to re-energise me to turn and continue with the mission. I could quite easily sit down on the overpowering carpet, rest my back against something and close my eyes for half an hour or so, or maybe more.

My eyes catch a glimpse of the Thames in the distance, and I feel a spike of energy when I think about Josh and Alice waiting for me on the river. The small amount of energy gives me enough strength to release the runner and move my hand to my radio.

"Josh. Come in, over," I say into the device.

"Receiving, over," Josh replies almost immediately.

"I've cleared floor ten and I am just about to retrieve Karen and Jim. Do you have anything to report? Over,"

"Nothing to report. Holding station and awaiting your arrival. Do you have an ETA? Over."

"Not yet. Will check in when we leave floor ten. Out."

"Copy," Josh confirms that he understands. My eyes leave the far-off river, my head turning towards the offices on the other side from me.

Feeling slightly better having spoken to my son, I pull the M4 up from my side and get into position to cross over to find Karen and Jim. As soon as I step away from the smashed window, a timid voice says 'hello', from my right, startling me.

My rifle swings around with my body and I find the face of a young woman poking out from the barely open door of the end office on this side of the room. My gun points straight at her and I can only imagine what my deranged face must look like, but the young woman's eyes bulge in terror as if I might shoot her dead. I quickly lower the M4 slightly and try to ease the look on my face, to show her I am not going to shoot her.

"Hello," I eventually respond, almost forgetting.

"Please help me," the young woman asks, her eyes welling up with tears that will quickly start to roll down her tired and haggard face.

"Who's in there with you?" I ask bluntly.

"Nobody, it's just me," she blurts back trying not to break down completely, and who can blame her. She must have been hiding in that room alone for days, probably thinking it would be the last thing she sees.

I step towards her and she retreats away from me afraid, the door closing until she nearly disappears completely.

"It's okay," I tell her, softening my demeanour. "My name's Andy, I'm here to rescue Karen and Jim. We will be leaving shortly if you want to come, but it's going to be dangerous."

"Yes, take me with you, please take me with you," the woman says, the door opening back up without a second thought, her face showing a glimmer of hope that must have seemed lost to her.

"Okay, what's your name?"

"It's Tanya," the young woman tells me, the door widening. *She can't be much older than Stacey*, I think, as she reveals more of herself.

"Get behind me Tanya and we'll go and get Karen and Jim," I tell her, nodding behind me.

"Where are they?" she asks as she finally emerges from her sanctuary to fall in behind me.

"They are in one of the offices over there," I tell her pointing with the M4's muzzle. "You need to be quiet now and stay behind me. If anything happens drop to the floor and find somewhere to hide, understand?" I order.

Tanya's fearful face nods at me, her body crouching to mirror mine. I am pleased to see that the young woman is wearing sensible shoes, even if they don't seem to match the formal, but worn, office trouser suit she is wearing.

I move out and Tanya does as she is told, she stays silent and follows close behind as I stalk across the office. I scan the entire area as we move, but the M4 points right, towards the enclosed offices, and more importantly towards the entrance off the reception area. I am incredibly nervous that the commotion that has taken place in here, especially the exploding pane of glass, will have given away our position to other Rabids in the building. I have no confidence that the plastic tree wrapped around the adjacent office's door handles will lock one zombie inside, much less a horde of zombies. I have visions of them bursting through to overwhelm us at any moment.

Tanya and I manage to cross over to the other side of the open-plan office before the imaginary army of the undead rain down on us. *Maybe, I haven't given the plastic tree enough credit*, I joke to myself, but know that actually, I have.

Phil Matlock's nameplate is mounted on the third door from the left, which is painted in a 'lovely' shade of blue. I usher Tanya to the left of me, out of direct line with the door, and once she is in position, I tap on the door with my knuckles.

Before my knuckles have had a chance to complete their third tap, the door handle is depressed from inside and a crack of light appears next to me. A beady eye looks at me through the crack for a second before the crack widens.

"Andy, thank God! It's so good to see you," Jim announces with a broad, grateful smile cracking his dirty, tired face.

In his excitement, he tries to leave the office and I see Karen behind him, almost pushing him out of the door in her eagerness to leave.

"Hold on," I tell both of them, my left hand moving to Jim's chest to stop him. "Back inside, we're not leaving yet," I explain.

Jim's expression changes to one of disappointment and confusion as he comes to a stop, as does Karen's behind him, but she reverses back inside the office and she pulls Jim back with her.

An awful smell drifts out of the confines of the small office, the stagnant air is thick with the smell of body odour and human faeces. I almost regret telling my two friends to back up and I debate whether to change my decision.

I don't change my mind and usher Tanya inside the office before I follow her in, leaving the door open as long as possible. As I shut the door behind me, I feel a gag building in my throat, but manage to control my stomach and cover my reaction with a couple of coughs.

"It must be rank in here, sorry Andy," Jim says. Obviously, I didn't cover my reaction as well as I had hoped.

"That's okay, it can't be helped," I reply, trying to regain my composure.

"Tanya, thank God you're okay," Karen says upon seeing her young colleague.

Tanya goes straight over to Karen, upset getting the better of her after her ordeal and Karen opens her arms and takes Tanya straight into them to comfort her.

"We need to wait a while and let things calm down," I tell everyone.

"What was the loud crash?" Karen asks from above Tanya's head.

"One of the windows shattered from gunfire," I reply as Karen's eyes fix on the M4 across my midriff. *She has probably never seen a real-life assault rifle before,* I think as her eyes widen upon seeing it. "That's why we need to wait, let things calm down before we leave the building. We'll give it ten minutes and if everything's quiet then we'll go."

"Okay, Andy, whatever you say," Jim says, as I look around the room.

As I thought, the office is small with no ventilation of its own, apart from one air vent in the ceiling which has stopped working. The only desk inside has been pushed against the left wall to open up the floor space to sleep on, which is where we are all standing. Under the desk is a waste bin that has a folder strategically placed over the top of it. I have no doubt what the waste bin has been used for and my nostrils twitch to confirm it.

"How was Stacey when you left her?" Karen asks.

"She was okay. Anxious as you can imagine, but okay," I tell her.

"Were things bad outside on the streets?" Jim asks.

"They weren't good," I tell him honestly, without going into any detail. There is no point scaring the shit out of everyone before we go. "That's why I'm so late, but I am hoping I've dealt with the main threat."

"What was that?" Jim asks.

"It doesn't matter," I reply as I skirt around him to have a look out of the window. Phil Matlock's office is positioned on the side of the building, overlooking another tower close by. I can just about see the edge of the Lloyds building, which is down on the right. Luckily, the section I can see of Lloyds includes the side of the building with the entrance I went into and escaped from. Smoke still drifts out of the side of the building and rises into the sky above where the entrance is. I am relieved to see that there aren't any Rabids near the entrance, and with any luck, the three grenades I left them with have put them all out of action.

"When we get on the streets we need to move swiftly and as quietly as possible," I tell them all as I turn away from the window. "The river isn't that far, but we will run into trouble, I am sure of it. Everyone needs to keep calm and let me deal with it, okay? If you see me giving you this signal," I pull my fist down from head height, "then get down and take cover. Do you understand?" I ask, and everyone nods their understanding to me.

"Jim, I am going to need your help to cover our rear. Do you think you can do that?" I ask as I put my rifle down, standing it against the wall so that I can get the rucksack off my back.

"Yes Andy, I'll try. How do you want me to do it?" Jim questions.

"Basically, I'll lead us, and you follow on behind. Karen and Tanya will be in between the two of us. If you see anything, you will tell me, but you will need this just in case." I tell him as I pull a Glock handgun out of the rucksack and present it to him.

"I've never used a gun," Jim says, taking a step back from the weapon as if it might shoot him accidentally.

"I know you haven't, and it's only for emergencies. The first thing you do if you see anything is to make me aware of it. My rifle is silenced, this gun is not, and if you shoot it, the sound could attract more trouble, okay?"

"Okay," Jim says nervously, not making any attempt to take the Glock off me.

"Take the gun Jim," I tell him. "Or should I ask Karen to have it?"

Jim glances at his wife and then quickly reaches for the weapon. There is nothing like challenging a man's masculinity to convince him to step up to the plate.

Jim holds the Glock and looks down at it like a child. The gun looks oversized in his grasp. Perhaps Karen would have been the better choice after all?

"Hold it properly," I tell him with frustration, "by the grip. That's it, hold it up."

Jim's fist closes around the grip of the weapon and finally, he looks as though he might actually be able to wield it.

"The safety catch is on," I show him. "Try to pull the trigger now, with it on," I tell him making sure the weapon is pointed away from anyone. He does and nothing happens, the trigger will not depress.

"If you absolutely need to, flick the safety off, like this," I show him, reaching over. "Then point and squeeze the trigger. Don't yank it. Understand?"

"Yes Andy, I understand," Jim replies.

"Don't take off the safety unless you mean to fire the gun. The trigger is easy to press unintentionally, and we don't want any accidents.

"If you do have to fire, aim square into the chest," I tell him jabbing my hand into my own chest to show him. "A shot to the chest won't kill these creatures, but it will slow them down. Only a headshot will kill them. If you think you can hit the head, then do it. Okay?"

"Yes okay. Don't worry Andy, I can handle it," Jim says, with some confidence at last, as he raises the Glock to aim it.

"Good, keep your arms fixed, out straight," I encourage.

"Are we going to look for anyone else, before we go, Andy?" Karen asks, with Tanya now stood beside her. I assume that Karen has quickly told the young girl what is happening.

"No," I tell her bluntly. "If anyone else was still alive they would have come out to make themselves known, as Tanya did. It's too risky to start opening doors and asking for trouble. I can't cover a big group of people either, not effectively."

"I agree, totally," Karen tells me, her self-preservation coming to the fore, which I am pleased to see. That is the mindset we all need and in spades.

"Good, this is going to be extremely dangerous, with just us, especially when we are out in the open. So, do exactly as I say, when I say. Don't think you know better because you don't, believe me. If we get separated, our boat is waiting on the river. On the right of London Bridge, there is a small wharf down there. I take it you all know where that is?"

"Yes, we know. Don't we Tanya?" Karen says, and Tanya nods.

"There are steps down off the bridge on the left if we have to use them. But we will be taking the road right of the main junction on the way and then left to take a small road down to the wharf. Do you all know the way I mean?" They all nod to confirm.

I dare say that they all know this part of the city well, better than me. I could imagine myself taking a walk down to the river on my lunch breaks if I worked in this area, and I bet they have all done the same.

"Okay, good," I say slinging the rucksack back onto my back and turning to pick up the M4. My left hand reaches for the radio on my chest. "Josh receiving, over," I ask.

"Receiving. Unchanged here, over," Josh answers quickly again.

"Good. We are just about to move out and make our way off floor ten. We have one extra civilian, so that is me and three others, confirm over."

"Confirm, four total, over," Josh replies.

"ETA, fifteen to twenty minutes. Out."

"Copy."

I look at the three civilians, who look extremely nervous, but determined. Jim's knuckles are beginning to whiten on the grip of the Glock, and I tell him to relax as I skirt back towards the office door, which he does.

"This is it," I say turning to face the others. "Keep calm and stay behind me. If any of you see anything, Jim in particular, then tell me, as quietly as possible. If I pick up the pace or slow down, then so do you.

"There is going to be hideous scenes on the way, blood, and guts. I shot several creatures in the stairwell on the way up and it will be gruesome, so prepare yourselves. If you can't handle it, then don't look, keep your eyes fixed on me. We cannot afford panic; panic will get us killed. So, concentrate on getting out of here and concentrate on me. Any questions?"

"We are ready, Andy," Karen speaks for them all, after a moment's silence.

"Good, then let's go."

Chapter 18

Welcome air from the main office fills my lungs through the crack in the door that I make to check outside the small rancid office. The room is just as I left it minutes before, it seems that we have got away with the exploding window.

I signal for the others to stay where they are and pull the door wider so that I can slip through. Behind my rifle, I move down the room at double-time to take up a position at the entrance to the reception. Nothing moves, so I wave my hand behind me to signal to Karen to lead the others down to my position.

Glancing back to see them come, I notice the two women have copied my stance and stay low while they scurry over to me. Behind them, Jim brings up the rear, he too has his head down, with the Glock gripped in both of his hands, the gun high up next to his head. His stance reminds me of Clint Eastwood in his old Dirty Harry cop movies, but at least Jim has the barrel pointing upwards where he can't shoot any of our group.

Jim does a good job covering the rear as I move across reception arriving at the company's double-doored entrance. Staying on my feet, I push against one of the doors to give me a view of the foyer beyond, and I am pleased to see that the plastic tree, I derided, is still in place and that the foyer is empty. I tell Karen to stay put and I slip out of the entrance, the door closing behind me.

I am wary of the door to the Gents on my right and the other to the Ladies farther along the foyer. Either doorway could suddenly open, bringing with it a Rabid attack. The doors swing inward though, and I rely on that keeping any creatures that might be inside, trapped there.

Quickly, I move double-time past the doors and into the corridor that leads to the stairwell. The route is clear, so without delay, I return to get the others. I hold the door to Cole & Co open to let everyone out, my rifle pointing right, covering the threat from the toilets. With Jim out last, I follow the group, covering the doors the whole time. This means that I can't be upfront to lead the way, but I can't be in two places at the same time and right now I consider the foyer to be the biggest threat.

We reach the entrance to the stairwell without incident and after taking the obligatory look through the glass panel in the door, I open it.

Death is in the air of the stairwell; it rises to assault both our noses and our confidence. Everyone's complexion has taken on a shade of sickly green, something that I cannot hide either.

"This is going to get gory," I warn everyone before I move to the first flight of steps down.

There is no hiding the slaughter when we reach the floors of my fight with the undead, but at least they all get a warning that we are entering the carnage, blood-splattered walls give them the signal, as well as my words.

My speech, warning them to avoid looking at the ripped flesh and mangled bodies, if they didn't think they could handle it, sounds ridiculous as I play it back in my head. I can barely handle it myself as I reach the bodies and certainly cannot avoid looking at the carnage once again.

A whimper comes from behind me, as somebody struggles with the horror show, and that sound is quickly followed by a sickly urge from someone else. All our eyes must look upon the twisted bodies strewn across the stairs to avoid stepping on them or putting a foot into the large pools of dark congealed blood.

I point the M4 forward and try to get us past the slaughter as quickly as possible. I can't help myself taking one last look at the petrified face of the man whose guts have been fed upon as I go, brain matter still slowly running down the steps, as they will until the air overrides gravity and dries them out.

Just as I allow myself to think that the worst is over, my eyes fall on the screaming female Rabid, her face frozen in that desperate scream. Blood crowns the wall behind her and the body that has tumbled onto her cannot hide the bones jutting out of the skin of her crumpled, thin legs.

"Steady now," Jim's voice sounds behind me.

I turn to see Jim quickly move to put his arm around Tanya's waist, helping to hold her up. The poor girl's face is white as a sheet from the horror, and her legs are unsteady beneath her. I stop and wait just past the crumpled legs on floor six to see if Jim needs help, but he tells me he can handle it.

"That's the worst of it over," I tell everyone as we reach floor five and stop to take a breather.

"That was horrendous," Karen says, panting deeply to get oxygen back up to her dizzy head.

"I'm sorry but it couldn't be avoided," I reply, breathing heavily myself.

"No, I expect the other stairwell would have been just as bad," Karen guesses.

"I didn't even know there were other stairs," I reply.

"Yes, on the other side of the building," Karen tells me.

"They would have been too dangerous anyway, I haven't cleared them."

"Did you kill all of those… people?" Karen asks innocently.

"Yes, I'm afraid so, but they weren't people. They attacked me," I tell her defensively.

"Oh, I'm sorry Andy. I didn't mean it to sound like that. Of course, they weren't people," Karen says, looking mortified at her choice of words.

"Don't worry, Karen. I know what you meant."

"My heads all over the place," she tells me rolling her eyes.

"How are you feeling, Tanya?" I ask, changing the subject.

"Better," she manages to reply, but she still looks ill.

"Are you okay to continue?"

"Yes, let's get out of here," she replies trying her best to stand straight.

"I've got her," Jim tells me, nodding his head forward, the Glock waving in the air behind him. He is eager to leave the rank stairwell behind, as we all are.

We descend the remaining floors slowly and steadily, and I check each level as we reach it and glance to check on Tanya intermittently. Her colour begins to return, and she is climbing down the stairs unaided as we close in on the bottom of the tower.

When we reach the door that I entered the stairwell through, we stop again to take another breather. I retrieve a bottle of water from my rucksack, take a swig and then offer it around. Everyone shares the bottle gratefully and Jim gulps down the last of the water while I peer out of the glass panel in the door.

"Okay," I say turning. "The stairwell was horrific, but this is where the real danger starts. We are going to be out in the open with multiple points for us to be attacked from, which can't be avoided. We will move in stages, from one point of cover to another, wherever I can find it. We will move swiftly but carefully from one covering position to another. When I stop for cover, you all stop behind me and get down until I am ready to move again, understand?" Everyone nods with worried expressions on their faces.

"Keep your eyes peeled for anything that moves. If you see anything, let me know and point in the direction of the movement. Jim don't fire unless you have no choice, because of the noise. But if you absolutely must, then do it and aim for the body.

"If I start firing, that is not a signal for you to stop, only stop if I do. I could start firing before we have reached cover, so keep moving. Stay behind me, okay?" Again, they all nod.

"Stealth is the name of the game, we don't want to be seen, or heard. Are you ready?" I ask.

They are as ready as they are ever going to be, so I turn, check through the pane of glass in the door once more and then begin to ease it open.

Nothing has changed outside, so I open the door and go through. The way forward is clear, so staying low, I move double-time across and to the top of the escalator. As soon as I reach the escalator, I duck down and take a knee behind its side, my M4 pointing over it, resting on the handrail.

My three companions follow me across in good order and duck down behind me when I stop. *So far so good*, I think as I peer down the escalator.

From my vantage point, I can see the outside foyer area of the tower, with shattered glass and bodies covering the concrete. Beyond the foyer is the road and on the other side of the road, I can see one side of the Lloyds building.

The bodies, in amongst the shattered glass below are frozen as they were when I passed them on the way into the Cheesegrater. That might change when my companions' step onto the shattered glass and I curse myself for not taking the time to kill any Rabid threats down there before I stepped onto the escalator.

I calculate that two bodies might be an immediate threat, the two near the exit, at the bottom of the escalator. Lining the head of the closest one up in the sights of my M4, I pull the trigger and put a bullet into the top of its head. The body jerks on impact from the bullet and a dull thud echoes up to our position. I quickly move the rifle to get the other's head in my aim and take the shot. This bullet enters the back of the head, with another jerk and a dull thud.

Across, nearer the road, I notice another body lying in the glass that could pose a threat. The corpse's head is hidden behind one of the steel girders reaching up from the ground, however, and I have no headshot. I debate for a second whether to put a bullet in the bodies leg but decide against it. If the body is a Rabid and not just a corpse, shooting it in the leg might stop it from getting up but I've no doubt a deathly screech would quickly follow the injury. We don't need that exposure; I will deal with the body if I must when we get down there.

No other bodies are in the immediate vicinity of the bottom of the escalator, so I pull in my M4 and push myself up to mount the escalator. Behind me, nobody asks what I was shooting at or voices any concerns, they simply follow me, one by one onto the escalator.

Three-quarters of the way down, I stop and aim the M4 out over the road. The descent has given me a good view of the area around the entrance to the Lloyds building and I check it for any movement. I notice behind me that they have all ducked down behind the sides of the escalator, which is encouraging. Nothing moves near the entrance across the road, so I continue down the last few steps.

Stopping again at the bottom I quickly scan around before I step off and onto the shattered glass. No matter how much we all try to ease across the glass quietly, crunching noises meet every step we make and the sound echoes around the foyer. Each crunch grinds on me, the noise seemingly getting louder and louder, putting me on tenterhooks. The M4's muzzle darts in every direction, expecting an attack at any moment as the crunching sound continues from our four pairs of treading feet. Eventually, however, the carpet of glass begins to thin out and with a little care where we are treading, the noise starts to diminish.

As we go, the M4 spits out one bullet into the head of the body that was hidden by the girder, as it comes into my range. The roof high above comes to an end, so does the carpet of shattered glass. Thankfully, we finally reach the pavement at the side of the tower, where I stop behind one of its thick girders to scan the way forward.

I am fairly confident that the carnage on the road leading away from the Cheesegrater building was almost entirely caused by high-velocity rounds fired by the military. That would mean that most, if not all the bodies should not pose a threat and are simply corpses. There is no guarantee of that of course, but I haven't enough bullets, never mind time, to methodically put a bullet into each of the heads of the masses of bodies strewn out across the entire area. I will have to deal with any bodies that begin to move as they present themselves, if needed.

The M4's muzzle swings back in the opposite direction and I take another look towards the entrance area of the Lloyds building once more before we move. The building and what might still be contained inside is making me extremely nervous. I am not convinced that three exploding grenades would have been enough to deal with the amount of Rabids that appeared before me in there.

"Prepare to move, stay right," I order, as nothing moves on the other side of the road. "There are dozens of mutilated bodies along this road, so be prepared."

With that, I push myself away from the girder and break right onto the pavement in front of us. The first piece of cover I use is a burnt-out car by the side of the road, ten meters along the pavement. As soon as I stop, the other three lower onto their haunches next to me.

Unfortunately, the position is right next to a body in the road that has the left half of its head blown away. Flies buzz around the fleshy red and white innards and the smell emanating from it is disgusting. I scan the way ahead as fast as possible to check it is clear and to identify our next piece of cover. As soon as I am satisfied, I move to get the group away from the body as rapidly as possible, not that there is any guarantee our next stop will be any more inviting.

The stink of death at our next stop is overpowering, it hangs in the air like a thick soup. In front of the building's pillar I stop against, bodies are piled up on top of one another, and do my best to ignore the carnage spread out in front of me where a swarm of flies move across the bodies like shadows. The narrowing pavement up to the pillar obviously congested the poor souls into a throng where they were cut to ribbons by a shower of bullets.

Groans rise behind me as the full power of the smell of rotting flesh hits my companion's noses, there is no escape from it. We need to get onto the other side of the road, to the path that Alpha used. That path was not as bad as on this side and we cannot go forward here, there is no pavement to step onto, only corpses.

I look desperately across the road for another position for us to go to, but I suddenly see movement from ahead.

We will have to endure the rank smell a while longer while I deal with the figure that is shuffling along on the opposite pavement.

There is no doubt that the figure is a Rabid and I quickly have it in my rifle's sights. Just as I'm about to pull the M4's trigger, the Rabid disappears behind a bullet-ridden delivery van parked against the kerb on the other side of the road. *Fuck*, I say to myself, as I am forced to draw in yet another breath of contaminated air and wait for the Rabid to reappear from behind the van.

I move the muzzle of the M4 across to the rear of the bullet-ridden van where I expect the Rabid to reappear, my finger tense against its trigger.

"Andy," a sickly sounding Jim says from below me just as the Rabid reappears. Ignoring Jim's protests, I squeeze the M4's trigger and watch the Rabid drop to the ground.

"Let's move," I order quietly, stepping away from the pillar and into the road.

I see Jim and Karen get to their feet, but Tanya stays down. Jim, wobbling himself tries to get Tanya up but he flounders. I scan the area ahead to check nothing is coming before I quickly step back to help get Tanya up. Jim has hold of one of her arms but is barely moving her. I thrust my arm through the front of her armpit and keep pushing until I feel her other armpit which my hand goes under and then I yank her up and to her feet.

"Take her Jim," I order as I pull my arm free and get it back onto the M4. "Karen, help Jim."

As soon as I see Karen go to help, I am moving forward praying that they follow. They are slow bringing Tanya across the road, but they manage it, and they join me at the next covering point which is in a deep doorway just up from the bullet-ridden van.

"Put her down there at the back," I tell Karen and Jim as they come under the cover.

"I'm okay," Tanya says, trying to be brave, but she isn't, her legs are still unsteady.

"Get your breath back, Tanya," I tell her. "We can stay here for a minute."

I leave Karen and Jim to mind Tanya while I cover us out of the front of the doorway.

"She is looking better," Karen tells me after a minute.

"Tanya, how are you feeling?" I ask.

"Much better. It was that smell, I couldn't breathe."

"It was bad," I sympathise. "Are you ready to move?"

"Yes, I'm ready," Tanya says confidently.

I have already decided on the next covering position and I am ready to move, but I give them a second to get behind me. Once they are in position, I go, moving out of the doorway, going immediately left. I plan to get us all the way down to the main junction ahead and off this godforsaken road as soon as possible. Our cover is a car just short of the junction from where I should be able to scan all four roads that converge at the wide junction.

With the car only meters away, a creature suddenly tears from the right, it runs straight into the centre of the junction. The male Rabid comes to a skidding halt, to stare straight at me. Before I can fix the beast in my sights, the Rabid lurches forwards and into the air. I fire my first round, but the bullets skims past the flying beast which hits the roadside to burst at me like an oncoming vehicle.

I crash into the back of the car that I was heading for, my M4 coming thumping down across its roof to steady itself to fire again. I take my own advice and my next shot is aimed at the body of the beast that is no more than five meters away. This time the bullet hits, slamming into the right shoulder of the beast and knocking it sideways. Unable to catch its fall, the Rabid smacks into the road hard, headfirst. A whimpering cry escapes the creature's mouth as it raises its head from the roadside. My third bullet cuts the cry off dead as it shatters the Rabid's head, splattering its contents across the road.

Gasping for breath, I turn my rifle urgently this way and that, expecting more Rabids to appear to join in the hunt, but none do. Heavy breathing from around my legs tells me that the others are here and waiting for my next move. I concentrate and establish my bearings. The left turn off the junction, that is the road that leads down to London Bridge, the one we will be taking.

There is no movement, but little to offer us cover either, so we will have to make do with another doorway, even though I can't see a decent one from my position.

"Let's move," I say as I pull the M4 in and skirt around the left side of the car to leave the junction and the road of slaughter behind.

I concentrate to control my breathing and my heartbeat as I move, which are both becoming frantic. Frantic breathing and heart rate leads to frantic actions and decision making, neither of which we can afford right now. I slow my actions down, making them more deliberate, and equalise my breathing rate.

Gradually, my body slows down, and my thinking becomes clearer. I see a doorway that offers cover on the right of the road as we leave the junction and head for it. There is no indication of what the doorway is used for, I can't even tell if it is an entrance for a business or for residents of the block it leads into, not that it matters.

I stay on the outside, scanning the route ahead and let Karen and Tanya in behind me, but there isn't enough room for Jim behind, so he squeezes in next to me. In the distance, farther along the road, I can just about make out the junction in the road where it splits left and right, near the area where I had my episode next to the burnt-out cars. Waking up with Alpha and the pack standing over me seems surreal to me now, like it happened in another lifetime.

Concentrate, I tell myself, *what's your next move?* The street is all but devoid of decent covering positions but there is a car some distance away, past the opening on the left that leads into Leadenhall Market. The car is father than I would like to go in one movement, but we have little other choice.

"Let's move," I say and break cover, the car my target, unless I see a closer option as we go.

The M4 is trained on the opening to the market as I go past, its undercover walkway leads down and towards the Lloyds building so I eye it with suspicion. Nothing moves, however, and I turn my sight forwards, but just as I do… Jim shouts.

"Andy, in the market, they're coming!"

What is Jim talking about? I think urgently. *I have only just taken my eyes away from there.* I stop suddenly and spin to look back into the tunnel, which is lined with upmarket retail outlets and restaurants.

I see them immediately, shadows careering towards us from deep within the tunnel, and from the direction of the Lloyds building. Panic rising in my belly overrides my confusion as to why I didn't see the horde when my eyes meet the Rabid creatures. There are too many to engage with, I know that instantly. We need to run or hide and do it now, the beasts will burst onto this road at any moment.

"This way!" I shout when I see the opening to a narrow underpass between the building on the opposite side of the road.

My eyes meet with Karen's as I turn to see if the others are with me as I bolt for the opening, her face is in shock and close to sheer panic as she runs behind me. Undead screeches and cries of the hunt, echo at us from within the tunnel and the chilling noises are close.

I steal another look behind me just before I cross over the threshold into the underpass. Jim is bringing up the rear bravely, and I see the first Rabid burst into the road at terrific speed. For a second, I think I recognise the fearsome creature as one of Alpha's pack that took me in.

Other beasts pile out of the market, too many to count and they change direction instantly to follow us. As I enter the underpass, I cannot afford to stop or slow to let the others by. To do that, would slow us all down and mean certain capture by the horde, instead, I look ahead for cover or somewhere for us to hide, but all I am met with is concrete walls and steel fences. We must make it to the other side of the underpass and hope we find a sanctuary on the other side of it.

"Run!" I shout behind me as I near the exit of the underpass and pull a grenade from my combat vest.

A gunshot rings out of the underpass the moment I emerge from it and into the open air, the crack ringing in my ears takes me completely by surprise. I move slightly to the side and slam my brakes on to allow the others past and to throw my grenade into the narrow underpass. The confined space will create maximum exposure for the grenade and will take many of the horde out and slow the rest down.

Karen flies by me, closely followed by Tanya but Jim is missing. Another gunshot rings out from the underpass and then another. My eyes dart to see Jim has stopped halfway down the underpass and is firing at the Rabids just coming through into it.

"Jim, run!" I shout frantically, as I pull the pin out of the grenade.

Jim, with his back to me, fires the Glock again, his legs spread wide to steady his aim.

"Get them out of here," Jim shouts in reply before firing again.

I suddenly understand what he is doing, he is sacrificing himself to let us get away, he must know he can't hold so many Rabids back with just one handgun. There is no time to convince him otherwise, all I can do is respect him for his selfless actions. Jim keeps firing and I know he is going to run out of ammunition anytime now. *I should have fucking given him extra magazines for the weapon*, I think as I scan the courtyard we find ourselves in for an escape route.

There are several possibilities, I see as I look, but there is a narrow walkway off to the right that I decide on, the opening barely visible. Karen screams after her husband, her hysterical voice carrying over the sound of the gunshots.

I quickly look back down the underpass just in time to see Jim throw the empty Glock at the creatures closing in on him.

"Tanya," I shout pointing at the narrow opening. "Take Karen down there, drag her if you have to, do it now," I order and shove a hysterical Karen to try and get her moving.

Karen protests, but Tanya takes her by the arm and begins to drag her away.

"Think of Stacey," I shout at Karen and shove her again.

My words hit home with Karen, and she reluctantly turns and begins to follow Tanya. I spin back towards the underpass just in time to see Rabids take Jim down, his screams both chilling and heartbreaking.

Rabids engulf Jim in a feeding frenzy, but others slowly begin to move past the pile of withering bodies, and this time I horrifically recognise one of them. Alpha leads the horde towards me, its right side mutilated, the arm no more than a stump protruding from its right shoulder. Tattered flesh hangs down from the right side of its face and that side of the body is potholed from where shrapnel exploded into it. The gruesome injuries only seem to make the beast more terrifying and the look of despise on Alpha's face is paralysing.

I am suddenly conscious of the grenade in my left hand and without thinking, I roll it down into the underpass. The clink of metal bouncing pulls me out of my paralysing terror, I flick the M4 into automatic and begin firing constantly down into the underpass. While firing, I move right and behind a concrete wall just to the side of the underpass to take cover from the imminent explosion. I aim at Alpha, filling the beast with bullets and move my aim to the other Rabids coming at me and then the explosion hits.

The explosion in the confined space is extraordinary. The boom thunders out at me and I duck in reflex, my hand going to my ears. Beneath my feet the ground shakes and a cloud of dust and debris busts out from the opening next to me, to billow into the air. The moment the explosion dissipates, my head comes up, I take hold of my M4 and pull another grenade from my chest rig.

Just before I turn and run to Karen and Tanya, I pull the grenade's pin and throw it down into the smoke engulfing the underpass.

Chapter 19

I find the two women barely halfway across the courtyard at the same moment the second grenade explodes. Karen is slumped, distraught on the paving stones below her and Tanya is stood over her, trying to get her back onto her feet.

"Karen, we have to go," I tell her leaning now to drag her to her feet.

"Jim," she replies in tears.

"I know, but we can't stay here. We've got to get to the boat and back to Stacey." I pull at her again and finally, her legs begin to cooperate.

I look back at the underpass, but nothing is coming out, apart from billowing dust and smoke. We need to evacuate the whole area, quickly, the threat won't just come from the horde that followed us into the underpass, not after those explosions. Every Rabid in this part of the city will be converging on this area and they will have a smoke plume to pinpoint their destination.

"Dad, receiving, over," Josh's voice sounds from my chest, the explosions, unsurprisingly having carried right out to the river.

Tanya supports Karen while I reply.

"Receiving. We had Rabids in pursuit, but they have been dealt with. ETA, ten to fifteen minutes," I reply.

"Copy that, we'll be waiting," Josh tells me.

"Received, out."

In the distance, a Rabid cry rings out, an ominous warning of their impending arrival, if one was needed.

"Move, now. This way," I order.

I change my mind about which direction to go, the narrow passageway is in the wrong direction from the river, and I really don't fancy getting caught up in a maze of constricted alleyways with Rabids inbound.

Instead, I direct us left out of the courtyard which will take us south towards the river and we join a single laned road just off the courtyard that will take us down onto a main road. I am not exactly sure where we are, but we aren't far off my planned route and as long as we keep heading south, we will hit the river sooner rather than later.

A figure flashes left to right at the end of the single-lane road in front of us, I immediately pull my fist down at the two women and I drop to my knee, my M4 aiming in the direction that the figure disappeared. Karen, either not having seen my signal or not registering it in her current state, runs past me before she comes to a sudden halt. She turns around in surprise at my sudden stopping and quickly comes back to me.

The Rabid figure reappears behind her, but she is in my line of fire. I keep calm and lean forward to improve my angle, aim and fire. The bullet whaps into the Rabids face, the force of the bullet knocking it off its feet backwards to hit the ground.

I quickly push myself up and order Tanya to take control of Karen. We aren't going to make it to the river with Karen in this uncontrollable state and I come to an instant decision; we need to find shelter where I can speak to her to calm her down and get her under control. Just shy of the main road ahead, there is a building on the right with a wooden door.

"Follow me," I bark, crossing over to the door where I smash my foot into it, but the door holds firm. Stepping back, I aim the muzzle of the M4 at the lock and fire once into the lock mechanism. Again, I smash my foot into the door and this time it bursts open. After taking a quick look, I step inside and the women follow me in.

We find ourselves inside a medium-sized room that has three desks in it. With Karen and Tanya inside, I step back and push the door back closed, pushing the lock back into place as best I can. The door isn't secure, but I don't plan on being in here more than two or three minutes. I then turn, raising my rifle to check that the office is clear. I see that the door on the other side of the room is closed, and a quick check under the desks tells me that we are alone.

"Please sit down Karen," I say turning to her and pulling out a chair from beneath one of the desks.

Karen looks at me teary-eyed and does as she is asked, Tanya stands close by with her hands folded in front of her.

"I'm sorry," Karen says, snivelling, her sleeve going to her nose.

"There is no need to be sorry," I begin, after taking a breath, calming myself down and lowering to my haunches in front of her.

"My minds all over the place. I can't believe Jim is gone," Karen starts to get more upset, which is the exact opposite of what I'm trying to achieve.

"Yes, Jim is gone and I'm sorry about that Karen, truly I am. What he did was so brave, and he did it because he had to. He had to do it to save you, so that you can get back to Stacey. To see your daughter again."

"I know." Karen snivels again.

"Don't let his sacrifice be for nothing. If you don't get your head together straight away, we have no chance of reaching the river and getting back to Stacey. There will be a time to get upset and grieve for Jim, but that time is not now. Do you understand?" I say assertively.

"Yes, Andy, I understand, but it's difficult."

"Of course, it is. Don't dwell on it now, think of Stacey, think of seeing her again. She needs you, now more than ever. Are you up for it?" I say with all sincerity.

Karen's head rises and she takes a deep breath through her mouth, a breath that is quickly expelled through pursed lips and bulging cheeks.

"Yes Andy, I am up for it. I won't let you down again. I will put it out of my mind," Karen says confidently. "The important thing now is to see my daughter again."

"Yes, Karen. Yes, it is. That is all that matters."

"I'm ready," she tells me.

"And what are you going to do?" I ask.

"Watch you and do everything you tell me," she insists, looking me straight in the eye.

"That's all I ask. We are so close now Karen. Just a bit longer."

I push myself back up and Karen follows me up straightaway, her sleeve in use again, this time to dry her eyes.

"How are you doing Tanya?" I ask, looking at her.

"It's just so frightening," she tells me.

"I know, you're not the only one that thinks that," I reply.

"We will be okay, won't we?" Karen interjects, putting her arm around Tanya's shoulder. "We will follow your lead so that we can get the hell out of here, won't we Tanya?"

"Yes, let's get out of here," Tanya agrees.

"Good, that's what I like to hear," I tell the two women. "Let's see if there is another way out of here, I don't want to go back in the direction of that courtyard. Stay close."

I move towards the door on the opposite side of the room and quickly crack it open. Outside is another room, a small reception area and a set of stairs leading up on the far side of the room with another door at the bottom. The reception is clear, so I move out into it and see the main door on the left that must open onto the street.

Moving over to the stairs, I point the M4 up the stairs and listen, but there is only silence. I debate whether to check behind the other door, but it is closed and so I decide to leave well enough alone.

"Watch the stairs and that door while I check the front door," I tell the two women, who nod, their eyes darting immediately in that direction.

The front door is wooden, big, and solid, it won't be kicked open easily. In fact, I see that it opens inward and so it won't be kicked open at all. Positioned halfway up is a standard lever that can be opened from inside, but below the leaver is a deadbolt that can only be opened with a key. Shit, I think, the only way I am going to get this door open is to shoot the frame away around the deadbolt, that is going to cause noise and it will take more than a couple of rounds to break it.

The only other options are to look behind the door by the stairs or go out the way we came in, neither of which are good options. I decide to have a look to see what is in the next room and go over to the door by the stairs.

My reluctance to open the door turns out to be unfounded. There is only another empty office behind the door, there is no exit though, unless we start climbing out of windows, which is not going to happen.

That leaves me with either going back into the courtyard, where the two grenades have just exploded or dealing with the front door, which I decide is the best option.

The frame next to the deadbolt splinters with a thud as the first bullet hits the wood, the shot is aimed high. The next three shots are aimed in a line down from the first shot and the frame next to the deadbolt is in tatters by the time I lower the M4.

I approach the door in hope and reach up to the lever above the deadbolt. With the lever turned, I pull at the door, the sound of cracking wood accompanies the door opening slightly, but without enough leverage from just the lever the door holds. There is no door handle to pull on and so the only other place to grab hold of is through the letterbox.

With my hand stuck through the letterbox, I turn the lever and yank at the door with all my weight. More wood splinters and suddenly, the frame gives way and the door jerks open. I catch myself and the door before it shoots open too wide, exposing us completely.

"Well done," Karen says from behind me.

"Are you ready ladies?" I reply faking a smile.

They are and I gradually increase the gap of the door so that I can get sight of the street outside.

I don't know why but the view I get surprises me, I was expecting to see a wide road with cars and shops. The view I get is a dim narrow road, completely overhung by tall office blocks only meters away on the opposite side of the road.

Everything is quiet, even though the road leading up to the courtyard is just on the left, past the end of this building. I signal for Karen and Tanya to follow me out of the door, they do without question and we cross straight over the road taking cover in a doorway of the office block. A Rabid shriek echoes to us, bouncing off the buildings that reach straight up above us. I have trouble determining which direction the chilling noise sounded from, the echo seems to swirl around hitting us from every direction.

Stood behind me in the doorway, Karen and Tanya wait patiently for me to decide when it is safe to move. The M4 searches the road for the source of the dreaded noise and then it finds it. From the left, a Rabid jogs towards us, heading in the direction of the courtyard we have just evacuated. The beast, attracted by the thunderous explosions, resembles a local resident out for a leisurely run through the streets of London, its jog is that casual. Only the inhuman way it moves gives its real motive away, and I get the Rabid in the M4's sights.

As soon as the creature is within my range, I squeeze the rifle's trigger. The bullet explodes through the Rabid's head, its exit trajectory speeding the bullet through a window in a building behind the creature. Crashing into the road, the Rabid is dead, but now, echoes of smashed glass fills the area and I know instantly that the noise, which continues to reverberate, is bound to call other creatures into our vicinity, we need to leave, and fast.

"Move," I order, just loud enough for the two women to hear.

I don't want to go anywhere near the courtyard and so I break left out of the doorway, in the opposite direction. Only a few meters down, a road intersects onto this one from the left, leading south. I come to a stop at the end of the office block, using it as cover to check the new road before I decide to use it.

The road looks clear, and I turn onto it urgently in a hurry to get off this road and its echoes of smashing glass. Keeping low, we move down the road as rapidly as we can, the M4 out front, pointing our way.

My nerves begin to shred, the road is long and even narrower than the one we have just left behind. On each side of the road, tall buildings hang over us like daemons, threatening to envelop us completely. The farther we travel down it, the narrower it becomes, and the light diminishes. My rifle swings from one threatening shadow to another, I expect each one to suddenly come alive and burst forward to attack.

Yet another screech rings out from our near vicinity, but I have no idea from where. I steel a look behind, expecting to see a horde of zombies chasing down the road ready to pounce and to feed, but there is nothing there apart from the shadows we have already passed.

To toy with us further, the road narrows again, into a single lane, the buildings on each side towering and almost within touching distance. An abandoned car blocks the throughway, cutting it down to a slim pavement on each side of the vehicle. Obviously, the driver chose to ignore the large painted words on the roadside stating, KEEP CLEAR. *Fucking idiot*, I think in my frustration as I choose the left side to squeeze past.

With the car behind us, we finally approach the end of the eerie and claustrophobic road. Ahead, looks like a brighter and more open piece of London for us to tackle, with a wide road and lower buildings.

Just as we are about to emerge, a creature careers around the corner only feet away and on a collision course to hit straight into me. Adrenaline and shock flood my bloodstream, the beast's eyes wide in mirrored surprise.

Gasps of terror and fear sound from behind me from both Karen and Tanya, a fear that also shoots through my body. Moments before the Rabid rams into us, its face changing from surprise to a terrifying joy unable to believe its luck, my finger manages to yank at the M4's trigger.

A single bullet spits out of the M4's muzzle and by more luck than judgement it slams into the Rabid's chest bone with a sickening thud, it's face changes again as the force of the bullet knocks it skidding backwards, but not over and not dead. The couple of seconds of grace is enough for my wits to return and with the M4 pulled back firmly into my shoulder, I fire again.

This bullet strikes dead centre in the Rabid's forehead, killing the beast instantly. Only the fast-travelling contents of its head hit the ground before it does.

I must force myself to not break into a run and not to stop until we reach the river. Instead, I move past the twisted body in front of us and take cover at the corner of the closest building to check our route forward.

Directly in front of me is a smoggy main road, it is wide with two vehicle lanes and two cycle lanes, dismembered corpses litter the roadside, like leaves in Autumn and bullet holes pit mark the surroundings. I check left and right with my rifle and thankfully, there are no Rabids to be seen in either direction. Ahead of us, however, is another bloody building site, its perimeter a boarded wall cutting off a way forward. Only a zombie outbreak could have stopped the incessant rebuilding of London, I cannot think of anything else that could possibly stop the city's unstoppable march of progress.

To the left, the boards reach down to the next building along and join onto it. There is no way through in that direction, not without us having to go past the neighbouring building too, taking us away from our destination. I look right and I am relieved to see that the perimeter boards stop short of the next building, and there is at least a walkway and hopefully a road leading south. That is the direction we must go, but it is a good distance away.

"Let's go, stay close," I tell Karen and Tanya as I step out.

I stay right, not crossing the road, staying where there is some cover, even if it is only the side of an office block and the doorways cut into its stone façade. The other side of the road, with its boarding, devoid of any cover whatsoever.

In the event, I don't use any of the doorways, the way ahead is clear, so I keep going straight past them, skirting around fallen bodies, but eyeing them closely. Only when I reach the end of the office block which is directly opposite the route on the other side of the road, do I stop.

A stone corner pillar marks the end of the office block and I use it for cover while I scan the area before we cross the road. The area is quiet, too quiet but we cannot hang around waiting for something to happen, and with a quick signal to the women, we move.

The wide main road feels incredibly exposed as we rush across, avoiding numerous corpses as we go. I feel sure that we will be seen by the undead and a screech will cry out at any moment. Nothing happens though and we quickly reach the other side. I only stop briefly to check the new road off to the left before we step on to it.

We find ourselves on another narrow side street, but it is well lit due to the open building site adjacent to it. I proceed cautiously, slowing our pace right down as there are blind spots on either side of us, entrances into the building site on the left and into the multiple buildings on the right. The body count drops considerably on this side street, but they are still there to hamper our progress.

"How much farther?" a voice whispers from behind me.

I ignore the question as I see a flicker of movement ahead, down low, hidden in the shadow of one of the entrances into the building site. My rifles sights fix onto the threat, my body tensing. Slumped on the ground, its back resting on the board behind with its head flopped down, sits a figure.

I am instantly reminded of the bullet I shot into the head of the man under the desk back in Cole & Co's office. I almost wish I had gone back after the office was cleared to check to see if it was a Rabid I killed, or a man.

That thought stops me from pulling the trigger of the M4 so readily this time, and I edge down the street closer to the forlorn figure, trying to figure out what I am dealing with. Each step brings a better view, but with its head facing down it is difficult to determine if the figure has turned.

With only a few meters remaining until we are within striking distance, if the figure is Rabid, I purse my lips. Wanting to draw attention and hopefully tempt the lowered head up, I whistle gently. Conscious of any noise that we make I don't go for a full-on wolf whistle, that would only ask for trouble.

The head waivers, coming to life. *That's it*, I think, *wakey wakey, let's have a look at you*. Another gentle whistle breathes more life into the slumped figure and gradually, the top of the head moves back until a face is revealed.

Inhuman grey skin, broken with dark bloodied lines sits on the bones of the face like an unwanted membrane, telling me all I need to know. The Rabid fixes me in a haunting, hungry stare to confirm its undead state and its cracked black lips begin to part.

The M4's bullet whips the head ferociously backwards where it thumps into the boarded wall behind it. Only for a moment does the head stay upright before it flops back down taking the hideous face out of my sight. I see blood, pieces of bone and brain sliding down the painted boards of the building site's perimeter wall as I move past the creature's carcass.

"Sorry, Karen," I say quietly, having not answered her question. "No, it can't be far now."

"Don't apologise, Andy," I hear her reply.

I see another main road ahead as we near the end of the side street, and by my calculations, this should be the road I used to move up to the junction with the pile of burnt-out cars, filled with charred bodies. A grim sight that I daren't let my eyes fall on again.

I am right, the corpse laden road is the one I used. We now have only two blocks to tackle before we reach the wharf, where Josh and Alice will be waiting for us, floating on the river.

Wind your neck in, I tell myself, *that is still two blocks of Rabid infested city to get through*. This is not the time to get overconfident and think we have made it, the time to relax is when we have travelled back up the river and gone back through the military cordon. *Then and only then will it be time to pat yourself on the back*, I think, cursing myself.

I poke my head out from the end of the side street, the breeze deciding to change direction just as I do and the gust of air hits me directly in the face, bringing with it the stink of rotting corpses that number far too many to count on the roadside of our latest challenge. With my stomach trying to ignore the horrendous smell, I nervously look left, along towards the junction where I collapsed. I wonder how Karen and Tanya would feel if they knew about my fragility. Would they have stepped onto the tightrope we are walking, so willingly, if they knew what was behind my mask? I seriously doubt it, hence, I have kept it to myself.

The junction is just out of my line of sight, and thankfully, so are the incinerated cars, only drifting smoke moves in that direction and it is the same when I look right from behind my rifle. On the other side of the road, I recognise the side street with the trendy wine bar I used on my way out. The street is to the left and towards the junction, but it's too close to the junction and I look elsewhere for a route south. Just on the right across the road, and away from the junction is another side street that I decide to use.

So many twisted bodies cover the road that I take a second to pick a path through them. A bit of zigzagging will be required to ensure we stay well away from any corpses that might suddenly reach out to grab hold of a fleshy ankle. The path is there though, and with a quick check behind, we move off.

"Stay away from the bodies," I tell the women as we approach the first of many strewn in the road, as if they needed telling.

An ominous quietness hangs over us as we begin our long winding route across the road. The M4 swipes through the air from left to right, searching for targets, stopping to look forward and into the side street we are heading for with each sweep. Each peak of its arch left reveals more of the junction and its monument of incinerated death to me.

Perhaps, I quicken my sweep when I swing left to avoid what waits, or perhaps my reluctance to look upon the carnage again makes me miss seeing the threat.

Whatever the reason for my lapse, what my vision blurs from my fragile mind, my ears do not.

Chapter 20

Despite our distance away from the junction, the first deathly screech rings out as though the Rabid was stood next to me. The noise, a call to arms to its kindred, rushes along the road to stop me dead in my tracks and I freeze, instantly, facing the route south that we are winding towards. My rifle floats in the air in front of me like a mirage. I must turn to the left and face my foe, but time stands still, as my mind reels in dread and shock.

A second chilling cry of the hunt ricochets off the surrounding buildings and I force my body to snap out of its stupor. My back twists to bring my rifle to bear left, the object suddenly feeling like the powerful weapon it is, once more. My heroic turn is ridiculed, it is met by a crescendo of ear-piercing Rabid noise, as dozens of the undead screech out to announce their readiness to attack.

My feeble fear at laying my eyes on the carnage of the incinerated cars is dispelled at once, as I finally look towards the junction. Any sight of my phobia is overwhelmed by the army of the undead racing away from the junction, the horde converging onto the road that we stand upon.

Once more, the power is stripped away from the M4 that I hold out front, the weapon no match against the terrifying mass of figures chasing towards us. My rifles bullets would be chewed up and spat out by the fearsome creatures unless I happened to hit one or two in the head. One or two dead Rabids will not make a dent in the horde and would not let us escape our fate.

My last single grenade hangs idly from the front of my combat vest. Another futile thought, one single grenade will not cut it, not this time. Maybe if I had a box full of the handheld explosives I would be in business, but I don't, I have only one.

"Andy?" a petrified voice asks from my right.

Karen's quivering voice forces me to drag my eyes away from our impending doom, the undead horde beginning to get close enough to come into sharp focus.

Karen and Tanya, cower behind me to protect themselves from the Rabid creatures that are about to stampede us and tear us to ribbons. They are fatally mistaken if they believe that I can protect them from such an overwhelming force, and their panic-stricken faces tell me that is not what they believe.

Both women look at me in desperate expectation to see what I am going to do next and in my own desperation, I shout my order at them.

"RUN!" I shout at the top of my voice in a fit of panic, spittle flying from my mouth.

My legs spring to life instantly, driving me forward, aiming for the side street that will take us south and to the river. Visions of Catherine and Emily waiting for me with bated breath in the cottage rush through my mind, I cannot let them down and leave them behind to fend for themselves. I must not die now, here in this godforsaken place, they need me to return to them, they need my protection.

My protection is what Karen and Tanya are relying on, at this moment. I glance behind to see if they are with me and I see Karen's legs split to hurdle over a corpse blocking her path, all caution thrown to the wind. Tanya is beside her, her legs moving as fast as she can muster.

We will make it into the side street, that much I am confident about, as I too spring over bodies in front of me to land onto the pavement. On landing, I race to the cusp of the street where I spin around to take cover behind the corner of the office block, firing the M4 into the oncoming horde that is now only meters away, desperately trying to win us a few seconds of time.

"Run!" I shout at the women as they arrive at my position. "Keep going!" I add as the M4's magazine empties itself into the undead.

One or two Rabids go down but they are only replaced by other ferocious beasts, as I knew they would be. I eject the mag and my muscle memory changes it out in a flash to get the rifle firing again. I keep my finger depressed on the trigger until the second magazine is spent, then I turn to run, ejecting the next mag as I go.

Karen and Tanya are a short distance in front of me as I push another magazine home, and I'm desperately trying to catch them up. The narrow side street's light changes subtlety as the chasing pack of zombies burst onto it behind me, their shrieks of death making sure I know that they are still coming to feed.

That is when I pull the last of the grenades from my front and pull its pin. With my legs pumping, I gradually catch up to Karen and Tanya who are neck and neck in front of me, sprinting for their lives.

The street narrows slightly, and the solid walls on either side of me to contain and deflect the explosion, indicate that is the time to drop my last grenade. The grenades destructive force is now our last hope of outrunning our hunters, who are closing in fast behind.

"Grenade… keep going!" I shout as the device hits the ground behind my feet. I can only hope that the women hear and understand my warning and don't break their stride when the explosion hits.

With the grenade dropped, I concentrate on running and increase my speed. Lactic acid pumps through my muscles, providing them with energy to catch up to Karen and Tanya and then to move past them. Ahead of us, the street is cut off by a building and the road turns sharp right and I look for cover as I sprint towards the latest obstacle.

The almighty explosion erupts behind, with a shattering BOOM, moments before I arrive at the right turn. I don't turn to see what damage the explosion has managed to create and how much time it has bought us, if any, until I reach the cover of the corner.

Pieces of rubble rain down into the road as I spin to watch the women chase by me. "Turn next left," I shout as they go by and I begin to fire the M4 blind into the cloud of smoke clogging the street where the explosion erupted.

Another magazine is emptied into the smoke and dust without me knowing if I have hit a single Rabid. I eject the mag but just as I reach for another from my combat vest the first Rabid comes through the dissipating smoke.

The creature stumbles out into the open, its torso cut to ribbons, the beast looking unsure of what its objective is. Other shadows move behind it and then emerge to join the first Rabid. A snarling sound emanates, and I turn to look at the creature making the sound. I find myself locking eyes with the culprit, its evil eyes drilling into me.

Launching forward, the creatures snarling escalates into a wailing screech and I turn to run, knowing that their deathly pursuit has resumed.

Only a short distance away is the turn left, that I told Karen and Tanya to take. I can only hope that the chasing pack don't see me turn before they round the corner. As I steal a look behind, I see the creature again for just a second before the building cuts off the view.

Ahead, the women have made good progress, they are nearing the junction with the main road ahead. Across the main road marks the last block of buildings before we reach the wharf. We are close but I have no idea what might wait for us on the main road and the women are about to rush out onto it.

"Left" I shout, with the hunting pack at my back. I was praying there would be a road straight ahead down to the wharf but no such luck, another building stands in our way blocking the final part of the route.

There is no time to stop and clear the way ahead, I will have to let the women run blindly onto the main road. The gamble pays off, I see as I round the corner to join them on the main road, it is clear.

"Right," I shout at the two women ahead, as they near a road that will lead us down to the wharf. I see them disappear behind the building as they turn into the road and I quickly look over my shoulder.

Terror rips through me. The swarm of Rabids, their fearful eyes fixed on me, are only a meter or two behind. I turn the corner, legs pumping and see the two women in front, the wharf beyond them and then the embankment wall.

We are so close to reaching the beach where Josh and Alice will be waiting ready to come in and pick us up, but we have no chance of making it. At any moment now the pack will catch up to me, take me down and rip me apart. Karen and Tanya might make it to the wharf, but where do they go from there? They will not know about the stairs to the left that will take them down to the beach, even if they had time to use them, which they won't. Their fate will ultimately be the same as mine.

I stretch my legs as far as I can, pushing off the tarmac behind and reaching for the next piece to use in desperation. My muscles burn, threatening to burst as I use every ounce of energy I have remaining. Our fate is sealed, I know it in my gut, a gut that will be greedily torn out of my stomach. Karen breaks through onto the wharf and into the light, but I look beyond her and I strain to increase my stride still further. If only I can get one last glimpse of my son over the embankment wall before the undead take me—doesn't my sacrifice deserve that much? *Please God let me lay my eyes on my son, one last time before the end!*

My pitiful prayers go unanswered, Rabids are upon me, snarling into my brain and I am still meters away from the embankment wall. *This is it;* I tell myself, *there will be no moment of joy before the excruciating end.*

A shadow interrupts the light of the wharf ahead coming to block any chance of me seeing the river and my son who waits there.

High-velocity rounds streak past my head, they thud into the horde directly behind me. A glimmer of hope brings me back to my senses and my fight returns. My legs push again as I look forward, expecting to see Josh firing, taking out the Rabids at my back. I told him not to get off the boat, he stands no chance of saving us from so many of the undead. This will be the end for him too, I begin to panic.

But it is not Josh that has made the shadow ahead, I suddenly see as I finally focus. Remarkably, the high-velocity gunfire is streaking down from a helicopter hovering just off the embankment wall.

Movement from the left as I near the wharf startles me, have Rabids somehow got in front of us? My arms lift the M4 to bear as I run to aim at the sudden threat just as tracer fire speeds past my head from the helicopter and into the pack behind me. My finger moves away from the M4's trigger as I see that the sudden movement ahead is not the undead outflanking us.

A team of Special Forces operators, dressed from head to toe in black ops combat gear stalk past me, their rifles ablaze. Miraculously, I emerge onto the wharf to join Karen and Tanya as the team shuffle past me. Keeping low, their rifles sweep deliberately to seek out new targets, the weapon's muzzles lighting up instantly as they identify and engage their targets.

My head spins as I try to come to terms with our incredible survival and my amazement at the sudden appearance of our military salvation. Karen and Tanya look on, clinging onto each other, eyes wide in astonishment. The downdraft from the helicopter behind us swirling their hair into the air.

Bullets fly from above and behind the three of us, and from the men on the ground ahead of us. The Rabid horde is not defeated; however, figures still stream into the fight from the main road beyond, no matter how hard the Special Forces press their advantage.

Gathering some semblance of sanity, I decide that it is time that I get into the fight and raise my M4. Just as I do, the roar of an unseen low flying jet engine streaks from somewhere above. The sound booms as it travels through the enclosed streets, echoing off the surrounding buildings.

Blinding light erupts from the direction of the main road, instantly flashing down the narrow street of the battle. The shockwave from the ordnance dropped from the fast jet slams into me as the eardrum splitting explosions shake the ground beneath my feet.

"Duck!" I shout at Karen and Tanya, not knowing if they will hear my cry as blisteringly hot air rushes down the enclosed street. I pull my head down and my knees bend to let the burning air burst across me.

Behind, the helicopter has already taken evasive action and lifted away from the embankment wall to let the explosion escape and erupt out over the River Thames.

The moment that the explosion dissipates, and before my arms have left my head, the sound of dull gunshots is already sounding, their volume feeble after the almighty explosion.

My head comes up to watch the professionals in front of me press ahead again, guns blazing. A downdraft buffets the three of us as the helicopter comes back in to continue its support of the troops, retaking its position off the embankment wall over the beach below.

My M4 sits idly in my hands as I watch the Special Forces in awe as they methodically finish off the Rabid horde remaining on the street. *If only the whole of London could be cleared as readily as this one small part of the city*, I think as the troops do their work.

Gradually, the gunfire begins to diminish as the undead are slaughtered one by one. Nothing is left to chance, the dozen or so troops move in amongst the bodies firing bullets into heads until each and every one is eliminated.

Josh. Alice, I suddenly think, my mind all over the place as the troops run out of Rabids to fire bullets into, and they begin to form a perimeter.

I turn away from the carnage, looking to check on Karen and Tanya as I go. The two dishevelled women are still clinging onto each other in astonishment and shock, their eyes wide looking at the troops, dressed entirely in black, shooting down at the last of the undead.

The downdraft from the helicopter hovering above thrusts into me trying to push me back, but I resist and push against it. I see the river, but the embankment wall still cuts off my view of most of it and I step over to the wall. Placing my hands on top of the wall, wind buffeting me, I apprehensively look out across the water to find my son.

It takes me a moment to get my bearings, the scene is not as I left it. Three black Special Forces rigid inflatable fast boats have been pulled up onto the sand of the small beach below. The boats sit close to the corpse of the first Rabid I killed early this morning after I had jumped onto the sand.

I turn away from the beach and look out onto the water where two military patrol boats are positioned meters apart from each other on the river. The two boats flank each side of another smaller boat, our boat, and I see Josh and Alice stood inside its hull.

Josh has his back to me and seems to be remonstrating with a sailor stood on one of the patrol boats. I wave across the river trying to get Alice's attention as she stands next to Josh, but she is looking everywhere apart from at me.

Suddenly, Alice's head turns in my direction and my waves become more vigorous. I see a smile spread across Alice's face and she urgently pulls at Josh's arm. Josh turns to Alice in surprise, and she says something to him excitedly, while pointing towards me.

Josh's head spins in my direction and he finally spots me up on the embankment wall and that I am alive. Josh, who must be overcome, drops down, bent over in the boat, his hands moving to his head.

Perhaps, somebody up above was watching over me after all, I think as I look out at my son, my eyes welling up.

Alice's hand goes to Josh's shoulder to comfort him, but as soon as she touches him, he pushes himself upright. He gives me a wave back and then quickly reaches for his radio.

"Thank God, Dad. Are you okay, over?" Josh's voice squawks from the radio on my chest. I just about hear it over the roar of the helicopter.

"Just about champ. But if it wasn't for these guys, we wouldn't have made it. When did they turn up, over?" I ask.

"About five minutes ago. Are the others with you, over?"

"I've got Karen and one other. I'm afraid Jim didn't make it, over," I tell Josh sombrely.

"Shit," Josh replies. "Fill me in later, over."

"I will. What are those guys saying, over?"

"Nothing, they won't tell me anything, apart from we cannot come onto the beach to get you, over," Josh replies.

"Okay, I'll see what I can find out from up here. I'll let you know. Out," I tell Josh.

"Copy."

I turn away from the embankment, my eyes falling on the colossal carnage reaching up the street in front of me. The Special Forces troops have formed their perimeter. One or two walk between the fallen undead, double-checking none pose a threat, and there is a conflab going on between three of the black-clad operatives close by. These are obviously the ones I need to get some answers from, but before I get the chance, Karen comes over to me.

"Are you okay," I ask. She looks a bit broken, something I am not surprised by in the least. She comes right up to me and throws her arms around me, taking me somewhat by surprise.

Karen squeezes me tightly in silence for a moment and I belatedly put my arms around her to give her a reassuring hug in return. Tanya stands close by watching on, she looks completely drained. I can only feel admiration for the young girl after her ordeal of been trapped in that office for days and then dragging herself through this nightmare. She has an inner strength that I am sure she knew nothing of before and I hope she finds some peace now.

"Thank you, Andy," Karen says as she breaks away from me to look me in the eye.

"It was rough. I'm sorry about Jim," I tell her.

"We knew it was a gamble Andy, so don't blame yourself. It will be tough, but I will get over it. Stacey and I will be together," she tells me, and I think that they will be as I look at Karen.

"Andy, fucking Richards," a voice asks from my left. I am not sure if I am being asked a question or being addressed.

"Yes, and you are?" I reply as a tall, burly, black-clad operator approaches me.

"You're a fucking loose cannon," the man says as he reaches to pull up his black balaclava, his helmet under his arm. "You always were."

The black material rises to reveal a face I know well, a face I had hoped I would never see again.

"I don't know what you mean, Sergeant Briggs," I answered.

Briggs and I had a long history of butting heads. I was his Captain for a short time before I left the SAS and the military. Briggs passed selection two years after me and the man is a complete arsehole. Luckily, the two of us were never posted into the same troop together, but we completed plenty of operations in the same field together and we never saw eye to eye. But when I was fast-tracked for promotion, he did everything he possibly could to fuck-up my command. He took pride in trying to make me look bad to the top brass, at every opportunity. Not that I ever let him succeed.

"You don't know what I mean?" Briggs says in amazement. "Just look at your little escapade today, for example."

"I'm here to help some friends, that's all," I tell him.

"And how was that going before I turned up to save your ass?"

"We haven't got time for this Sergeant," I say changing the subject, and not only because this dickhead has a point. "We need to evacuate the area, the enemy could be regrouping as we dick swing, Sergeant."

"My men have us covered," the Sergeant grins, loving every second of his time in the spotlight.

"Nevertheless, Sergeant, we are leaving," I insist, without really having a leg to stand on. We are in their hands, it seems.

"Corporal," Briggs shouts to one of his men, who comes to heel immediately.

"Get the women down to the boats," Briggs orders.

"What is going on here, Sergeant," I demand.

"What can I tell you Richard's. It's on a need-to-know basis, and you don't need to know." Briggs grins.

"Where are you taking them?" I ask urgently. "Am I going with them?"

"The women will be safe, don't worry. But I have different orders for you, my friend."

"Come on, Don. I know we don't see eye to eye, but that's in the past. What's happening?" I resist referring to Briggs by his full first name. Calling him Donald will only wind him up even more, I know he hates it. I'll keep that in my pocket in case I need it.

"Sorry, Richards, I can't help you," Briggs replies.

"Andy?" Karen asks worriedly as Briggs's men try to usher her towards the steps down to the beach.

"Go with them, Karen. They will look after you and I'll see you later." I hope that my words might resonate with Briggs's men if not with him, about the women.

"Okay. I'll see you soon, Andy. And thanks again," Karen says as she turns to leave.

"Thank you, Andy," Tanya tells me with a worried look on her face. I try to give her a reassuring smile in return.

I watch Karen and Tanya walk towards the steps for a moment, two black-clad operators escorting them along.

"What now?" I ask turning to Briggs.

"Now you take a little flight." Briggs smiles sarcastically. With that, he turns and whistles sharply, raises his arm above his head and winds it around in the air.

Immediately, the rest of Briggs's men begin to close in their perimeter, stepping back towards us, their rifles still pointing outwards, covering the rear.

Before my radio is confiscated, which it undoubtedly will be, my hand snaps across to my chest.

"Josh, they are taking me. I don't know where, but I won't be coming back with you. Tell the girls I love them, and you."

Briggs steps angrily towards me, his hand going to my chest. This is not the time for a fight or a scuffle, so I let him, my hands spreading out in surrender. The radio is ripped off my combat vest just as I hear Josh's panicked voice sound.

"Think you're so fucking clever, don't you Richards?" Briggs says as he drops the radio to the ground. He looks at me for a second before he stamps his size ten boot down onto the radio, cutting off Josh's voice with a crack of breaking plastic.

"There is no need for this," I plead to Briggs, who looks back at me with disdain.

"Take his weapons," Briggs orders his men.

Reluctantly, but voluntarily, I unclip and hold up my trusted M4 to the masked operative who steps forward at Briggs's order. I feel bare without the weapon, especially considering we are still in harm's way.

"Your sidearm," a muffled voice comes from behind the mask, handing the M4 to his colleague.

This time I pause to look at Briggs, he knows very well that surrendering my sidearm is the ultimate show of defeat. Any notion of honour between SAS comrades is quickly dispelled, however, as the Sergeant just stands watching my capitulation.

"Your sidearm, Sir," the operative repeats. I do notice that this time he adds 'Sir' at the end of his demand.

Deliberately, keeping my eyes on Briggs, I slowly reach for the Sig, pull it out of its holster, before handing it over. I then pull my combat knife from its sleeve on the opposite side of my holster and hand that over also. I don't give Briggs the satisfaction of it having to be demanded from me.

"Satisfied?" I ask Briggs.

"Secure the prisoner, Corporal," Briggs orders, completely ignoring my question.

"Sergeant?" the masked face questions sounding doubtful.

"You heard me, Corporal," Briggs orders, once again.

Reluctantly, the Corporal's hand reaches behind his back and pulls a pair of plastic zip cuffs off his utility belt. He then walks around the back of me to tighten them around my wrists behind my back, the plastic tightening against my skin with a fast-clicking sound as they zip closed.

"Sorry, Sir," the Corporal whispers in my ear, ensuring the Sergeant won't be able to hear his words over the sound of the helicopter.

With my humiliation complete, I turn my back on Briggs, deciding to let him have his moment. Instead, with my hands bound behind my back, I look over the embankment wall to see what is going on.

Josh and Alice are still blocked in a pincer movement with the two patrol boats, and Josh has his back to me again. He has taken up his complaints with one of the patrol boat crew again, not that it will get him anywhere, I am sure of that.

Low down, on the shore of the beach, I see that Karen and Tanya have been loaded into one of the black fast boats. They look lost as they sit tight-lipped in the middle of one of the boats, waiting to see what will happen to them next.

I glance behind me and see that Briggs's men have closed right in behind me, and any moment now they will start their evacuation from the wharf and down to the beach to join Karen and Tanya in the boats. The only thing they are waiting for is for me to be loaded into the hold of the helicopter which is beginning its approach to the embankment wall.

I take a few steps back from the wall as the downdraft and overpowering noise from the helicopter begins to close in. A strong hand closes its vice-like grip around my upper arm behind me and I look to see that Briggs is unsurprisingly, the owner of the hand that has taken hold of me.

"Going somewhere?" Briggs asks with a smile of victory spread across his lips.

Looking away from his smug face without giving him the satisfaction of an answer, I simply stand and watch the helicopter come down, its door gun still pointing straight down the street behind me.

The pilot brings the helicopter down, slowly but surely, until its hold door is within reach. Pain shoots through my bicep muscle as Briggs applies pressure, ensuring any thoughts of me making a break for it is quashed. I don't know where he thinks I am going to run to, there is nowhere to go, certainly not without a weapon and with my hands tied behind my back. On the other hand, and more likely, the bastard just wants to cause me pain, but I don't show him he is succeeding.

Briggs's grip relaxes slightly, but at the same time, he shoves me forward and then releases my arm and I stumble forward towards the wall. Is he expecting me to climb on top of the wall without the use of my hands, wouldn't it be much easier all around if he released them?

No chance, two of his men close in either side of me and grab both of my arms, their grip is strong but forgiving. They lean me backwards supporting me so that I can get my feet up on top of the wall, then push me back upright with the help of the door gunner who jumps down to get involved and helps me upright.

Getting into a hovering helicopter can be dicey at the best of time, never mind with your hands tied behind your back. Thankfully, the door gunner mounts the helicopter before me and helps steady me as I step across the void and into the helicopter's hold. He keeps hold of me and directs me over to one of the seats where I plonk down.

Down on the wharf, I see Briggs shout his orders to his men, but cannot hear a word he says, he then turns his back away from his men who begin their retreat towards the steps and down to the beach.

I am extremely disappointed not to see Briggs lead his men away down to the boats, and it can only mean one thing; he is getting into the helicopter.

Sure enough, as his men disappear right out of my view, Briggs mounts the wall with ease and confidently steps across and into the hold, where he drops into the seat next to me. *Great,* I think, as two of his men, one of which I am sure is his Corporal follow him up and climb on board to take seats opposite me. The only bonus is that I see my M4 is coming along for the trip.

With everyone now on board, the helicopter immediately begins to hover sideways away from the embankment wall before lifting us up and out over the river.

I cannot slide back into my seat because my hands are still tied behind my back, instead, I have to sit forward, perched close to falling out of the seat, which I am sure Briggs takes great satisfaction in.

As the helicopter rises, my mind races to think where Briggs could possibly be taking me, what orders is he following? One thing I know for sure is that it has something to do with my missed appointment at the hospital.

Epilogue

With the helicopter gaining height, I look out of the hold's window next to me. As the pilot brings us about, I see the Special Forces troops filing down the beach, aiming for the fast boats; at least that means Karen and Tanya are about to get out of harm's way.

I feel for Karen, she has lost her soulmate in Jim, the two had the closest relationship I have ever witnessed, they were inseparable. To live with someone and then to also work all day with them, you must be more than just close, right? Karen will take it hard, there is no doubt about that, but I think she will come to terms with her loss, in time. Jim sacrificed himself to save her so that she could live and be with their daughter once more and Karen will come to understand the deep meaning of what he did, and why he did it.

I am confident that the men will make sure they are looked after, not all members of the Special Forces are complete arseholes like the man sitting next to me. In fact, most are the complete opposite and good people. Even if Briggs has given them suspect orders with regards to the women, those orders will be bent to make sure the women are treated well.

If I were to be asked, was the mission a success, I would have to say yes. Jim is a big loss, of course, but we rescued one of Stacey's parents from certain, and indeed, impending doom. And then there is Tanya, we might have lost Jim, but we saved another.

I strain my neck to try and catch my last glimpse of Josh and Alice on the water below and manage to catch a fleeting one, but they already look so distant. I know Josh, he will be going absolutely ballistic at this turn of events and I can only hope that Alice manages to keep him in check and get him out to safety.

A vibration starts against my right thigh, someone is trying to ring me. I look around the hold to try and find a willing volunteer to retrieve my phone out of my pocket so that I can see who is calling. I feel so helpless with my hands out of action, for fuck's sake. Odds are on that it is Josh, with a hat full of questions for me, none of which I will have an answer for. The other possibility is that it could be Catherine. Perhaps Josh has called her already to tell her what has happened, and she means to give somebody a piece of her mind.

Whoever it is, they are going to be as frustrated as I am, because the vibrating goes unanswered. I am not inclined to ask any of the men for help, and Briggs would shoot down anyone who tried to help me, in any case.

I suddenly have a terrible thought. What if the military doesn't just let Josh and Alice sail off into the sunset? What if they decide they have other plans for the two very capable soldiers? Both Josh and Alice could easily find themselves press-ganged back into active duty, and who knows what terrible consequences that could result in and what about Catherine and Emily, who would watch out for them?

Fucking hell, I think and debate whether to try and get some intel out of Briggs. *Don't waste your breath*, I tell myself, *he won't offer anything to ease my mind.* I decide to wait until we get to wherever it is that we are going and try my luck with whoever is in command there. It is very doubtful that Briggs would know anything anyway. Despite his superiority complex, Briggs is a small cog in a very large wheel, a dogsbody trained to follow orders, I know, I used to be one.

Opposite me, the two other Special Forces guys take off their helmets and begin to pull off their balaclavas. I am surprised, but not stunned to see that I know one of the men, Corporal Simms sits opposite me, looking at me gingerly. I had an inkling that Briggs's Corporal was one of the men who took part in the operation to retrieve Sir Malcolm's safe from the Orion building, his body language and the use of the word 'Sir' had raised my suspicions. I wonder what the likelihood is that any of the other men who were on the wharf were part of that team?

"Corporal Simms," I say, nodding in acknowledgement at the trooper.

Briggs will know full well that Simms and I have history, so there is no point trying to hide it. I am sure the Sergeant's actions in ordering Simms to disarm me and then to bind my hands was quite deliberate by Briggs. I imagine Briggs got quite a trip out of giving the orders.

Simms nods back at me but says nothing, and I leave it there. Simms is obviously uncomfortable and there is no point trying to rile Briggs up.

The helicopter's pilot has taken us over the north of the city, I see as I turn my head away and look out of the window. I cannot guess which part of the country I am being dragged off to for certain, but if I had to put my money on somewhere, it would be Porton Down, the government's Top Secret research facility, where, I am sure, they have some extremely uncomfortable plans for me. My only confusion is, if we are heading there, why is the pilot flying north? Perhaps there is a connecting flight to take me that distance?

I am just lamenting about having to fly that distance with my hands tied behind my back when the helicopter slows suddenly. *Surely, we can't have reached our destination already*, I think, *we are still over North London and inside the quarantine zone?*

Briggs and the two other Special Forces operatives begin to make movements to get their kit together, as is natural when a journey nears its conclusion. I look out of the window again in confusion to see if we are where I thought we were. The view confirms that we are still over North London, St Pancras train station is clearly visible below, which dispels any doubt.

The pilot brings the helicopter to a stop, hovering over what I see is the red-bricked building of the British Library, then we begin to descend. I am totally confused, why on earth would we be stopping at the British Library? I am sorely tempted to ask the question, but I resist, knowing Briggs will only toy with me.

We touch down, not in the grounds of the library but on its highest roof. Simms and his partner are up and out of their seats immediately, he pulls the hold door open and both men jump down onto the roof and take up covering positions, their rifles scanning the rooftop area.

Briggs is out next and the only person left in the hold with me is the door gunner who helps me up out of my seat and down onto the library's roof. Briggs takes hold of my arm and leads me out from beneath the helicopter's rotors.

Simms moves past us and heads to a doorway jutting out from the roof. Behind us, as soon as we are clear, the helicopter powers its engines and lifts straight up before dipping its nose and flying off.

Simms stops next to the door and looks up towards a camera positioned just above the door frame, a green light flashes and he moves aside for his partner to do the same. Another green light is shown and then Briggs looks up to the camera. A buzzing noise sounds before I get a go at looking up to have my eyes scanned, and Simms pulls the door open.

Briggs and I are last through the door which swings shut behind us. Inside is a stairwell, and without pausing we start to descend two flights down into what was once a doorway that must have led into the library. The exit has had a thick steel plate fitted over it, however, sealing it completely. In fact, every exit out of the stairwell is sealed off, I see as we continue down.

One set of stairs follows another, and I begin to pant from the excursion hoping that I don't slip and fall, especially with both of my hands out of action. Eventually, Simms comes to a stop at the bottom of the stairwell and faces a door, he reaches for the door handle just as another buzzing noise sounds, and pulls it open.

Beyond the door does not lead into the library but to another stairwell which Simms starts to lead us down. I notice that the previous floors sealed exits have now disappeared, and I start to wish I had counted how many flights of stairs we have descended. I am sure we must have descended far deeper than the structure of the library, as it isn't that tall, and suddenly realise we have gone beneath the ground level of the library. We must have, and the last door we entered through was the threshold.

All at once, while I am still trying to figure out what is going on, we reach the bottom of the second stairwell. Yet another door buzzes which Simms pulls open, and then to my surprise I find myself walking horizontally along a tunnel, one that I cannot see to the end of.

The roof of the tunnel is just above my head and the sides just wide enough for two people. I have lost my bearings and have no idea which direction we are travelling; all I can do is keep following.

After around ten minutes of walking, I can finally see the end of the tunnel ahead and it looks like we are approaching another doorway. As we get closer, I see words painted in red on the door and what looks like another camera above it. I squint, trying to read the letters, but it isn't until Simms stops in front of the door that I can finally read the red-painted words. They read, STATION ZERO.

The fight continues in

CAPITAL FALLING 5 – ZERO

If you have enjoyed CAPITAL FALLING, be sure to leave a review. Amazon reviews only take a minute and are so important in building a buzz for every book.
Many thanks, every review is appreciated!

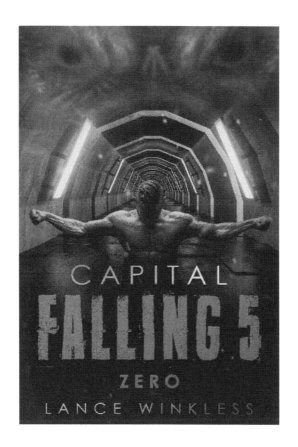

CAPITAL FALLING 5 – ZERO

As chaos deepens, the fight for survival is relentless!

Having shown their self-serving hand, the merciless authorities are scrambling to find a solution, aiming at last to contain the viral outbreak that has wholly ravaged London. No quarter will be given, and Andy Richards is their quarry.

The focal point remains ground zero, where every form of brutal experimentation is still on the table… in the frantic struggle to stem the rise of the ferocious undead. With desperation surging, grasping for a remedy may stand, instead, to poison mankind. Though down, however, Andy is not out. His resolution knows no bounds. As driven by an unrelenting mission—securing a future for his loved ones, and possibly for mankind itself—he'll soon be forced to prove himself . . . and face impossible choices.

Capital Falling* — *Zero marks a vital stage in the battle to wake from a spreading nightmare of ferocious infected creatures. A resolution could be possible, but so might the unthinkable.

Again, Lance Winkless raises the stakes, and pushes readers to the brink . . . *it will be impossible to look away!*

THE Z SEASON - TRILOGY 1

3 Novels - A #1 Best Seller - 650+ Pages -
Infectious to its Very Core

A trilogy of standalone and unique novels that don't
hold back and all with a zombie - undead twist.......
YOU HAVE BEEN WARNED!

KILL TONE

A festival of feverish, exhilarating tension with a rock 'n roll crescendo that unleashes hell itself, this is not for the faint-hearted. KILL TONE proves the perfect blend of decadence and undead carnage, whilst never losing sight of its predominant humanity.

VOODOO SUN

Caribbean Voodoo may have caused this nightmare, and nothing short of a miracle will help Max get out alive. A tale of undead carnage and mayhem, VOODOO SUN embarks for bliss but lands in true perdition.

CRUEL FIX

CRUEL FIX is a terrifying trip through the labyrinth of loss and lunacy. Bleak and sinister it may be, but spirited humanity retains a twisted shard of hope …. Though all that glitters isn't gold, and all that walks is not alive.

Read these novels in any order, you choose. Each is a tale of its own and completely unique, but be warned they don't hold back and are not for the faint-hearted or easily offended!

For more information on Lance Winkless
and future writing see his website.

www.LanceWinkless.com

By Lance Winkless

THE CAPITAL FALLING SERIES

**CAPITAL FALLING
CAPITAL FALLING 2 – DENIAL
CAPITAL FALLING 3 – RESURGENCE
CAPITAL FALLING 4 – SEVER
CAPITAL FALLING 5 - ZERO**

THE Z SEASON – TRILOGY

KILL TONE
VOODOO SUN
CRUEL FIX

Visit Amazon Author Pages

Amazon US - Amazon.com/author/lancewinkless
Amazon UK - Amazon.co.uk/-/e/B07QJV2LR3

Why Not Follow

Facebook www.facebook.com/LanceWinklessAuthor
Twitter   @LanceWinkless
Instagram @LanceWinkless
Pinterest www.pinterest.com/lancewinkless
BookBub www.bookbub.com/authors/lance-winkless